A N N I E
J O N E S

"Annie Jones writes about characters we all know and—despite their quirks—love. Sadie Pickett is an endearing character whose foibles and charms will leave you smiling as you think, *Yes, life is just like that.* Carry on, Sadie, and thanks for inviting us along for the ride!"
—Angela Hunt, Christy Award-winning author of *The Debt*

"...Annie Jones...a top-notch creator of love and laughter."
—*Romantic Times*

"Annie Jones writes with a heart, humor and soul that holds the reader hostage till the last page. Don't miss Annie's newest!"
—Linda Windsor, Christy Award-winning author of *Along Comes Jones*

"Annie Jones never fails to draw in readers with delightful characters, snappy dialogue, humor, emotion and a story that lives in your heart long after the last page is turned."
—Diane Noble, award-winning author of *Phoebe*

"Annie Jones has a proven ability to bring to life characters with whom we can identify, and whose trials and triumphs become our own."
—Hannah Alexander, bestselling author of *Safe Haven*

"With her unique blend of humor, poignancy and perceptive insight into human nature, Annie Jones gives her readers a book to treasure."
—Sharon Gillenwater, bestselling author of *Twice Blessed*

ANNIE JONES

Sadie-in-Waiting

TM
Steeple
Hill
Café

Published by Steeple Hill Books™

STEEPLE HILL BOOKS

ISBN 0-373-78531-3

SADIE-IN-WAITING

www.SteepleHill.com

Printed in U.S.A.

During the course of writing this book I often found
myself turning down some metaphoric dark alley and
in need of someone to light a candle to show me the way.
Thank you to my many candle lighters, who include:
Chi-Libris KC Mini-Retreaters
PQALs Prayer Sisters
My agent, Karen Solem
The kind editors who caught my mistakes
And my family who almost never complains
when I lose track of the time and end up
sending out for pizza for dinner—again.

❧ *Chapter One* ❧

Sometime in her childhood Sadie's daddy made a point of telling her, "If you pray for patience, you will be sent adversity for a teacher."

So she never prayed for patience. Not *once*.

And yet for some reason she still seemed to get dished out more than her share of adversity.

It seemed to follow her around, in fact, like a lovesick pup. A pup with the sleepy-eyed gaze of her husband, Ed, the persistent whine of her children's teenage angst and the maddening bite of her sisters' habitual bickering. To top it off, that puppy traveled with a pack, constantly nipping at her heels.

President of the contentious Council of Christian Women—*contentious* not being part of the official title, though she often thought it should be. *Nip.*

Unpaid, unnoticed, as-needed, fill-in employee at her husband's pharmacy. *Nip.*

First person everyone in town called to report about the often exasperating actions of her father, Solomon Shelnutt. *Nip.*

And ever-present gnawing that made it all the more difficult for her to shake it all off—the seemingly silly, self-indulgent empty ache of being a mommy to teens and no longer having any little babies to mother.

Adversity, in her case, loved company. For Sadie, more often than not, the biggest helping of it—adversity, not company—came in the form of her seventy-one-year-old father's never-ending pursuit of what he called "authentic individualism." That was Daddyspeak for "Nobody tells Moonie Shelnutt what to do."

He'd said those very words to her this morning, so she should have had an inkling that this was the day trouble would go out of its way to find her. Find her? It had already phoned her three times! Well, three people had already phoned her trying to pry her out of the house to come down and "deal with your daddy."

Not today, she had decided. Today she would hide out from the relentless responsibilities of her life.

She had planned to let the phone ring.

She had planned to ignore the petty problems people piled at her feet daily with the expectation "Sadie can fix it."

She had planned to let somebody else learn from adversity today, even if it meant she never, ever, *ever* mastered the noble virtue of patience.

Adversity, she discovered this fine May Monday morning when she flung open her front door—dressed in high-water overalls, shower shoes and a freebie windbreaker a pharmaceutical rep had given her husband, no less—had other plans. It had come in the form of a brand-new, never-expected variety right there on her doorstep.

And it had a proposition for her.

She heard him out impassively before saying, "Earl Lee Furst, I know you've been elected mayor of this little slice of

Kentucky paradise an unprecedented thirteen times." Sadie quoted directly from the ruddy-faced man's mayoral-campaign ads, knowing he'd never allow himself to acknowledge the sarcasm in her doing so. In fact, because he'd got her up out of her safe, comfy easy chair when she was definitely not in a mood to do so, she laid it on extra thick. "And that the Furst family has roots so deep in Wileyville that they not only helped found the town, they grew themselves into the very character of the place, but—"

"It's true, Mrs. Pickett." He beamed, his hand on his low, round belly. "Me and mine have long been pillars of the church, the chamber of commerce and the community at large."

"And don't forget primary sponsors of the Tri-county Bass-travaganza Fishing Tournament," she droned.

"Ah, yes, the Bass-travaganza." His eyes shone with a distant light usually reserved for talk of Mother, God and country. "That sucker really hauls in the cold hard cash."

Sadie cleared her throat.

"That is to say, it's a real boon to you business owners, Mrs. Pickett. And like most things that keep this town's head above water—all *my* idea."

"Well, you've had some, um, *doozies* in the past, I'll grant you that." And even though the local paper had predicted a scorcher of a day—going so far as to remind the parents of the children taking Lollie Muldoon's town walking tour to slap extra sunscreen on the kids—Sadie wrapped Ed's jacket more tightly around herself and took a deep breath. "But I hope you understand, Mayor, that all I can ask about this latest brain-child of yours is…"

He leaned in close like a kid getting a whiff of pie—or like a thirteen-time mayor getting wind of a palpable piece of praise. "Yes, Mrs. Pickett?"

"Are you out of your cotton-pickin' mind?" She plunked her hands on her hips.

He gave her one of his polished politician's chuckles, shifted his feet on the chipped-paint floorboards of her old porch then smiled. "Mrs. Pickett… Sadelia… Sadie. May I call you Sadie?"

She didn't want him to call her anything, but she did prefer Sadie over her legal name of Sadelia, or the more formal Mrs. Pickett, which even after nineteen years of marriage still made her think someone was talking to her mother-in-law. "Yes. Fine. Sadie is fine. Though I don't think we need to bother with a lot of these niceties, because we just don't have anything more to say to one another."

"Oh, but I hope that's not true. I very much hope that this is only the beginning of a very long, very productive working relationship and perhaps…yes, even a friendship, Sadie."

She tried to hold back a shudder, failed miserably, then mustered up a meek smile and murmured, "Somebody must be walking over my grave."

Instantly she regretted introducing the *g* word into the conversation.

The mayor leaped on the opportunity and motioned toward her open door. "Speaking of graves— I was hoping we *could.* Speak of them, that is."

Wileyville Parks and Recreation Supervisor and Superintendent of City Interment Locality. Sadie could hardly catch her breath to think of taking on such a title much less the implications of the job the mayor had come to quite literally lay on her doorstep.

"All right, we'll talk about it." She drew a deep breath trying to force her mind to form a cogent, clever, well-worded argument as to why she could not possibly even consider his offer. After a few seconds when no such argument materialized, she simply shook her head and, her voice cracking, said a bit too loudly, "The cemetery lady? You want *me* to be the town cemetery lady?"

"Don't forget the park."

"The park is just four swings and a slide. What you are, in truth, asking of me is to take on managing Barrett and Bartlett Memorial Gardens. And since, despite that lovely name, there are only a few shrubs and wild rosebushes to be found on the premises, it's plain to see you want me to oversee the graveyard."

"Maybe if we sat down and talked this over sensibly…" He stepped toward her half-open front door.

Manners dictated Sadie ask the man inside, but…

A home reflects the people who occupy it. Chaos in the home meant chaos in the family. That's one of the first things a girl learns growing up in a small town. Always keep your house—or at least the part seen from the front door—in order, and people will know that you manage the rest of your life with the same sense of style and grace.

Sadie glanced back over her shoulder into her living room.

Empty pizza boxes left over from Saturday night lay on the coffee table. Her fifteen-year-old son's video game system tangled in a heap in front of the TV. Her daughter's clothes draped up and down the stairs and dangled over the banister—the aftermath of yet another mother-daughter heart-to-headphone talk.

And next to the chair where Sadie had been sitting this Monday afternoon? A bag of jelly beans with all the black ones picked out and eaten, crumpled tissues lying on the floor in drifts around a virtual tower of unread self-help books. And the cordless phone peeking out from a mound of magazines and throw pillows where she'd tried to suffocate the poor thing to keep from hearing another plea to come and…

"Actually, Mayor Furst, you caught me at a bad time." She finally stepped fully out onto the porch and closed the door behind her. Choosing the lesser of two evils, she believed they called it. "I was just on my way out, there's been kind of a little…emergency."

He slid his glasses off and rested the tip of one earpiece alongside his thin lips, a pose he employed for almost every photo they ran with in the *Wileyville Weekly Citizen.* "Nothing serious, I hope."

"No, no. Just a little…misunderstanding."

"Ah." He nodded and slid his glasses back into place, obstructing the expression in his eyes when he added, "So how *is* your daddy?"

"I never said…" She looked out at her quiet street lined with refurbished turn-of-the-century houses then sighed. "He's fine. I just need to get over to the VFW and collect him."

"Wonderful. I'll walk with you over there, then." He swept his arm out, inviting her to go ahead of him down the steps, through the morning glory–covered arched gateway and out onto the sunny sidewalk.

"Oh." She curled her bare toes against the thick rubber soles of her pink-and-orange shower shoes. "I…I need to change."

Into an entirely different person. *This* Sadie wasn't about to go strolling through town looking like a walking laundry pile with the mayor at her side. Though it might finally be the one thing she could do to make her daddy proud.

No, Sadie could practically see Lollie reveling in the role of president of the Wileyville Historical Society, pointing Sadie out to the grade-schoolers taking the town tour today and saying, "What we learn when we study about the people who have built our fine town, children, is that some folks are a lot like the big oaks that line our fair streets. The nuts don't fall far from the trees." Then she'd nod to the mayor, smile big at Sadie and add, "On your way to see your daddy today, sugar?"

"I'm sorry, Mayor. I can't just up and go with you right now. I hope you understand."

"Of course, Sadie. It seems I've got you at a bad time. I don't want to press you to make a decision under these circumstances."

"But I think I can safely say I've already made my decision and it's—"

"Don't say it." He held up his hand. "Don't say no. Not yet. Talk it over with Ed and get back to me."

To protest meant to prolong his presence, so she simply smiled and nodded, telling herself she didn't actually agree to anything. The door creaked as she opened it just wide enough to slip through, and before doing so she turned to the mayor and mumbled the expected, "Thank you for thinking of me."

"No, thank *you*, Sadie." He grabbed her right hand in a vigorous shake then leaned in, still holding her palm to his and whispered, "You know, given all you've been through lately and all you have had thanklessly thrust upon you over the years, I think a new job, a *real* job, would do you a world of good."

"Oh." She had no idea what to say to that. So she murmured, this time with some actual connection to the sentiment, "Thank you. Thanks…for…for showing faith in me."

She shut the door and fell back against it, unable to make perfect sense of what had just happened.

A new job? A *real* job?

Sadie didn't want a new job. She wanted her old job—the role of wife and mother, just the way it used to be when everybody still needed and relied on her. That was her *real* job, the only one she ever really wanted.

But with the kids growing older and more independent, and the Lord having seen fit to deprive her of another chance at holding a new baby in her arms ever again…

Not that she blamed the Lord. She told herself it was part of His plan. She told her family and friends that He knew what was best and she had to accept it. And times like these, in the dimly lit stillness of her all-too-quiet home, she told the Lord…nothing at all.

She had nothing to say to Him. She could not pour her heart out to Him, because ever since she'd lost the baby, her heart had been as empty as the tiny crib in the closed-off nursery upstairs.

That had to change.

Every day she woke up and waited for that change to come.

And it had.

Slowly.

To some extent.

Most days now she was…fine.

Or functioning, at least.

But she still didn't feel like her old self. She just felt old. That her time of being somebody, of making something remarkable of her life, had passed her by. She felt bereft, devoid of the possibility of ever becoming her *best* self. Not an easy concept to convey to those who looked to her to keep their little worlds in orbit. And she knew no way to express it to them anyway, short of confessing that most mornings when she looked at herself in the mirror, one overriding, inescapable thought filled her mind—*here is a woman who will never be good enough.*

Never.

And on days like this, it seemed that life—and the likes of Daddy and now even the mayor of her hometown—conspired to prove her right.

✦ Chapter Two ✦

"Wileyville was founded by three main families: the Bartletts, the Barretts and the Fursts." Lollie Muldoon made generous gestures toward the three mansions standing across from Monument Circle where her walking tours always began.

One of the once-impressive houses had fallen into disrepair. One had found its purpose housing the Home Extension Offices, the Wileyville Historical Society and the county food bank. The third, and most opulent of the trio, remained the home of Mayor Furst and his family.

The sight of the Furst mansion made Sadie want to run in the opposite direction—home. But knowing that route held neither answers nor respite for her, she simply put her back to the house and decided to hurry past the tour and get on with her mission.

Two historical society members of long standing—there, no doubt to offer their opinions on Lollie's practiced patter—stopped her cold.

"Sadelia Pickett? 'S that you?" a woman in a wide-brimmed sun hat asked.

"It is. It's her." Her companion raised a hand to wave then called out, loud enough to cut into Lollie's well-rehearsed tale about the founders divvying up the town like a pie, "Did I miss out on you having a young 'un?"

Sadie tensed. She placed her hand over her midsection and told herself to keep breathing, slow and steady.

"Having a child in this class is not a prerequisite to taking the tour, ladies. *Some* people come along to learn." Lollie tilted her head up, which smoothed out the soft folds of her double chin just a little.

The two tour detractors sniffed.

Sadie relaxed. She wouldn't have strictly called Lollie's sly smile that followed triumphant, but it did have that air about it. Sadie mouthed a thank-you and started to wind her way around the group when the white-haired matron with the brass name badge on her chest motioned to the small crowd to head down the street.

Before Sadie could clear the cluster of children completely, Lollie called back, "We're tickled to have you along, Sadie."

"Well, I wasn't—"

"Most of you probably know that Mrs. Pickett's family owns the Downtown Drug, there." She pointed to the three-story wedge-shape building that Sadie's husband, Ed, had owned for the last twenty-three years. "Of course, we all call it 'Pickett's on the Point.' And that's where we will be stopping for refreshments at the end of the tour."

Every head in the group turned toward Sadie bringing up the rear. Every eye gaped at her.

Stuck. She conjured up a lame smile. "Well, I can't stay for the whole tour, but I guess I could walk along for a ways."

"Wonderful! Mrs. Pickett is also in charge of the Council of Christian Women. So y'all had better be on your best behavior." Lollie laughed.

More head turning. More gaping.

For one fleeting moment Sadie considered sticking her tongue out at the whole curious lot. But, of course, she didn't. Instead, she sighed and trudged along as they moved up the familiar street.

Lollie's voice droned in the background.

Wileyville had not one, but two main streets, forming an elongated V with the cemetery, the city works-department storage, what was left of the town park and the building where Sadie would have an office if she took the job Mayor Furst had offered, all bordering the bottom edge.

Along the way lay the usual mix of stores and services. Owtt's Eatery still had the same basic menu and the same motto—Let's Eat Owtt's Tonight!—it started with in 1959.

Across the way, the signs in the window of Muldoon's Home Furnishings, proclaiming Once-in-a-Lifetime Savings!, had hung there so long that their vibrant red, white and blue had faded to pink, cream and periwinkle.

A-One Appliance and Repair with its shiny new gadgetry on display sat next to Szajkowski's American Hardware, which still sold nails by the pound and dispensed all the advice a person could handle for free.

Of course, just around the corner at Pep and Bobbie Jo Huckleham's Boys and Curls Beauty Salon and Barbershop, Pep was all too happy to tell you the hardware store advice "weren't nothing but a bunch of hooey" and gladly offer you some "rock-solid" advice of his own invention instead.

In fact, a stop in any of the businesses around town could yield a person myriad opinions on anything from politics to pan-fried chicken recipes. Maybe that's also why Wileyville had a full half-dozen law offices—in case the sum of all that learned counsel didn't quite add up to the whole.

Just down the way, tantalizing aromas from the Not By Bread Alone Bakery wafted out onto the sidewalk. Here and there stood empty old buildings with faded For Sale Or Lease signs in the windows. The courthouse, city hall and the library, all grand old buildings, each had a sign in front touting the need for public support for essential renovations.

"This here is the first church founded in Wileyville." Lollie jabbed her finger toward the small stone structure. The congregation had long ago outgrown the building and now it only held a small midnight service on Christmas Eve and a sunrise one on Easter.

Churches played a big part in life in Wileyville. The four biggest ones anchored the north, south, east and west sides of town. Two still had bell towers and they took turns playing evening vespers, two hymns at 6:00 p.m., and on the Fourth of July and Memorial Day, something with a patriotic flavor.

Their spires and crosses jutting above the town's rooftops sometimes seemed to Sadie like the wagging fingers of ostentatious old matrons, out of reach and out of touch with the daily goings-on beneath them. But sometimes, in the twilight of the day or in autumn when the leaves showered down around them, yellow and orange and crimson, or when they stood silently swathed in fresh snow, they reminded her, and everyone around them, that now and then it was wise to look up and acknowledge your part in something larger than yourself.

"And this place we're coming up to in the next block—" Lollie stopped at the corner, spreading her arms to keep the children from crossing ahead of her "—the Weed 'Em and Reap Garden Supply and Nursery is owned and operated by Sadie's older sister, April Shelnutt."

A little gasp slipped through Sadie's lips. Walking along, lost in her own thoughts, she hadn't even realized where they were. "Um, Lollie, this has been lovely. Very…um, enlightening. But I have to—" Sadie jerked her thumb over her shoulder, eked out a smile, waved goodbye then hurried off without further explanation.

What could she say, really? Sadie loved her sister—half sister technically, though Sadie never thought of her that way. Though they shared the same mother biologically, their childhood experiences had created a bond that felt no different from the relationship Sadie had with her younger full sister. Still, she had no intention of passing within eyeshot of April's place. The last thing she needed on this stifling late-spring day when she had planned to stay out of adversity's way (and already failed not once but twice) was to run into any more of her family than absolutely necessary.

Toward that end she zigzagged away from the second primary town thoroughfare, Wileyville Road, to bypass the medical clinic where her brother-in-law was finishing out his last year of residency and where her younger sister, Hannah, worked as a receptionist.

It took a few machinations to manage it but finally, tucked down a shady little side street, in what was once an old railroad tavern, Sadie arrived at the local chapter of the VFW.

She wanted to keep right on walking.

She wondered what would happen if she dared try it, if she ignored this unwanted obligation and just got herself to the pharmacy without anybody noticing. Maybe that would break the grip of whatever had her spirit in knots. Maybe, just maybe, if she rushed in breathless and beleaguered, Ed would take one look at her and say, "Sweetheart, you look frazzled. Let's hop in the car and just drive and drive until we find a nice little bed-and-breakfast where no one can find us. Then we can finally have that second honeymoon you so richly deserve."

And maybe Mayor Furst would roller-skate by to bestow on her a brace of flying pigs to pull her along in a rainbow carriage to her new job in the marshmallow gardens beside the gold-plated playground in the world's best city park.

One was just as plausible as the other, and she knew it.

Drawing a deep breath, she pushed open the VFW Hall's heavy glass front door and confronted her father, who was seated in the foyer lined with metal folding chairs and a fair number of curious onlookers. Wherever Moonie held court there were always curious onlookers. "Daddy, I do not have time for one of your shenanigans today."

The instant she crossed that threshold, her daddy's eyes sparked to life from under his charcoal-colored hat. He smiled, and the lines in his face fell into familiar folds. And like the perfect gentleman farmer that he definitely was *not,* he stood and gave a little bow. "Well then, tell me when you do have time, Sadie-girl, and I'll pencil my next shenanigan in at your convenience. Anything for my darling daughter."

No. She would not bend. She would not cave in at the sight of him brimming over with tenderness and tomfoolery.

"But it's a sad, sad day—" he shook his head and took his seat again, neither his gaze nor his broad smile faltering "—when an old man has to make an appointment just to get a little attention from his own flesh and blood."

Attention. Like everyone gathered around the silver-haired man with the twinkling blue eyes didn't know that getting attention was at the very heart of everything Solomon Shelnutt had done for most of his seventy-one years. And it had worked. It had worked on his mama and on his big sister. Young Solomon had been given his nickname by his sister, Phyllis Amaryllis—Phiz to all those who adored the redheaded Amazon, which was just about the entire human race, give or take a handful of people she'd caught mistreating animals and the odd embassy spokesperson in countries where she'd come close to causing international incidents.

"We called him Moonie," she tells it, "because we *had* to. Gracious, girls, back in the day when your daddy was coming up, why, everyone he flashed with that wicked grin and those angel eyes, well, they thought he just about hung the moon."

Sadie'd seen that effect firsthand. Her best friend adored her father. The widows at church fawned over him. Even her sister April's temperamental greyhound, Squirrel, sighed and rested her head on her paws when he came into the room. Polite and polished and absolutely unashamed of his adoration of every embodiment of femininity, no female seemed able to resist Moonie Shelnutt's charm.

Except for Sadie's mother. Some thirty-five years ago, *she* ran off in the middle of the night—probably to spare her heart the torture of looking into those eyes and resigning herself to the fact that this man always got his way.

No, not always, Sadie amended. Not today.

"Come on, Daddy." She waved for him to get up from the metal folding chair to accompany her home. "Memorial Day is only ten days away, and these nice ladies have enough to do to get ready for the festivities without you sticking your fingers in the pie."

"Pie? There's pie?" He sat up straight and turned to a plump woman in pink polyester. "Why wasn't I informed?"

The lady in pink giggled.

"I say bring us pie." He held his arms wide. "Pie for everyone."

"You're going to be eating humble pie here in a heartbeat, Daddy, if you don't—"

"Thank you for coming on down to pick up the old fool, Sadie." If charm were rocket fuel, Deborah Danes wouldn't have enough to hoist her hindquarters over a ramshackle henhouse. But she got things done. And in a town where the likes of Sadie's father constantly sought to "undo" everyone and everything, that made the six-foot-something, former Miss Maryland and Ladies' All-State Shot-putter a veritable bounty of blessings.

"Family matter, ladies." With a snap of her fingers, Deborah rousted the small group of women up out of their seats. In broad sweeping gestures she herded them toward the adjacent room where banners, bits of tissue paper waiting to be made into flowers, bags of candy and boxes of small American flags covered rows of long, sturdy tables. On her way out she pointed at the man sitting at the center of the musty-smelling VFW lobby and narrowed one eye at Sadie. "He's insisting we give him a slot in the Memorial Day parade."

"Oh, Daddy." Sadie rubbed her temple. "Why?"

"Why?" He crinkled up his nose and leaned forward, his age-spotted hands on his knees. "I think the better question is why not? There's going to be a celebration in town, and I say *why not* be a party to it?"

"Daddy, everything in life can't be your own personal celebration."

He laughed and adjusted his hat just so. "I'd have to ask you again, Sadie-girl, why not?"

"Because…" She raked her fingers through her hair, marveling that she didn't pull it out altogether in total frustration.

"Because…" Deborah spun around. Her hair, beautiful chestnut waves with a shock of blond in the front, which somehow looked relaxed and regal all at the same time, did not move even when she leaned out to seize the doorknob and bark, "It simply won't do! If I let all the people who wanted to be in this dog-and-pony show just up and join the parade, then *nobody* would be left to watch it."

The door slammed.

Moonie removed his hat and scratched his head.

Sadie pinched the bridge of her nose and looked at the floor. A pale reddish-brown wisp of hair fell forward over her eyes, and the play of the low-watt lightbulbs overhead highlighted a single gray hair. She sighed and got back to business. "Daddy, clearly Deborah wants me to reiterate to you that they reserve the honor of participating in the Memorial Day parade for veterans only."

"Is it my fault I couldn't put on a uniform and serve my country?" Hat in hand, he spoke softly. He always spoke softly. But that never kept his words from carrying the power of that proverbial big stick. "After all, I had to stay home and raise you three girls after your mama run off. And with your baby sister…"

"I know, I know, with my baby sister just three weeks home from the hospital." Sadie didn't think in her whole life she had ever heard her daddy refer to her mother's leaving without tacking on that bit about Hannah.

"Besides—" his grin spread out slowly in catlike satisfaction "—it's not just veterans. They let them girls in."

"What?" Sadie threw her hands up and shook her head. "What girls?"

"The ones with sparkly doodads all over and the high hair that they perch up on the back seat of open-air cars."

"They perch their hair on the back seat of cars?"

"You know what I mean." He did a passing fair imitation of a beauty queen in all her glory giving the regal wave to an adoring audience.

He didn't have to act it out for her, of course. She had once been one of those girls gone gliding through town with a smile as immovable as her lacquered hairdo. And because of her former glory, she was still asked to join the annual float.

Dogwood Blossom Queen. An honor bestowed on "the sweetest bloom of the senior class, a girl lovely of face and fair of temperament," or so the Wileyville High School yearbook always touted her. Wholesome. Chaste. And dutiful to a fault.

In other words, if the good folks of Wileyville had been a passel of heathens instead of, as the monument across from the Point proclaimed, "A community built on four faiths: God, family, patriotism and self-reliance," being chosen Dogwood Blossom Queen would have been the equivalent of getting selected "girl most likely to be thrown into a volcano."

"They have to have the queen and her court in the parade, Daddy. They're like…" She pictured her sweet, obedient, younger self jumping into a smoking crater and managed to muster up a half shrug. "They're like old-fashioned apple pie."

"Half-baked?" He winked.

"Oh, excuse me, but that's a bit of the pot calling the kettle black, isn't it?"

"You the kettle? Because you're one of them girls, and I don't recall you ever serving in any wars."

Wars? She fought one daily just to get by, and his nonsense did not make it any easier on her. But she couldn't say that out loud, so she just sighed and muttered, "Daddy, that's just a tradition. They ask that every woman ever elected a Dogwood Blossom Queen ride on the float. And honestly, I don't consider it any great honor, either, to be hauled through town on the back of a flatbed truck wearing a faded prom dress under the banner Our Bygone Blossoms."

The humor of that had not been lost on the town. Every Fourth of July the eldest members of the South and Central Civic Charities Club made an appearance in that parade, standing in the back of a pickup decked in toilet-paper "gowns" while someone walked ahead carrying the sign Our Old Queens. Given an option, Sadie would rather have ridden with them.

"Your sisters can be in the parade. Is April a veteran? Is Hannah? Hardly."

"They were Petal Maidens." The all-girl court that attended the Dogwood Blossom Queen each spring. "And they don't do the parade, Daddy."

Something for which Sadie admitted a grudging admiration.

"Maybe *they* don't, but what about our towheaded little pistol of a pal? Martha Tatum Fitts McCrackin."

Moonie loved to say the whole name of Sadie's best friend, who rented the back half of the Downtown Drug building to run the Royal Academy of Charm and Beauty. He loved the cadence of it, he said, especially since she married Royal McCrackin fifteen years ago. And he never missed a chance to shout it out to the woman everyone else called simply, Mary Tate. Mary Tate egged him on, waving and cooing and blowing him big exaggerated kisses whenever or wherever he called to her.

"Now, our Martha Tatum waltzes her brood down the street every year, doesn't she?"

"Daddy, I've told you a thousand times those are not Mary Tate's children. Those are some of her students doing what she calls a salute to our American service people in tap dance and precision flag twirling."

"I don't care if she calls it Betsy Ross and the Star-spangled Supremes. It's a bunch of rhythmically impaired youngsters with glitter glued on their gym clothes waving ribbons on sticks, clomping down the street in shoes that sound like they got bottle caps stuck to the soles." He brandished his hat in the air, caught up in the pure joy of the image he'd created. "And all the while that sweet pixie of a gal walking alongside carrying a boom box bigger than she is, blaring music so loud and distorted she might as well be hauling along a trash compactor in a rusty wagon."

If he hadn't just described the ragtag troop to a tee, Sadie might have had a bit more conviction when she jerked her chin up, crossed her arms, narrowed her eyes and said, "Fine. You want to be in the parade with the rest of the little children? I'll arrange with Mary Tate for you to march with them."

He stood at last, his smile lighting all the way to his eyes, and asked, "You think I won't do it?"

"Daddy, I don't think there's anything you won't do." She dropped her arms to her sides, turned toward the front door, then paused. She should probably just let it go but… "What I don't understand is *why*. *Why* are you the way you are?"

His hand flattened warm and soothing against the small of her back. "Sadie, honey, I could ask you the same question."

"Maybe you should ask *yourself* that. Doesn't it say in Proverbs, 'Train up a child in the way he should go…'"

"'And when he is grown he will not depart from it.'"

"Old."

"What?" His faded plaid shirt rasped against the sleeve of her shapeless denim dress.

"When he is *old*," she corrected. "Not when he is *grown*. The verse says, 'When he is old he will not depart from it.'"

"Well, maybe that's my problem, then." He pulled her close to his side, his cheek to hers, and took her hand in his. "I grew, but I never have let myself get old."

"You mean you're still very childish?" she muttered.

"Childlike." He kissed her cheek and drew away, his hand still clinging to hers. "Filled with joy. I thought…I most surely did hope…that I had done my very best to train you up that way, Sadie-girl. To always be a child of joy. But these days when I look into those world-weary eyes of yours…"

"I know, Daddy." She gave his rough fingers a squeeze. "I'm just tired, that's all."

It wasn't really a lie. She *was* tired. But that did not tell the whole story, and she could see her daddy knew it.

"Sadie, honey, you can't go on like this."

"Don't start, Daddy."

"*Why not?* Someone has to start, Sadie. Whatever you're doing isn't working—surely you can see that? If you won't do it for yourself, someone has to start—start talking the truth, start looking at things in a new light, start reaching out."

"Thank you, Daddy." She touched his cheek, shut her eyes a moment and drew in the damp aroma of fresh pastry from the Not By Bread Alone Bakery. "But no. No, thank you."

"But, sweetheart, I wonder…maybe there's something I can do to help."

She pulled her shoulders up, opened her eyes and forced a smile. "What will help right now is to get you out of here before Deborah pokes her nose out that door and offers to toss us both out on our you-know-whats."

"Our ears?"

She looped her arm through his. "Somewhere decidedly south of our ears, Daddy."

"Oh, then we'd better scoot." He pushed the front door open. "If I hit that unforgiving pavement anywhere but my hard old head, I might just suffer an injury."

"Then as often as folks threaten to toss you out of places, maybe you should invest in some iron-lined britches for protection."

"Iron britches. Oh, I do like that notion. Imagine the epidemic of throbbing toes when I tell all them around town who say I need a swift kick in the pants, 'Go right ahead and give it all you got!'"

The bright daylight made her squint and the picture of her father getting the last laugh on his critics made her wince.

"Now, that's what I like to see." He swiped his knuckle over her cheek. "You should smile more, honey, it really suits you."

She didn't have the heart to tell him the truth, so she obliged him with a nod, then pinched the fabric of his plaid sleeve between her thumb and forefinger. "Now, Daddy, please, *ple-e-ase* promise me you won't get into more trouble today."

"I'll go you one better than that. How's about you won't hear a peep out of me for a good…oh, three or four days?"

"Why? What do you plan to get up to?"

"Get up to? Me?" His dentures made a soft whistling sound as he grinned and chuckled at the same time. "I can't win for losing with you, girl. One minute you warn me to stay out of mischief for a while, and when I promise to do just that, you accuse me of ulterior motives."

"Well?"

"Don't you worry none. For the next few days you won't even know I'm in town."

She studied his expression for any hint of monkey business, but when her eyes met his, she saw there such love, such compassion, that she felt a twinge of guilt for having even considered doubting his good intentions.

She kissed his cheek and with a gentle shove sent her father off for his home in the section of Wileyville lined with tidy little tract houses built in the sixties that people still referred to as New Town. After that she inhaled deeply and held her breath. What to do now? Should she head back to her house, back to the soft old chair where she had intended to spend her day?

She chewed her lip and gazed at the pharmacy down the way.

...someone has to start—start talking the truth, start looking at things in a new light, start reaching out.

More than a few people considered her daddy a crackpot, but sometimes he did say some awfully wise things.

Her hard-earned, perfectly awful day had already gotten off track. Maybe...

Why not, Sadie-girl?

Why not, indeed. It wasn't a big deal, no giant leap for lonely-wifekind, but somehow Sadie's stride took on a whole new air of importance as she headed off to surprise her husband and maybe, just maybe, do as her daddy suggested—and start something!

❦ *Chapter Three* ❦

Sadie rapped on the huge glass window of the Royal Academy, then motioned for her best friend to meet her at the open door.

"Right foot step, feet together, pause. Heads high. Slowly, smoothly, glide, ladies, glide! No peeking at the ground and, remember, if you move too fast, you're going to wobble!" Mary Tate demonstrated the modified waltz step all the way over to Sadie's side, then slipped through the door, calling back, "Keep it up, maidens. Dogwood Blossom Queen gets crowned in five days, and I will not have my name associated with a bunch of peekers and wobblers."

Sadie gave her friend a quick hug, jerking her head toward the goings-on behind them. "Processional practice?"

"What else?"

"Got started on it kind of late, didn't you?"

Mary Tate blew a tuft of pale blond hair off her damp forehead with a puff from her cotton-candy-colored lips. "Bunch of the girls got the idea they didn't need to practice walking this year."

"What changed their minds?"

Mary Tate folded her arms and leaned back against the door-frame, smirking. "The shoes arrived."

"Don't even mention them." Sadie rolled her eyes. "I still have nightmares about those vile things."

The shoes—pointed-toe satin pumps that had gone out of style the same time as pillbox hats and bouffant hairdos—came ready to dye the exact color of each girl's frothy pastel dress. They had 3¼ inch heels, because anything less would look downright dowdy, and anything higher…well, as Mrs. Cummins, the high school principal put it, "High heels and hoop skirts, can you imagine anything more common than that? We're feting our girls here, not throwing some Hollywood version of a trashy yee-haw Dixie teenage wedding!"

Waynetta Cummins was Wileyville's equivalent of Miss Manners. When she decreed something "too tacky to abide," you could pretty much count that that dog didn't hunt in any event over which she held sway around town. There existed, of course, one glaring exception to that rule.

"You'll never believe this, but my daddy wants to walk with your troop in the Memorial Day parade."

"Okay."

Sadie blinked. "Easy as that?"

"Sure? Why not?"

There was that question again. "You aren't mortified at the prospect of crazy Moonie Shelnutt walking along with your group?"

"Naw, I'll just dress him up as something vaguely military and let him loose. Maybe I can round up a costume for Uncle Sam or General Lee. Or…if all else fails…Colonel Sanders." She laughed. "The kids will love it."

"Of course they will. All kids love Daddy. I think they recognize him as one of their own kind."

"You're too hard on the old man, sugar. Too hard on your sisters as well, but then why would you treat them any different than you do yourself?"

"Ha! The last thing I am is hard on myself. In fact, if anything, I totally overindulge my moods and bad habits, and you know it." Sadie tugged at the side of her dress in hopes of making her figure look a little less like a saggy old sack of potatoes. "But at least I finally broke that hypercritical cycle with my own kids."

"Sweetie, how many times do I have to point out that you can't call what you have going on a cycle? You are not repeating the mistakes of parents. You couldn't if you wanted to."

Sadie gazed down the tree-lined street in the welcoming town where her father had raised her in the best way he knew how. The place she had also chosen to bring up her children to the best of her own ability.

"I'd describe this whole hard-on-yourself-versus-not-so-hard-on-your-kids deal more as a pendulum." Mary Tate let her arm dangle limp from her raised elbow, then set it swaying in illustration. "And sending it swinging as far as possible in the opposite direction from your natural inclinations does not amount to the same thing as dealing with the problem."

Mary Tate had sung a variation on that tune so many times these last few months that Sadie had no problem jumping right in with the well-worn refrain. "Yes, yes. Olivia's seventeen. I don't have a lot of time left to make sure that she's prepared for the world beyond Wileyville. The clock is ticking, and so on and so on and so on."

"The clock *is* ticking, Sadie, ticktock, ticktock. But you don't seem the least bit inclined to hear it or to take a hard look at what's going on around you." Mary Tate paused and stared pointedly at a shiny red car with a white top that pulled up in front of the pharmacy.

Sadie glanced over her shoulder just long enough to see the poised and polished regional sales representative for a line of cosmetics Ed carried in the store.

"Ticktock, ticktock." Stepping out to the side for a better vantage point, Mary Tate watched the sales rep's clipped stride take her into the front of the building. When she turned to Sadie again, her eyes shone with concern, her usual smile set into a grim line. "Honey, listen to me, I know you feel bad right now, but you can't go on letting the world pass you by."

"Me? I thought the topic for today's sermon was Olivia."

Her friend shut her eyes and let out a long, weary breath. "Okay, you want to talk Olivia? Fine. How's this? You can't keep letting Olivia hold your entire household hostage to her whims."

"She doesn't hold the household hostage." *Just me.* Sadie didn't have the nerve to face her friend's response to that kind of admission. So she focused her attention on the girls at practice through the large window and pretended to check out her reflection by ruffling her raggedy hairdo. "Olivia is a good kid who's at that awkward age when she thinks she's grown up and no one else does. She just runs hot and cold, that's all."

"She runs white-hot hissy fits and cold shoulders to manipulate you into letting her have her way."

"The getting-your-own-way gene is strong in that girl, I have to admit."

"She's taking advantage, Sadie. And you let her do it because you're scared to death that if you dare to yank her in line, she might not like you very much."

Despite the caring touch of a hand on her arm, Sadie stiffened.

That did not dissuade Mary Tate, who only inched closer and lowered her voice to a raw, emotion-filled whisper. "And I know you, honey. If you thought anyone that you loved with all of your heart had stopped liking you, it would break your world in two."

Tears sprang to Sadie's eyes. She couldn't help it. Since she'd lost the baby, she had cried too easily…and much, much too often.

"And right now you think your world is too fragile to take that kind of chance." Mary Tate reached over and gave her a sideways hug. "But I'm telling you, for your daughter's sake, you *ought* to risk it. She might not like you, but trust her enough to know she won't stop loving you. Never, ever."

Glib advice coming from the childless-by-choice contingent. Sadie thought it, but she didn't even come close to voicing it. She loved this woman she'd befriended on the first day of junior-high gym class when Sadie couldn't even make it around the track without Mary Tate's encouragement and support. She would never say a thing to hurt her. Besides, Mary Tate had a valid point, and if Sadie weren't such a dunderheaded fool, she'd admit it right now, right here, right out loud.

Instead, she folded her arms and sniffled, her chin high. "That all? You don't want to tell me about how to do things differently with Ryan while you're at it?"

"No, but if I were to say anything, it might contain a few choice words about Ed treating you more and more like a loyal workhorse and less and less like a loving helpmate. And I might ask how you hope to grow your son up into the kind of husband and father his future wife deserves with that as an example."

"Ed doesn't treat me like a workhorse." Though she didn't suppose she'd call herself his helpmate, either. "That's just his way. After all, he's only a—"

"I know. I know." She shook her head. "A Yankee."

"I was going to say he's only a *man*."

"Oh, yeah. One of *those*, too." She rolled her big blue eyes. "You're preaching to the choir on that one, sister."

Sadie laughed. "Besides, Ed's no more a Yankee than I am a bona fide southern belle."

"Yeah, sure, I know. Not every woman born south of the Mason-Dixon is a belle." She was repeating the admonition Mrs. Cummins used as the launching point for her infamous "God may separate the wheat from the chaff, but it's manners that set the ladies apart from the riffraff" speech.

"Mrs. McCrackin?" a girl called above the clack of heels on the hardwood floors inside. "The music stopped. Should we keep walking in circles?"

Mary Tate shut her eyes and answered, "Why don't you just keep walking?"

"What do we do for music?"

"Hum!"

Mary Tate paused to collect her thoughts. "No, we are not all born belles." Mary Tate peered, squinty-eyed, over her shoulder at the young ladies tottering around her studio with all the grace of geese dancing on sawed-off stilts. "In fact, some of us are downright ding-a-lings."

Whether she intended that jab at herself for taking on this project year after year, or the girls for refusing to concentrate and get it right, or even Mrs. Cummins for her steadfast embrace of the most awful shoes in existence, Sadie didn't know.

"Ding-dong belles," Mary Tate singsonged under her breath. Her head shaking, she turned to Sadie and shrugged. "Well, guess I'd better get back to *chime* school. So where are you off to this fine afternoon?"

"No place special. Just thought I'd pop in and surprise Ed."

"Hold on a minute there." Her friend banged the heel of her hand against her temple, her face scrunched up on one side. "Something's wrong. I thought I just heard you use 'Ed' and 'surprise' in the same sentence."

"Oh, ha-ha." Sadie interrupted her phony laugh with an even more phony yawn.

When Ed first moved to Wileyville from Michigan to take over the town pharmacy, he'd told everyone he had come South to thaw out. Nearly a quarter of a century later, and despite the fact that in his work he had ministered to them in every conceivable situation known to man and medicine, a lot of folks around town would tell you they still found the man's demeanor a bit…glacial.

But they didn't know him the way Sadie did. They didn't know the warm and funny, private man who had courted her all those years ago and cared for her all these years since. Their marriage had set tongues wagging all over Wileyville. After all, she had hardly been twenty years old, and Ed more than a decade older, a businessman set in his ways and *not from around here.*

"Joke all you want," Sadie said. "I realize how many people see my husband as not much more than the balding head lowered over their prescriptions at the back of the drugstore. But *I* know that when he lifts his head and looks up, he still only has eyes for me."

"Now, that's the kind of confidence I like to hear. Go on in there and make him look up." The shove in the right direction Mary Tate started to give Sadie suddenly turned into a grab at her arm and backward tug. "But let's not startle the life out of him when he does. Wait here a sec."

"What? Why?"

Her companion had already darted inside. "Not bad, girls, not bad. Now each of you grab a chair and practice taking your seats in unison. Remember, no plunking down like you have rocks in your pockets. Lower yourself to the edge of the seat and *perch!*"

Chair legs scraped over the floorboards.

Quarrelsome voices rose, then just as quickly fell.

Mary Tate appeared from the back room dragging behind her a canvas tote on wheels. It thumped and bumped along over the threshold and onto the sidewalk.

Sadie stared at it. "You plan on moving in with me, the better to do a total makeover?"

"This? This is just the bare necessities." The heavy brass zipper ripped open, and Mary Tate began to rummage around inside. "If I ever did put my mind to doing a makeover on you, sweetie, you'd have to clear the driveway and set up a delivery ramp, because I'd haul stuff in by the truckload."

"Truckload? Do I really need that much?" Did she have to ask? Anyone paying the least bit of attention could have seen how she had let her appearance slide. And at thirty-nine, she'd already been on a downward slope to begin with.

She made a quick survey of the woman looking back at her in the window. Hair—blah. Complexion—blah. Outfit, attitude, overall physical condition—blah, blah, blob.

"Would you look at me?" She leaned forward and pulled her cheeks back with both hands, hoping that might help her look a little less like a basset hound with a sleep disorder. "No wonder when Mayor Furst needed to fill a slot working among the living impaired, he thought of me."

"Start the music again, girls, and walk it through from the beginning. I may be a minute," Mary Tate bellowed. Then she turned and cast a worried gaze at her friend. "Sadie, what in the world are you talking about?"

"The mayor offered me a job this morning—running the cemetery."

"A new job!" She handed Sadie a hairbrush and went to work applying blush in quick decisive strokes. "When do you start?"

Sadie tamed the worst of her dull tangle of curls down and tossed the brush back into the case. "I don't."

The plastic blush case snapped shut. Mary Tate frowned. *"Why not?"*

She wished people would quit asking her that. "Because…well, because…did you not hear what I said? He wants me to run the *cemetery*."

"I heard. Do this." She opened her mouth and looked up.

Sadie complied.

It was a true validation of the depths of their friendship that Sadie willingly stood right out there in public, giving free rein over her face to a woman who did her own makeup in such a way that she seemed always in a state of perpetually flushed surprise.

"Sadie, it seems to me that God has seen fit to bonk you on the noggin with this blessing, and you don't even have the good sense to embrace it."

"Bonk me on the noggin?"

"That's what I said."

"Some hear a still, small voice. Others see a heavenly host of angels. Me, I take a blow to the head? Though, come to think of it, that does sound like the kind of blessing I'd have bestowed on me."

"That's because when the Lord has to deal with the chronically mule-headed, even He sometimes has to do something to get their attention."

"But the cemetery, Mary Tate?"

"Yes, the cemetery, Sadie." She stuck her tongue out from the side of her mouth and doggedly whisked the mascara wand repeatedly over Sadie's skimpy lashes. "I think it's the perfect job for you."

"*Why?*" Sadie blinked and backed away before her eyes got caked shut with the inky stuff. "Because I'm unfit to work among the living?"

"Because you've experienced your share of grief and loss. Stand still, will you?" Mary Tate withdrew three shades of lipstick, surveyed them, then handed Sadie an elegant black-and-gold tube. "When people in pain come to you, whatever you say or do will carry real meaning. You could help a lot of people in that kind of job, Sadie."

How? she had wanted to cry out. How could she help other people when she hadn't even been able to help herself?

"No. No, I couldn't." She applied the neutral-color cream over her dry lips, pressed them together, then stood back and checked her slightly improved reflection again. "Could I?"

"Yes. You could and you should."

Sadie sighed. "If I really believed that…"

"Then what? What would you do, Sadie, if you let yourself dare to believe in your own potential?"

Her pulse quickened. She couldn't even imagine the possibilities.

Once upon a time her younger self might have come up with a staggeringly fabulous list of dreams and goals and the sacred secret hopes of her heart's fondest desires. But she wasn't young anymore. Hadn't the doctor used those very words when she begged him to give her some reason why she had lost her baby?

She shook her head. "I'm not a kid anymore, and this is not taking laps around the school track, Mary Tate. No matter how much you try to build me up into thinking I have it in me, I'm not taking the job."

"Why not?"

"Why would I?"

"Aside from providing comfort—for yourself and others—it would provide you with a more independent lifestyle."

She folded her arms. "That's what they say about adult diapers, but I'm not rushing out to get me some of those just yet, either."

"A job would make you feel useful again."

"My family finds me quite useful, thank you very much."

"Used and useful are two very different things."

Sadie answered with a warning glare.

"If nothing else, taking that job would get you out of the house."

"In case you hadn't noticed, I'm out of the house already."

"Okay, okay then. How about feeling productive? A sense of accomplishment? How about feeling appreciated?"

"My family a...uh...um... I *am* out of the house."

"Terrific. That's a start. Now all you have to do is build on it."

A start. Just what Daddy said she needed. Just what got her heading over here from the VFW Hall to begin with—to see if she could start something.

"Go inside the drugstore and tell that husband of yours you're taking that job."

That wasn't the something she had in mind.

"If that doesn't make Ed lift that balding head up from filling prescriptions and look at you—really, really look at you—I don't know what will."

Make Ed really look at her? Wasn't that what she'd been longing for?

"You're right! Why didn't I think of that?" Sadie gave her friend the briefest of hugs and hurried off, calling, "Mary Tate, you're brilliant!"

"Hear that, girls?" Her friend's voice trailed out behind her as she stepped-halt-stepped back to work. "I'm brilliant. If y'all aspire to the same, I suggest you learn to glide-pause-glide like the regal maidens you're supposed to be—and for land's sake, quit peeking!"

Brilliant. She'd begun the day with her only plan to sit in the dark and hide from the world, and now she had a whole new objective. She'd tell Ed she was taking the job.

Not that she *wanted* the job. But to tell Ed about it—what a jolt that would provide.

The kind of jolt that could set a man thinking about all he had taken for granted. That could make him look at his wife with new eyes, with new gratitude for all she had done for him. It just might work.

❧ Chapter Four ❧

The old tin bell jangled when she pushed open the glass-and-wood front door with its gold scroll letters proclaiming: Downtown Drug. With a deep breath and a lighter heart than she'd had in quite a while, Sadie stepped into the cool quiet of Ed's domain.

"Mrs. P."

"No time to talk." She breezed past the newly hired employee, trying not to dwell on the look of total shock on his freckled face. "Is Mr. Pickett in the back?"

"Mr. Pickett?" The boy's voice crackled. "He's not... Mr. Pickett went to lunch."

She stopped in her tracks. "Lunch?"

Ed Pickett never left the store in the middle of the day. Not to attend the children's school functions. Not to check on her when she had the flu or worse. Not even to go to the doctor when he cut his hand and needed stitches. That day he'd wrapped up his wound, waited until five and then showed up at the clinic blustering to his brother-in-law to take care of it quick so he could get back in time to close out the cash register.

Sadie glanced around at the tidy rows of over-the-counter remedies, foot-care products and hair dyes. No sign of forced entry. No strange blast marks or eerie lights that the cable-TV shows described as characteristic of alien invasion. It would have to be something that wild and unbelievable to pry her husband from the store at this time of day.

"Are you sure he *went* to lunch? Because I've been standing outside the Academy for the last fifteen minutes." She jerked her thumb toward the right side of the pie-slice-shape building. "Seems I'd have seen him leave, just like I saw Carmen Gomez come in."

"Carmen?"

"Yes. Surely you know who I'm talking about, the cosmetics sales rep? I saw her come in not ten minutes ago. Didn't you see her?"

"Oh. *Carmen.*" He laughed unconvincingly. "I—I forgot, she's in the stockroom setting up for a, uh, product demo."

"I see." Since when did they start doing product demos in the storage room? Maybe the same time Ed took actual, leave-the-pharmacy-floor lunch breaks. "And Mr. Pickett is…?"

"On lunch break?"

"On lunch break at…?"

"On lunch break at…" The kid's lips moved but he hardly made a sound. His gaze roamed the ceiling like someone struggling to mentally piece together the jackpot puzzle on a game show. "Oh! Mr. Pickett is on lunch break…at this very moment."

The kid grinned.

A knot rose in Sadie's chest. She thought of going to check with Carmen to see if she had a more satisfying answer, then hesitated.

What would charging in on poor Carmen, asking questions about Ed's whereabouts, do? Make Sadie look like a jealous middle-aged shrew, that's what.

She trusted her husband. He had never given her reason to think he'd so much as bent his wedding vows, much less broken them.

Ed loved Sadie.

He honored her.

And if he knew what was good for him, he also obeyed her.

Not that she ever ordered him around, of course. Just that Ed was the kind of man who implicitly understood the meaning of the old phrase *If Mama ain't happy, ain't nobody happy.*

Not that Sadie could qualify as happy, but that had nothing to do with anything she could lay at Ed's feet. Her gripe with him wasn't that he'd hurt or betrayed or even so much as toyed with cheating on her. It was that her husband hadn't seemed to even notice whether she was happy or sad or even in the room in such a long while.

Inattentiveness, yes. But capable of infidelity? Not Ed.

"I can tell Mr. Pickett you stopped by, and when he has the time maybe he can just reach you at home," the young clerk offered, sweeping his arm out to shepherd Sadie toward the door. "You know—that you'll just be hanging around until you hear from him."

Sadie blinked and cocked her head. "You make me sound like a loyal spaniel waiting for my master's call."

"No, ma'am. I wouldn't call you a dog, not by no means."

"Well, thank you for that." She smiled, sighed, then let her gaze wander to the street beyond the door. Guess she had no choice but to go home and resume her vigil in the chair until somebody needed something else from her. "When Mr. Pickett returns, tell him—"

"Don't you dare do that, Ed. I've finally got you just where

I want you." Carmen's lilting Georgia accent coming from behind the closed stockroom door rang through the quiet storefront like a hammer shattering glass.

"Was that Carmen talking to Ed? *My* Ed?" Sadie asked it aloud but did not intend it as an actual question.

"Nothing is going on, Mrs. P., I promise." The clerk's heavy footsteps thundered along behind Sadie as they both went flying toward the storeroom.

Or was that relentless pounding the sound of her heart?

Ed and Carmen.

How could he?

How could she?

How could Sadie not have seen it coming, and how would she ever cope with the aftermath of this ugly turn of events? Hadn't she already suffered enough? How could God heap more on her now just when—

Sadie flung open the door.

Carmen jumped as if she'd taken an electrical charge.

Ed sat up. "Sadie!"

"Ed?"

He stood up, yanking the yellow terry-cloth towel from around his neck as he did. "I didn't realize you were... I just let Carmen... I hope you didn't think..."

Plip.

Slimy purple gel dripped from the tip of his nose to splat on his shoe.

Sadie didn't know whether to laugh or cry. "A facial, Ed?"

Ed wiped his chin with the big towel now draped around his neck. "I can explain."

"You can explain?" Sadie plunked her hands on her hips. The rush of sweet relief she should have felt in finding nothing more untoward than personal grooming going on behind the closed door did not come.

Sadie was mad.

She had every right to be mad.

And she wanted Ed to know about it.

"Letting another woman give you a facial? This from a man who once spent an entire beach vacation without ever once getting into the water because he had pronounced my pink-bottled depilatory 'too girlie' to use—" she should have stopped there but she had to take it all the way, concluding with her eyes narrowed "—on his back hair!"

Carmen showed the good form to stifle her laugh at that. "Honestly, Sadie, I've asked him to let me show him this line of men's products for a year, and now the company is having this contest—an all-expenses-paid trip to Cancún—for the rep who gets the most new accounts this quarter. But Ed said—"

"I said I knew the men in Wileyville, and they wouldn't see the good of slapping a bunch of goo on their faces to look nice for the hogs." He swiped away the last of the facial gel and grinned.

Carmen's eyes glittered and when she smiled, not a single line formed in her young, soft brown skin. "So I told him I could change his mind about that if he'd just give me an hour of his undivided attention…."

"An hour? An hour of your undivided attention, Ed?" That newest bit of information hit Sadie like a sucker punch.

"Just a little bit of time, Sadie, that's all."

"A little bit of time out of the middle of the day. An *hour* for my husband to laugh with and joke with and discuss his work with and…and…and give his attention to—and don't take this wrong, Carmen, I think the world of you—a woman who sees him mainly as a means of hitting her sales quota and winning a quarterly contest. While I sit at home day after day literally pining my heart out for someone to notice me, someone to talk to me."

Ed hung his head.

Carmen looked at her shoes.

Only the sound of brakes squealing out in the street broke the silence.

Sadie turned to storm out.

"This is ridiculous." Ed threw the towel to the ground. "Sadie, wait!"

Wait? She stopped in her tracks and jerked her head up. Wait for what? Hadn't she waited long enough?

In fact that's *all* she had done. As the years went by, Sadie had become nothing more than a lady-in-waiting.

Waiting on her teenage children to stop looking at her as if they thought she had the brain capacity of a half-stuffed sock monkey. For them to, as it says in Proverbs "rise up and call her blessed."

Waiting for the day when the man she'd married would finally decide he'd worked enough, come home early, sweep her into his arms and tell her how much he loved and appreciated her.

Waiting for things to settle down emotionally and perk up romantically, to work out financially, and for her tummy, hips and thighs to finally, finally, fit into the fabulous, electric-blue size 8 summer dress she'd splurged on more than two years ago.

Sadie was waiting, basically, for her "real" life to begin.

She had not deluded herself. She had expected to be in for a long wait.

But then she had *been* waiting most of her life.

Waiting for her wayward mother to one day come walking back through the door.

Waiting for her two sisters to stop acting like wounded, bickering children and be a real family.

Waiting for her daddy…

Daddy. After all these years, Sadie was still waiting for her daddy to grow up.

Well, maybe she had waited long enough. Maybe it was time, at last, to take action, to start something, as she'd been advised.

Sadie drew a deep breath and turned on her heel. "Ed, I came here to tell you something. Mayor Furst has offered me a job, and I—"

The bell dangling from the front door clanged to cut her off.

"Sadie! Ed! Y'all better get outside quick!" Panic edged Mary Tate's voice, and then she was gone.

"Come on." Ed had his arm around Sadie in a heartbeat, guiding her toward the door.

Carmen and the new clerk didn't linger behind, either.

The old floorboards shook with the combined weight of the four of them practically running for the front door.

Ed reached the door first and pushed ahead of Sadie, probably thinking to blunt the impact of whatever Mary Tate had beckoned them out to see. "What's wrong? Are Ryan and Olivia okay?"

"It's not the kids." Mary Tate motioned to Sadie that it was safe to come on out to the sidewalk. Then she pointed to a spot halfway down the block. "It's the big child."

"Martha Tatum Fitts McCrackin!" Moonie climbed from the front seat to the back of his prized vintage yellow boat of a convertible Cadillac, waving like a castaway sailor signaling a rescue ship. He took a seat at the back, in a position not unlike "the girls with high hair" who rode in the holiday parades, and pointed to the crumpled fender. "Looks like I had a bit of trouble at the drive-thru bank."

The blonde cupped her hand to her mouth and hollered back the perfect setup for the ornery old man who had just promised Sadie he'd behave for a good three or four days. "That branch doesn't have a drive-thru, Moonie."

"Does now," Ed muttered seconds before her daddy gave the same reply.

By then two police cars had arrived, and the officers practically scrambled all over one another trying to do the honors of giving Moonie both a stern talking-to and a hefty traffic ticket.

Meanwhile, the president of the bank had come outside with a handful of customers trailing on his heels. The bank staff stopped short of the sidewalk, but each did manage to find a spot near the plate-glass windows to feign working while they watched their boss make wild gestures and rap his knuckles on the hood of Moonie's car.

The ruddy-faced old man finally hopped out amid it all, tipped his hat and began handing out his business cards, probably with a caveat that they'd better spell his name right when they reported the incident in the paper.

Sadie leaned her head back on her husband's chest, letting the vibration of his gentle laughter ease away all the emotions she'd struggled to cope with a moment earlier.

Ed leaned down and brushed his lips over her cheek. "Forgive me?"

She dug her elbow into his side. "No."

"Yes, you do." He buried his nose in her hair and inhaled slowly.

"Things have to change, Ed," she whispered.

"I know. For starters, sounds like you're going to have a new job."

"No, for starters, I'm going to have to meet with my sisters and decide once and for all what we are going to do about Daddy."

"And then you're going to have a new job?"

"Who knows? If I can get my daddy straightened out, then I might just have myself a whole new life!"

"If you wait until you get Moonie straightened out, darling, you may be too old to start a new life."

He'd intended it as a joke, she knew, but that didn't make it sit any easier with her. Maybe she had already been waiting too long. Maybe she'd never have the kind of life she dreamed of. Maybe God had other plans for her.

And all that she could do about that at the moment was…to wait and see. *Wait and see.*

✎ Chapter Five ✎

"Are y'all praying for me out there?"

From her seat on the floor, Sadie easily laid her head back against the door and answered the voice behind it. "You know we are."

Of course, she was praying for her sister. What Sadie could not do for herself she could easily do for others, especially those she loved as much as she loved Hannah.

"Well, cut it out, will you?"

The oldest of the sisters, April, looked up from her perch on the nearby window seat. "Why?"

"Because it's making me nervous," came the muffled voice from behind the pristine white door. "I can't accomplish my goal in here knowing that you two are on the other side of the door praying over the outcome."

The look on April's face moved from stunned indignity to sudden and delighted enlightenment. She burst out laughing.

Sadie clenched her teeth but could not contain her own laughter. She'd tried to hold back but how could she? The image of Hannah—prissy, "conniption fit waiting to happen" Hannah, she of the "manicured nails and trips to Atlanta to buy only the best of the best for her wardrobe" Hannah—sitting in her cavernous bathroom with her two fretting sisters outside, backs to the door in fervent prayer while she tried to do what she must to take an at-home pregnancy test cracked her up.

"You two cackling like a couple of hens is not helping, either!" The bathroom tile amplified Hannah's complaint.

And it only made them laugh harder.

"Y'all…*please*," Hannah nagged.

"Okay, okay." April stood and held her hand out to help Sadie up. "We'll take it into the kitchen."

"I'd very much appreciate it if you would." Abruptness barbed Hannah's courteous words.

So much so that Sadie couldn't help getting in a jab of her own as they headed out into the hallway. "Call us when you've…had a breakthrough."

More girlish giggling bubbled up from the two women old enough to be above that kind of silliness.

"Just go and wait in the kitchen for a while," Hannah said from behind the door.

"Mind if I brew some herbal tea?" April asked, her soft brown braid bouncing against her back as she hurried ahead of Sadie.

"Tea, coffee, get that roasting hen out of the fridge and stuff or glaze or presoak or whatever you're supposed to do to one of those things, if you have the inclination. Just leave me be for a while." The hinges on the door between the master bedroom and bath whined and Hannah's next order came out loud and clear. "No matter what the results are, I want a minute alone and then a minute to call Payt and tell him the news. I want him to be the first to know."

"Yes, ma'am," April and Sadie called out together as they headed down the stairs.

April's sandals hit the hardwood floor of the foyer first. She paused there only long enough to grab her backpack and half turn to ask Sadie, "Was Ed the first to know about your babies?"

"Was he?" Sadie held on to the faux antique finial at the bottom of the handrail and cocked her head. "I don't remember. I do know it didn't come as much of a surprise when I told him."

"Of course not." April chuckled and headed off for the gleaming black-and-white kitchen.

"Of course not? Why do you say that?" Sadie hurried to catch up.

"Well, you have to admit, Sadie, as far as your life has been concerned, things have pretty much run along the tried-and-true steady course." She clunked the hunter-green backpack onto the glossy imitation-marble countertop and began opening drawers and taking out spoons and napkins.

"Tried-and-true?" Sadie sat on one of the mismatched kitchen stools Hannah had gotten from the church thrift shop and so proudly painted, following instructions from a magazine. "What do you mean by that?"

"You know, college, marriage, babies." She filled the teakettle with water. "I'll never forget how you told me after the Christmas Eve candlelight service that you and Ed had decided to start a family. Olivia arrived in time for Advent the next year."

"You make me sound so predictable."

"No." She shut the water off and set the kettle on the stove, flipping on the heat then stepping back to make sure that everything met her standards. "I wouldn't call it predictable. More that when you set your mind to something, Sadie, it happens."

Sadie rested her cheek in her hand. "I think you're describing yourself. You're the planner. The planter. The one who has seen her goals and aspirations take shape. I'm the one who rushes headlong here and there and lets other people make my mind up for me, remember?"

"I remember a lot of things, Sadie. In fact, sometimes I wonder if I remember too much, or if…" She drummed her fingertips over the protected handle of the teapot then straightened her shoulders and turned to face Sadie. "Well, the point is, you're the one who has so much to show for her life. I have a business and, of course, our family, but you're the one who's got it all together."

The praise rang hollow in Sadie's ears. And on top of the longing in her sister's tone, it almost broke Sadie's heart. If she were made of sterner stuff and if her sister weren't the stoic type, she might have gone to April then, put her arm around her and…she had no idea what.

So she sighed and shook her head and bent down the corner of the napkin in front of her. "Me? I don't have anything together that didn't already come prepackaged. Having it all, that's Hannah's bailiwick. She's the organizer. Her Imperial Highness delegating, always delegating."

"Not anymore." April pulled a dented cardboard box from her bag and took out two tea bags that smelled of chamomile and peppermint. "She isn't going to delegate someone to have this baby for her. Though—"

Footsteps overhead cut her off.

They both waited and listened.

More footsteps. Then quiet.

Sadie curled her fingers into tight fists. "This is killing me."

In a heartbeat, April's hand fitted over Sadie's. "I wondered about that. Are you…are you okay with all this?"

"Not really." She leaned back and tilted her head up to look at the ceiling in the approximate spot where the results might even now be being revealed. "You know me. If

I had my way, I'd have my ear pressed up against that door listening."

"No, I mean are you okay with…with the whole baby thing?"

"Oh." The baby thing. She cleared her throat, tried to make herself revisit any and all of her feelings on the matter but, finding that impossible, simply lifted her shoulders and said, "Yes."

"Do you want to expound on that?"

"No." Okay with it or not, Sadie would not risk spoiling Hannah's moment by letting her own too-long-unresolved grief intrude.

"You want to talk about something else?"

"Please."

"All-righty-then, tell me about this new job."

Sadie shut her eyes, pressed the heel of her hand to her forehead and groaned.

"What?"

"What made me even consider running the cemetery?"

"The *park* and cemetery." An important distinction to someone like April.

"You mean what's left of the park. Have you checked it out lately? They've let city storage all but take over. Old trees, equipment, piles of mulch, bent-up old street signs, they're everywhere."

April reached up into a cupboard and pulled down two oversize ceramic mugs. She set them down decisively and smiled. "Maybe that's why you've been placed in this position, to stop the takeover and restore the park to the way it looked when we played there as kids."

"April, we never played there as kids."

"Didn't we?" She tipped her head to the right, her forehead creased and her eyes moving as though speed-reading the story of their childhood. "Seems I remember a park with red-and-yellow horses on springs?"

Sadie shook her head. "Slide and swings. All we've ever had here."

"No monkey bars? No wooden teeter-totters?"

"Nope."

April hooked her finger in the neck of her soft, baggy T-shirt and ducked her head. "You're sure?"

"There are pictures all around the superintendent's office of the land as it appeared in every decade. No springy horses. Not a single teeter or totter."

"But I remember those teeter-totters and how happy I was when you were born, because I thought I'd finally have someone to sit on the other side, and Mama said—" She gasped the faintest little gasp possible then covered her mouth, her eyes wide.

"Mama?" The very word took Sadie's breath away.

Sadie had so few recollections of their mother. A stolen moment sitting in her lap, a summer day in the yard of a house she had only seen in her mind's eye. In truth, over time she had begun to doubt the validity of those images. Were they memories or dreams or something in between?

Daddy refused to talk about it. He didn't want to dwell on the past, he said. No good could come of it.

And April, who had been seven when their mother left, had never defied him in that. She kept whatever she recalled locked tightly away. But with this little slip, perhaps a door had opened, and if Sadie prodded, gently, maybe she could learn something about the woman she had never known and yet always missed.

"And Mama said…?" she prompted her sister.

April pressed her lips together, her chest rising and falling with every shallow breath. Her cheeks flushed with a ruddy glow in marked contrast to the rest of her fair, freckled complexion.

"April?"

April opened her mouth.

The teakettle cried out with a blast of steam.

Both sisters nearly jumped out of their skin.

Then April spun around to lift it from the heat.

She hunched her shoulders protectively, and Sadie knew there would be no talk of Mama and the past today.

When her sister turned around again, a practiced calm masked her features. "No. It couldn't have been the park here in Wileyville, then could it?"

"April…"

Her sister's gaze lifted and met Sadie's for only a moment. Pain, then confusion, then sober resolve took over again.

She tipped the kettle up and the water cascaded and swirled into the mug. "Well, whatever reason this job came to you, I, for one, think it's… Hmm, how would I describe it?"

"Creepy?" Sadie suggested, dipping the tea bag into the steaming liquid in front of her.

"Inspired."

"By madness?"

"No."

"Well the more I think about it, the crazier it sounds to me."

"What does Ed say? What about the kids?"

"Ed and the kids? They don't say much of anything, least not to me."

"Something wrong at home, Sadie?"

Something was wrong at *heart*. But how did you express that to a sister with whom you had never truly opened up? It was probably too late for that kind of relationship now.

"Everything at home is, you know, the way it always is."

"Then what's keeping you from that new job? What are you afraid of, Sadie?"

When did she sprout a sign proclaiming: *Please feel free to butt into my life?*

"Afraid?"

"You worried about what people will think if you take that job? Or that you might actually excel at something besides the things you decided ages ago should be your life's work?"

"You mean my marriage and family?" She hit the words a little too hard, realizing too late it smacked of tossing in April's face the very things she had not cultivated in her own life. She did not apologize, though, because that might make things worse. "My 'life's work,' as you put it, seems to me very much a work still in progress. I'm not sure I'm ready to tackle more, especially now in the midst of the high drama of taking away Daddy's Caddie."

"When does it get out of the shop?"

"We have another week's grace before we have to do the dirty deed."

"He won't surrender those keys without a fight."

"Three of us and one of him," Sadie reminded her, tapping her spoon against the edge of her cup.

"We may have to call in reinforcements."

"Or get sneaky. You ever tried your hand at firing tranquilizer blow darts through a bamboo stick? Digging tiger pits? No-holds-barred Ninja fighting?" She curled her fingers and moved her arms in first slow then rapid circles, as if she might strike at any moment.

April withdrew her own spoon from her mug dripping tea on Hannah's tabletop. "You're saying we can get those keys if we use our heads."

Sadie ducked then winked. "And maybe our teeth and feet."

Quicker than a skinny minute, April grabbed a sponge and wiped up the almost imperceptible mess she had made. "We could sell tickets and raise enough to fund Daddy's retirement."

"What about Daddy?" Hannah walked into her own kitchen the way a debutante might walk in to a ballroom, perfectly groomed, totally confident and wavering on the very verge of getting sick and blowing the whole effect.

"Forget about Daddy." Sadie forced more buoyancy into her tone than she meant to, but somehow couldn't seem to deflate it as she added, "What about the mommy?"

"I refuse to answer on the grounds that Payt was with a patient and I haven't spoken to him yet." Hannah's smile trembled. Tears brimmed just slightly above her lashes.

She didn't have to say more.

"Oh, Hannah." Sadie and April both went to her, folding her into their arms.

Sadie sniffled. She had prepared to hear only good news. She hadn't even imagined another outcome. But suddenly this turn of events reopened her own pain, the very real pain of wanting a child with all her heart, and her own body unable to provide.

A sob caught in the back of her throat. She could not give in to her traitorous emotions now. Hannah needed her. She had to stay strong.

Hannah stepped away from them.

"You can try again," April murmured.

Sadie stiffened.

"It's too soon to worry anyway." Flicking her long brown braid over her shoulder, the oldest of the sisters rubbed the youngest's back. "It'll happen in God's time. You've only been trying for four months."

"Six months," Sadie corrected. It had stuck in her mind because when Hannah first talked openly about getting pregnant, elated Sadie had prayed they might have their babies within the same year. Shortly after that she had miscarried. "It's been six months."

"A year and six months," Hannah whispered, her gaze lowered to her entwined fingers.

"What?"

In one brief but deep breath, Hannah regained her compo-sure, glanced at the steaming mugs of tea then headed for the refrigerator. "Technically, I suppose you could say that for the first year it was less a case of thinking in clinical terms about cycles and conception and more a case of leaving it in God's hands."

"Not a bad place to be." April took a sip of tea. "In God's hands."

"Yeah, I know." She withdrew a cut-glass pitcher of iced tea and a delicate plate of cut fruit, took a side step to gather a tall fluted tumbler then set them all on the kitchen counter. "And in the end, for all our calculations and calendar counting, that's where it all will always rest—with the Lord. But still…"

"You have your concerns," April said.

"Yes, I do. We waited for so long now, trying to get Payt through med school and his internship, holding out for just the right time to start our family. Now every time I see that negative on the pregnancy test strip, I can't help wondering if we waited too long."

"Thirty-five's not that old," said the woman who felt ancient at thirty-nine. "Not these days."

"I hope not. Payt wants so badly to have children. And he *should* become a father, he'd make such a terrific one."

Payton Bartlett was what well-brought-up people around here kindly called "a late bloomer." Drummed out of military school, washed out of the Coast Guard…and after he ran his uncle's printing business into red ink, Payton's father called him a bad seed. Probably worse if there were no ladies pres-ent.

Then, while "taking a break to find himself" young Payton had landed on a mission trip to Nicaragua, trying to impress a girl whose name he conveniently couldn't summon to mind anymore. The romance didn't last, but as is often the way things go, his lifelong love found him. Working with children in dire need awakened in Payton a drive and ability that no one had suspected he possessed. He came back from that trip with the desire to become a doctor, a pediatrician.

Old man Bartlett had amassed a fortune, but lacked foresight and forgiveness where his greatest earthly treasure, his family, was concerned. He cut Payton off, refusing to fund another impossible dream that would surely fail.

About that time Hannah entered the picture. She was working toward her degree in journalism at the time. They dated and married and later went off to his eighth-choice medical school, a small, obscure place in a western state—but that did not mean it came cheap.

So Hannah left college a few credits shy of attaining her degree and went to work anyplace she could. Payton studied. And when the time came for him to do his residency, Hannah suggested they return to Wileyville, where the Bartlett name had some cachet. With that to build on, she had hoped he'd get an offer to join a prestigious medical practice someplace in Kentucky where they'd have a lovely home and she'd have a houseful of babies.

"Yes, Payt will make a good dad." April poured tea. "And you'll be a great mom."

Hannah picked up a lemon slice and stared at it for a few poignant seconds before raising it above her glass and squeezing the juice into her drink. "I suppose."

Neither April nor Sadie seemed to have anything to say to bolster her opinion of her abilities. What could they say, after all, to reassure a sister who had lived her whole life reminded that as soon as she was born her own mother had run away?

And so, like so many times in their lives, since they could not quarrel about the situation, they remained silent. Leaving things unsaid, Sadie had decided a long time ago, helped maintain the delicate balance among them. It kept things safe. Talking meant revealing one's self, and that meant none of them could keep up the pretext that they accepted their mother's leaving as just one of those things that happens in life.

"You'll keep trying." April issued the statement like a decree from the eldest.

"Either that or—" Hannah plunked the lemon into her glass, then wiped her fingers on the cotton towel by the sink. "I haven't said anything to you two because it's not a sure thing by a long shot, but there is another way we might start a family."

"You're going to adopt!" April gave voice to what was also Sadie's best guess for her sister's plans. "Hannah, that's wonderful."

"No, not adoption, not exactly." She tucked her rich auburn hair behind her ears, not once but three times, in slow, meticulous strokes. Then she wet her lips and fixed her attention on her glass of iced tea. "Payt has a second cousin he hasn't seen since high school. The two of them spent summers together up until then, so they have a history, a bond."

The legs of Sadie's stool wobbled as she shifted her weight forward and asked, "And?"

"His wife died in an automobile accident six years ago. He was driving and suffered severe injuries, as well. He's never fully recovered, physically or emotionally."

April hugged her mug to her chest, her head bent. "That's just awful."

"It gets worse. This is where Payt and I come in. This second cousin has a child, passed around from one family member to the next and…and now it's our turn."

Sadie leaned in farther still. "A child?"

Hannah nodded. "A seven-year-old boy."

"Seven?" April didn't cluck her tongue, but she might as well have.

Hannah cast her green-eyed gaze heavenward. "And a *boy*."

"Nothing wrong with boys." Sadie sat back again at last and laughed, thinking of her own son, Ryan, at that age. "Well, nothing wrong that a little patience, love and earplugs won't help."

"But what would *I* do with one?" Hannah said.

Sadie placed her hand on Hannah's wrist. "Be his mom."

"That's the catch. Even though he can no longer care for the boy, this cousin won't give up his parental rights. I can't blame him for that, but it puts us in a tentative position at best. He wants us to become foster parents."

"Fostering a child in so much need, Hannah, I can't think of anyone better suited to do that than you and Payt." Again April spoke in such a way that it seemed just her speaking of it made everything indisputable.

"On the one hand it's ridiculous. Me? *Mom* to a seven-year-old boy?" She spread her hand over her heart, her delicately painted nails bright against her creamy skin and silk knit top. "Then I stop and think—this is my chance to be the only mother some child has ever known." Her hushed voice broke. She raised her gaze to first April's, then Sadie's. Her hand closed. She sniffled. "That really gets to me, you know?"

They both knew so well, they did not dare try to put it into words.

Hannah's perfectly plucked eyebrows crimped down. "I really hate it when things get to me."

"Oh, admit it. You're just a big softie." Sadie crinkled her nose up.

Hannah responded silently in kind.

April took another sip of hot tea before asking, "When do you have to decide?"

"We have to take some classes, and we want to be settled in our new house."

"I like *this* house." April made a show of looking around them at the sparsely furnished house in the part of town officially called Furst Heritage Hollows but that everyone jokingly referred to as Debt Valley.

"Payt and I want one someplace else. Wileyville is quaint and all, but he's not the small-town type."

"What about you?" April crossed her legs at the ankles, the thick soles of her sandals thudding quietly together. "If you're going to start a family, one way or another, don't you want to be close to us?"

"Close is one thing. Practically on top of one another in the same town?" Hannah pursed her lips in an implicit *No thank you.*

April sighed. She uncrossed her ankles and crossed them again. Then she plucked her braid from her shoulder and began flipping her fingertips through the soft frayed end.

Finally, without making eye contact with either of her sisters, she raised her chin and said, "No matter which you chose, though, that leaves the Daddy thing up to Sadie and me."

"And just why is that?" Not a single human being on earth who knew her would think Hannah wanted to be a party to doing anything that might even slightly upset her much-adored daddy. But the women in this room knew that if it came down to it, she'd ruffle every last one of the old rooster's feathers in a New York minute rather than be excluded from anything she saw as a sisterly decision. "I am just as much a part of this family as you two. I have as much to contribute as either of you."

"Don't start that whole runner-up-sister routine again, Hannah. We're talking about seriously taking care of Daddy here. It's not a contest."

Runner-up sister. Hannah loved to bandy that ridiculous title around whenever she and Sadie competed for anything, most of all when vying for their daddy's approval. In Hannah's opinion the fix was in. Sadie always won. And Hannah always felt like the runner-up, the sister named to step in should the Miss America sister be unable to fulfill her duties. Sadie hated the expression not only because it kept a hurt alive in Hannah that Sadie could not ease, but it also must have been an awful blow to April. If Sadie was always the star sister and Hannah next in line, what did that make their older half sibling? Not even in the running?

"Sadie's right," April chimed in, with a sure hand on Hannah's shoulder. "There's no contest here."

"Just a decision worthy of King Solomon himself," Sadie said. Making their father do something he did not want to do could wreak havoc on all their fragile relationships. "How do we divide up *our* Solomon's care without tearing the family in two?"

The ice rattled in Hannah's tea glass as she tipped it slightly back and forth.

April tapped her spoon against the side of her cup.

Sadie jiggled her foot and, in time to it all, asked quietly, "Who…gets…Daddy?"

"I do," Hannah said.

"But you're moving," April reminded her.

"That's not settled yet," Hannah retorted. "And in the meantime—"

April clunked the spoon down lightly on the countertop. "In the meantime you can use taking care of Daddy to keep you from having to make a decision about becoming a foster parent?"

Hannah's green eyes sparked, but she did not meet either of her sisters' gazes when she proclaimed, "April, that is a low and despicable thing to say."

"Which doesn't make it any less true," Sadie murmured.

"And I suppose you want Daddy, too?" April folded her arms. "Miss 'anything to avoid taking the job that everybody knows you were born to do'?"

"I refuse to believe I was born to run a cemetery!" Sadie evaded a real answer with enough phony huff-and-puffery to rival anything Hannah could produce. "Why shouldn't *I* take care of Daddy?"

"Because like I said, it's no contest," April spoke up. "I'm taking Daddy."

"You, April?" Hannah set her glass down hard. "Why do you think it should fall to you?"

"He's not even your—" Sadie found the sudden good sense not to finish that statement.

The only topic more off-limits between the three sisters than their mother's abandonment was April's birth father. Even if they did allow themselves to broach the subject, they wouldn't have had much to say. They had a name, David Bock, and the information that he and their mother had met in college, and when he'd found out about April's impending birth, he'd disappeared. Moonie and Mama had married when April was a toddler, and he was the only father she had ever known.

So who was Sadie to throw the past in her sister's face, when all she wanted was the same chance at being bedeviled by Daddy that she and Hannah claimed.

"I'm taking Daddy and that's that." April's eyes flashed, but when she spoke, emotion did not rule the moment. "Because he took care of me when Mom left. I know he's not really my father, not biologically, but he's still my *daddy.*"

It was the kind of argument no human being with even a hint of a heart could have stood up against.

"So it's settled. Daddy lives with me." April clapped her hands together, and smiled big as all get out at her sisters. "Which leaves my two favorite siblings free to explore the new

avenues stretching out before them and the many new blessings—"

"You mean bugaboos," Hannah corrected.

Sadie held up one finger. "I prefer brouhahas."

April folded her arms and finished with a confidence Sadie,
for one, certainly did not share, "...the many new *blessings* that
await, if they only have the courage and faith to go after them."

∽ *Chapter Six* ∽

"Hope y'all are ready for this." With both hands in oven mitts, Sadie gripped her best platter, one of the few things she owned known to have belonged to her mother.

She swallowed hard to chase away the lump rising in her throat but that did nothing to abate the gnawing conflict warring within her. Should she or should she not waltz into the dining room belting out "On Top of Spaghetti"?

She drew in a deep breath from the steaming mountain of pasta in homemade marinara sauce that had taken the better part of the day to prepare. The swinging door that divided the professionally updated kitchen from the do-it-yourself disaster of a dining room creaked softly under the weight of her leaning back against it. Who was she kidding? Taking the light road with a cornball song had no place on the menu this evening.

Tuesday evening. Every Tuesday since—well, for so long Sadie had forgotten when it actually began—had been family night. No eating at friends'. No grabbing fast food after a soccer game. No pizza ordered in so everyone could cart a slice off to eat in front of the TV or computer. No sandwiches gobbled down on the way out the door to a school play or choir practice. No slow-cooking something to dish up whenever whoever showed up, showed up.

For the Pickett family, Tuesday night had Reserved stamped all over it in big red letters. Granted, they'd gotten lax about it lately. The past nine or ten weeks, Sadie thought. Maybe…maybe six months? Okay, they hadn't had an honest-to-goodness-family-night meal for over a year.

But tonight was different.

She had reminded Ed and the kids no less than three times each that this Tuesday they would be getting back into the old habit and eating as a family again. On this last night before she started her new job, she had some things she needed to get off her chest.

"Better enjoy this. It may be the last really big family meal I fix for y'all for a while." Using her hips for leverage, she set the door swinging open.

"Because, you know, after tonight, things are going to change around here." She strode into the dining room and stared at the empty chairs she had known would greet her. "Or not."

Sadie plunked the platter down at the end of the table and surveyed her very private little kingdom bathed in warm late-afternoon light.

Overhead, the ceiling fan Ed had installed after a fourteen-hour workday, whirred, sputtered, whined, then whirred again.

Layer upon layer of half a century's worth of bad taste in wallpaper fluttered in its intermittent breeze. Fox-hunting scenes in vignettes of red, gray and green peeked out from beneath a textured tan background dotted with aqua boomerangs, pink atomic stars and gold flecks. Three whole panels—one of them obviously hung upside down—of a sickly-yellow cabbage-rose pattern on a field of violet stripes had refused to budge. Meanwhile, some seriously ugly seventies disco-era metallic stuff had come off in thin, ragged strips that left shiny bits of silver paper everywhere.

Staring at the evidence of such mixed and meaningful personal histories, Sadie couldn't help but wonder about the people who had lived here before her. Had any of the moms of the many families that had sat down to dinner in this very room ever felt the way that she did now? Did those other women of eras past sometimes long for just a little gratitude?

Recognition?

Company?

And what about now? If she went door-to-door in her own neighborhood, would she find a sisterhood of lonely hearts, or would she find herself alone in her feelings, too?

If other women shared her experiences, she decided, they sure had kept it a pretty good secret.

In fact, she couldn't think of a single woman she actually knew ever having admitted to feeling so lost in her own home. Not the older women at church. Not the other moms in the neighborhood. Not even her aunt Phiz, the designated make-do mother figure of the family.

And since there had never been a subject the twice-widowed, multilingual, single-mindedly self-sufficient archaeologist Phiz didn't dare broach, Sadie couldn't help thinking that maybe everybody else had homemaking experiences straight from the mold used on old black-and-white TV shows.

Hi, honey, I'm home. Corny as it sounded, Sadie would have loved to hear those words shouted from the entryway. And children pitching in to help. *No, Mom, that's too heavy for you, let me get it.*

And the phone *not* ringing with someone trying to sell them something just as they sat down to eat.

The silver rim on the good china winked at Sadie in the soft candlelight. She exhaled slowly and picked up a plate from the stack to her right.

If her family were here, she would certainly have something to say to each of them.

"For Olivia." She ladled up a dainty portion. "Regardless of your complaining that the next year's senior-class commitments commence as soon as the graduating class does—um, commence, that is—you cannot completely ignore your role as part of this family. Got that?"

The dish clunked against the tablecloth, and some noodles dangled over the rim. Sadie reached to tidy it up, then stopped. Why bother? Who would notice anyway?

"And Ryan. Dear, sweet, 'I promised the music minister I'd learn a new piece on my guitar' Ryan. Earnest, reliable, 'Oh, didn't I tell you that I'm learning the piece to back up Amy Furst, and the only time she can get together to work on it is Tuesday and please, please don't make me ask her to come to our house because have you seen *her* house? And her *parents*? You and Dad are great and all, but I don't think you're ready to, like, interact with Amy, okay?' Let's just hope you don't get any big ideas of your own about interacting with Amy, because if you think Dad and I are the king and queen of uncool now..." A heaping scoop went sloshing onto another plate, and when she plunked it down, sauce slopped over onto the knife and part of the napkin.

Clean that up? She thought not.

"And Ed." She lifted the ladle as if in a toast to the man who had told her not half an hour ago that he was literally out the door on his way home. On his twenty-minutes-tops-if-you-walk-it-on-your-hands way home, she corrected.

Pasta and sauce hit gleaming white china with all the elegance of an overripe tomato tossed off a two-story balcony.

Splat.

She stood waiting for the sense of satisfaction she thought this futile act of sarcasm would bring. It didn't come.

For one brief shining moment, it flashed through her mind to just cut loose and send the plate and its slapped-down contents flying. She supposed when somebody asked her about it, she could just tell them, "Well, they say that you should throw pasta against the wall to see if it's done. Turns out it was—and so was I."

She was. Done, that is.

She settled Ed's plate in front of his accustomed chair, then helped herself to two full mounds of the delicious-smelling concoction.

The silverware by her own chair clanked as she rolled it up in the cloth napkin. She bent to blow out the candles, then turned to take her dinner upstairs to her room.

Ed would show up before too long. Probably. Or Ryan. Or Olivia. Let one of them clear the table and wrap up the leftovers.

And if they came tapping at her door, seeking her out to ask why she hadn't waited for them, she knew just what she'd say. "You are healthy, able and intelligent human beings. You know how to operate a telephone, a wristwatch and a microwave oven. Why didn't I wait on you? Maybe the question you should be asking is why don't you ever wait on yourselves?"

"You actually *said* that?"

"Oh, of course not, Mary Tate. The Lord would never grant me the gift of being both that bold and that clever in the same breath." Sadie clutched a box of cookies from the Not By Bread Alone Bakery and turned toward the park. "But I sure do wish I *had* said it."

"Someday you will. You have the fire in you, Sadie. I saw it the very first day we met."

"That must be why I love you so much, Mary Tate. You see fire in me where everyone else sees a nice comfy footstool."

"Well, maybe that's because you only show them your footstool side, honey."

"I can't help it." Sadie glanced over her shoulder at her own backside. "It's bigger than both of us."

"Oh, stop it. You still look good, girl." Mary Tate bumped Sadie's shoulder with her own. "But that's a fine example. Making a joke about yourself, that's the footstool Sadie talking."

"Maybe people see that because that's all there is—did you ever think of that?" Sadie asked.

"Thought of it and rejected it out of hand, thank you very much." The wheels on the little red wagon Mary Tate had volunteered to bring to carry the cooler of soft drinks rattled and squawked. "Maybe it's as simple as people not seeing what I do because they don't bother to look—really look. That's what friends are for, you know. To look beyond the flesh and the failings and see the you that God means for you to be."

Her friend's words touched Sadie, but she covered up quickly to avoid getting blubbery. "Girl, you are cornier than forty acres of Iowa farmland, you know that?"

"That doesn't make what I said any less true."

They walked on toward the town park where Sadie had scheduled the first meeting of her presidential term for the Council of Christian Women. She had hoped for one of the members to volunteer a home, a workplace conference room, a church basement—at one point she'd have settled for a centrally located tree house. When one by one the excuses rolled in, Sadie had to make a decision.

Her house?

She was a footstool, not a doormat.

So she chose to hold an outdoor meeting on what Mary Tate dubbed "her turf." And with the early-summer evening cooperating, she did not regret it one bit.

Yet.

"Oh, I forgot to tell you." Mary Tate snatched at the sleeve of Sadie's simple print dress. "I have gotten a ton of positive feedback about your daddy's appearance with us in the Memorial Day parade."

"Me, too. How could anyone filled to the eyeballs with orneriness look so innocent and adorable wearing an army camouflage shirt, red pants, blue suspenders with silver stars and a foam Statue of Liberty hat?"

"Got to admit it, sugar, the man has style. Just reeks of it."

"Yeah, well at least for now he's reeking over at April's, where I don't have to get wind of it."

"How's that going?"

"Who knows?" Sadie shrugged and the cookies shifted forward. Gently she tilted the box to set them right again, sighing. "Neither April nor Daddy has said a word."

"Then they must not have any complaints."

"Well, if April did have a complaint, I don't think for one minute she'd tell me. You remember when we were growing up how Daddy picked out admonitions from the Bible for each of us girls?"

"Wait on the Lord, Sadie-girl. Wait on the Lord." Having heard that booming through the household over the years, Mary Tate could do a better-than-passing fair imitation of Moonie's simplified counsel.

"For April it was 'gird your loins.' The single most closed-off, cautious human being I have ever known, and Daddy spent her childhood reminding her to always stay on guard."

After half a block, Sadie's friend made an obvious show of looking dead ahead toward good old Pickett's on the Point and asking, "So did you forgive Ed yet for the great facial fiasco?"

"Forgave and forgot, what else could I do?"

"Pout and punish?" She flexed her wrist and wriggled her fingers to set her jewelry sparkling. "Always worked for me."

"Put your hand down. You forget who went with you when you bought most of that stuff?" She pointed to herself.

Her friend tucked a strand of blond hair behind her ear, her eyes sparkling to rival the diamonds she'd just flashed. "You know I talk big. Just my way of, you know, keeping my spirits up. No harm intended."

"But...?" There was more. With Mary Tate there was *always* more.

"I still say you can't let Ed get off scot-free. You did catch him alone with a very attractive younger woman. If nothing else, he is guilty of using very bad judgment."

"If wives started punishing husbands every time they used bad judgment, or caused hurt feelings through carelessness, or took their wives for granted while spending too much time on other things, well, then..."

"Well, then maybe men would start acting better, ever think of that?"

"Hmm, seems like I recall someone around here just confessing they were nothing but a big talker. I don't see you trying to ride roughshod over Royal the way you suggest I do Ed."

She wrinkled her nose sheepishly. "I was hoping you'd go first, so I could see how it worked out."

"No, Mary Tate. Wives bullying husbands is not biblical. It's not wise. And it's not going to happen, okay?"

"Oh, all right."

"Besides, I'm too old now to start trying new tricks on poor Ed just because he acted like some clueless kid."

"Clueless? You sure? Carmen is awful pretty, and you know her nickname at her corporate office?"

"I don't want to know."

"Go-Go Gomez."

Sadie frowned. She could have lived a lifetime without having that wedged into the tangled knots of her thoughts and emotions.

"On account of she's such a go-getter," Mary Tate went on.

"Ed says she's a live wire. And no, I am not worried one bit about that." All right, she was a little worried. The statistics regarding fidelity, even among people of faith, were scary. But not half as scary as having your best friend plant ideas in your mind that had no business being there. "And I won't have you read anything into it, either."

"You're right. Right. Not my place to speculate. I'm sorry. You know me, not satisfied to accept the boring truth when something much more interesting might fit, right?"

"Right."

"Of course," Mary Tate singsonged softly as they turned the corner. "It could have been much worse."

"Oh, it's worse all right. Much, much worse." She played up her friend's insinuation with a shake of her head, then broke into a wry smile. "The man now struts around the house puffed up as a peacock because he thinks *I think* I caught him on the verge of committing an indiscretion when it hadn't even crossed his mind."

Mary Tate groaned. "Putting you in the most dreaded of all marital situations."

"Right. In the *wrong*."

"But you're not."

"I know. I *know*. He just doesn't get it."

"If he were my husband, he *wouldn't* be getting it—not for a long time, I'll tell you that."

"I'm going to get *you*, Mary Tate. Get you some help."

"Oh, please do, sugar. I've needed help a very long time now—hopefully in the form of a couple of buff, beautiful cabana boys from a culture where they venerate older women."

"What for? You're married."

"Yeah, but I'm not *dead*."

They stopped at the light.

Sadie shot Mary Tate the finely honed "Don't make me climb out of my comfort zone to drag you back to the straight and narrow because I'm the mama and you *will* not prevail with me" look that only a mother of teenagers could rightfully pull off.

"Oh, sugar, I'm teasing. You know no man alive holds a candle to my Royal."

"Holding a candle to Royal?" They hurried across the quiet street. "Isn't that your job?"

"You bet. Something needs doing, I just hold that man's feet to the flame and it gets done ASAP." Mary Tate laughed, gave the wagon a jerk, and struggled to try to hoist it over the curb.

"Sap being the operative word?" Sadie muttered under her breath, bending down to lift the back of the wagon and help out her friend.

"What?"

"Nothing." In fifteen years she couldn't recall ever having seen Royal do anything for his wife that his wife could do for herself. And since Mary Tate could do practically anything… "Can you get the wagon from here on out?"

"Got it. Let's go. Looks like Lollie and Waynetta beat us here." She waved to the women standing in the shade of the park's lone surviving oak tree.

Though the official roster listed nearly twenty members of the council mission statement: To unite churches and community through fellowship and service—Sadie had never attended a meeting with more than a dozen women present.

She expected far fewer than that tonight, and had not really planned a highly organized or particularly coherent agenda.

So it stood to reason that the first two to arrive would be the town's self-appointed social maven and the best-intentioned busybody in the county.

"Hi, Mrs. Muldoon, Mrs. Cummins! Hope y'all haven't waited long." Sadie gritted her teeth and prayed she had not just said "y'all" in front of Waynetta Cummins. She had, of course, and a lecture on "People judge us by our words" surely would follow.

To avoid that and the inevitable looking like a child in front of people she had come to preside over, Sadie slapped on her biggest slopping-sugar expression and settled the cookies on the picnic table. "Please do excuse me a minute, won't you? I have to run into my office and sign the group in as using the park this evening."

Sadie bowed. She *bowed*. Or maybe it was more of a curtsy. Anyway, her body bobbed up and down, she flung her hands out and stepped backward, all with her teeth bared in a smile that had to have resembled something between the maniacal grimace of a black-and-white movie vamp and the glaring high-beam smile of a game-show spokesmodel.

"Isn't she too cute?" Mary Tate hugged Lollie and nodded to Waynetta. "*My* office. Two whole weeks on the job, and already she talks like a bona fide career woman."

If the other women had an opinion about anything from her cuteness to her career, Sadie missed it. She'd already hightailed it away from there, as fast as her stubby little middle-aged legs could carry her.

❧ *Chapter Seven* ❧

"You'd better get back out there, sugar." Mary Tate bounded into Sadie's office with a cookie in one hand and a can of soda in the other. "Deborah Danes just swooped down on the group with an idea for our fall service project. She outlined it, made color computer printouts and stuffed them in little plastic page protectors for each of us. 'Course, you know how that went over with Waynetta and Lollie! We may have on our hands the very first all-female ultimate-fighting wrasslin' match in the history of the Council of Christian Women."

Sadie looked up from her desk and put one hand to her suddenly throbbing temple. "And how is running in here to tell me that going to stop it?"

"Stop it? Honey, I think you owe it to yourself to get out there and *watch!*"

"I'll be there in a minute." She flipped up one corner of the calendar that all but covered the top of her battered old desk.

"In a minute you might have missed it all. What's taking so long in here, anyway?"

"I can't find the paperwork."

"Look for it later, girl. You have three queen bees circling the hive out there and the end result will not be sweetness and honey."

"You don't understand. I thought for sure I'd left the Private Use of Public Property form right here." Paper whispered over paper in her in-box. She stepped back and opened her top drawer. "And now it's nowhere to be found. Tell me I'm not that careless, Mary Tate, or worse, so distracted or so...so...so old that I've become completely unaware of where I'm putting things."

"Old? Take that back! You're younger than I am."

"Two months."

"My December to your February, honey, it gives us entirely different birth years."

"Can we deal with your vanity crisis later? This really troubles me."

"Okay, calm down. I'll help you look." Mary Tate set her drink down, then held the cookie by one edge in her teeth and stood on tiptoe to peer over the bookcase on the far side of the tiny, dark-paneled office. Muffled by the cookie in her mouth, she asked, "What's it look like?"

"Nothing fancy. White paper, lots of blank lines to write names and times, on a brown clipboard with a red pencil on a string tied to the clasp."

Mary Tate rested her cookie on top of the old metal file cabinet in the corner. "Did you check in here?"

Before Sadie could tell her not to bother, she yanked at the handle of the top drawer. The squeaky wheels clattered along their runners and then clanked to a stop.

Sadie's pulse picked up. "How did you unlock that?"

"Unlock? It wasn't locked in the first place."

"It most certainly was. I double-checked it before I left this afternoon because…" She held her breath, glanced around the room, then exhaled and shut her eyes. "Okay, this may sound nuts, but at least three times since my first day on the job I've found things not quite right around here."

"Not quite right?"

"Amiss."

"A Miss what?"

She massaged her temple again even though it didn't produce any more of a satisfying response than talking to Mary Tate. "Messed up. Vanished. Out of place."

"Ooo-wee-oo. Strange happenings at the graveyard." She nibbled her cookie again, probably to hide the mischief in her grin as she teased, "Think it's the work of restless spirits?"

"I don't believe in ghosts, Mary Tate."

"What about some other kind of restless spirit? You believe in your daddy, don't you?"

"Why would Daddy—" She stopped herself, knowing that with Moonie involved one never asked "Why?" Instead, she shook her head and said simply, "'Why seek ye the living among the dead?'"

"You trying to ask why someone as full of life as Moonie would do mischief in a graveyard?"

"No. It wouldn't hurt you to open a Bible a little more often, you know that, girl? That's what the angel said when they came to look for the body of Jesus in the empty tomb. 'Why seek ye the living among the dead?' It's what Daddy always says about going to funerals and visiting grave sites."

"Funerals and grave sites are *for* the living, to help us deal with our grief." Mary Tate folded her arms, clearly not getting all the pieces to fit in her mind.

"I'm just saying, that for once in my life, the things gone totally wacko around me absolutely cannot be the work of

Moonie Shelnutt. He doesn't do cemeteries, and he doesn't have any plans to until he's brought to one feetfirst."

"Okay, if you've ruled out the occult and the obvious, what's left?"

"Overactive imagination, according to the chief of police." She picked up the phone and stared at the black bulky thing.

"Is that who you're calling?"

"No." Her fingers hovered for a moment over the numbers before she began to slowly punch them in. "I think maybe this time I'll try Kurt Muldoon."

"Breaking and entering on city property? That's police business, not the sheriff's."

"Yeah, but…" She chewed her lower lip, and aware of the quiet ringing in her ear, met her friend's gaze and whispered, "I can't call the police."

Mary Tate's eyes grew wide, her tone went hushed as one suddenly sucked into a potentially sinister mystery. "Why not?"

"Because…" Sadie straightened up and held the mouthpiece down so when the night dispatcher picked up he wouldn't hear her. "Because I've called them three times in two weeks, and every time they've come up with a perfectly logical explanation for whatever I reported. The chief of police has taken great pains to remind me that they do not have a large staff and time spent making like Scooby Doo out at the graveyard means time away from serious police work."

"Serious police work? Yes, Wileyville is a regular hotbed of crime. I'd wager that man has had to cut his coffee drinking time at Owt's down to only two hours a day."

The dispatcher in the sheriff's office answered. Sadie held one finger up to signal to Mary Tate to wait. In as few words as possible she explained who and where she was and why she needed to get in touch with Kurt. When the dispatcher put her on hold to see if the sheriff had left for the day, Sadie picked up the conversation where she and Mary Tate had left it. "It's his tone, you know, that pat-you-on-the-head, 'there, there, little lady don't worry your pretty self' way of his that made me want to just get right in his smug old face and say… Eeep!"

Sadie slammed the receiver into its cradle and practically leaped backward.

"Sadie, honey, what is it?" Mary Tate reached her side in two steps.

Just that fast the phone began to ring.

Sadie groaned and dug her fingers into her aching scalp.

"Are you going to answer that?"

"No!" She waved her friend away. "When the dispatcher couldn't find Kurt, he said it didn't sound like their jurisdiction, so he put me through to the police. That's got to be them calling me now just to give me grief."

"Okay, if you don't want to answer *that,* how about going outside, where your *other* duty calls?"

Sadie groaned, letting her head fall back. In doing so she caught a glimpse of the clock. "We have a full five more minutes before the meeting officially starts."

"But Deborah, not to mention Waynetta…"

"Circle this day on your calendar, pal. A new day has dawned for the council. As of today, that meeting will begin not when the bossiest woman shows up but when the president, *me,* calls the assembly to order."

"That *will* be different. And good for you for initiating it." Mary Tate gave her friend a hug.

Sadie patted her friend's hand and wondered how long she could keep up the brave face when what she really wanted to do was go home and hide under the covers. Aside from the odd and the unexplained incidents around her office, these two weeks had certainly taken their toll.

She was tired. But for once it was a good tired.

She was stressed. But at least she knew the source of that stress.

She was resolute. Though she did not have all the answers she needed to carry out her mission, for the first time in a long while, she had a mission to focus her energy on, if only...

She took a moment, thinking at long last the time might have come for her to utter a brief but heartfelt prayer for help. But before she could even begin to think of what to say, a gentle tapping on the office door demanded her attention.

"Yes?" she called out, already moving around Mary Tate toward the door.

It swung open. A man dressed in the familiar uniform of the Wileyville police poked his head in the office. Though she didn't recognize him, he obviously knew her by reputation.

"'Lo, Mrs. Pickett, I knocked because I know how skittish you can get."

"If you came over to tease me, Officer—"

"No. No, ma'am. No such thing." He stood fully in the open door and extended his burly arm outward. "I came by to confirm your qualms about all them suspicious goings-on 'round here."

She did not like the sound of that. Not one bit.

And when she edged carefully around the desk, over to the threshold and peeked out at the once-serene park, she did not like the *sight* of it any better.

"Oh, Daddy," she murmured.

"I thought you said he didn't 'do' cemeteries." Mary Tate raised her fist in the air. "Wooo! Go, Moonie, go!"

The officer laughed.

The phone rang again, and Sadie figured it was someone calling to tell her what they had just witnessed.

"Looks like we may have got straight to the root of all that monkey business around here that you keep phoning the station about, Mrs. Pickett."

Sadie covered her eyes with one hand. However, that could not blot the scene from her mind.

With the council members Sadie had just promised she would take in hand looking on, mouths agape, her father made his entrance. Foam Statue of Liberty hat flopping proudly on his silvery head, he grinned and waved, then pointed to the pile of luggage strapped behind him as he turned into the vivid green grass of the park, sitting astride April's shiny red riding lawn mower.

Chapter Eight

"Ran away from home." Sadie picked up the foil pan from tonight's frozen lasagna.

Instinctively, she started to immerse it in the hot sudsy water she'd run in the sink to presoak the dishes. But she stopped just in time. The very reason she'd stocked her kitchen with convenience foods was to save herself the trouble of washing pots and pans. She should just throw the thing out.

Really.

Just chuck it in the trash.

Instead, she stood there at the counter contemplating it along with her father's latest exploit. "Can you imagine that? Just up and running away from home at his age?"

Seated at the kitchen table, Ed rustled the pages of the *Wileyville Guardian News*. "Where Moonie is concerned, I can imagine just about anything."

"Mom, tell me again what they call you down at the police station." Ryan, with the cordless phone trapped between his cocked head and upraised shoulder, carried a precarious stack of dinner dishes to the sink.

"And on a lawn mower!" Sadie banged the used tinfoil pan down on the counter with a very disappointing *thwonk.*

Ed didn't even look up. "You should have seen that coming when you took away his car."

"Mom…Mom…what's the thing the cops call you?" From his vantage point, towering almost a foot taller than her, Ryan easily capped his mother's head with one splayed hand to hold her in place. "What's the name that officer said they gave you? I want to tell Amy."

"What you should tell Amy is goodbye." Olivia gathered the salad bowl and bread tray from the table and headed for the breakfast bar. "Your turn to load the dishwasher tonight and I don't want to get stuck with it."

Ryan waggled his head, then pretended to flip a strand of long hair over his shoulder in a dead-on impersonation of his sister in full snit-fit mode.

"I saw what you did." Olivia thunked the leftovers down. "Mo-o-om."

"That's 'Fraidy Sadie the Cemetery Lady to you, Miss Smart Mouth." Sadie slipped away from her son, who repeated the loathsome nickname to the girl on the other end of the line and shared a big belly laugh with her.

Ed uncrossed his legs, then recrossed them the other way. He exchanged one section of the paper for another, then sipped down the last of his iced tea. All without a single upward glance.

Sadie snatched up the disposable pan again.

Ryan then told Amy he had to go and hung up. He was still grinning from ear to ear when he popped open the dishwasher and yanked the bottom rack out to begin loading. "'Fraidy Sadie the Cemetery Lady. I like it, Mom. Very cool."

"I'm glad you approve. Here." She slung the crusty foil cas-serole container into his midsection with a wicked but harm-less *whack,* and smiled far too sweetly. "Wash this pan. And I mean *really* wash it, by hand."

"But you're supposed to throw these away," he protested.

"Then I'll throw it away clean."

He opened his mouth to argue.

She narrowed her eyes and frowned.

He thrust the pan in the sink, turned his back on her and went to work scrubbing.

Olivia gave a minor wiggle of teenage triumph to see her brother taken to task and tackled her own chore with renewed cheerfulness, singing, "'Fraidy Sadie the…"

Sadie tensed. "Don't finish that, please, Olivia."

"If the nickname bothers you that much, honey, quit the job," Ed muttered so low she wasn't sure he'd meant her to hear him.

"If the…what?" She came around the table and stood, commanding his attention. "Isn't that a bit like saying if your house is blue and you want it brown, burn it to the ground?"

"Just trying to be supportive."

"Supportive?" She pulled her shoulders up. "By implying I'm not strong enough to stand up to the good old boys' net-work, and at the first sign of them mocking me I should turn tail and run home?"

"Careful around those good old boys, Sadie." Another page turned. "We're going to need their good graces when the time comes to sell the pharmacy."

Sell the pharmacy. Ed had talked about doing that for the last five years. All the while he steadfastly turned down even the chance to *talk* to any of the prospective buyers who came to town every six months or so.

"Ed, all I'm saying is… Ed?" Sadie clenched her teeth in frustration. "Ed, would you please look at me when I talk to you?"

"Can't. Got these glasses perched just so on my nose. If I so much as hiccup, I won't be able to read another word."

She opened her mouth, then shut it again. Though the man couldn't act more irritating if he tried, the plain truth was that he wasn't trying. He just wanted to take a few minutes before he went down to close the store to leaf through the paper. And he looked so darling doing it, too, with his hair mussed up and those banged-up black reading glasses balanced on the end of his nose. How could she stay mad at him?

Sadie exhaled, leaned her forearms on the back of the nearest kitchen chair and shook her head. "I give up."

"What? What's wrong now?" He looked up at last, and true to his prediction, the glasses listed drunkenly to one side. "You want me to paint the house brown?"

"No, sweetheart." She laughed. "I want…"

Well, that was the million-dollar question, wasn't it? It had gone unanswered since that day when Mayor Furst had shown up on her doorstep and she started on this new, unknown path. What *did* she want? Until she could define it clearly, how could she ever hope to achieve it?

She ruffled her fingers through her hair, then folded her arms over her chest and gave it a stab. "I want everyone I love to just be happy."

She smiled because she thought she should after saying something so trite, it had an empty ring even to her own ears.

No one in the room said anything.

"Except maybe Daddy," she added, needing to fill the crackling quiet. "Maybe, just maybe, Daddy could stand to make himself a teeny bit less happy, especially if it meant the rest of us could have a day's worth of peace."

"I, for one, completely understand what Grandpa did." Olivia tore off a piece of plastic wrap big enough to mummify the half a loaf of garlic bread left over from the meal. "In fact, I'd go so far as to call it a noble act of rebellion, the powerless individual struggling against his controllers to reclaim his legally recognized and totally fundamental right to drive."

Sadie resisted the urge to take the bread from her child's hands and do the job for her. "Thus spoke the girl who earned her license but lacked the foresight to earn any money to pay for a car or for the added expense to our insurance, which we told her we would *not* pay if she let her grades slip below a B average."

"It's not fair." Olivia stared down at the wrap and the loaf.

Here we go. Hot-and-cold-running hissy fits or however Mary Tate had described it. For a second Sadie thought the girl would break into tears. And if she did, could Sadie hang tough and not rush to her and try to make it all better? She hoped so, but…

Luckily, or perhaps blessedly, Sadie never had to face that test.

Ed stood, cast his cattywampus glasses aside, then went to his daughter, putting a hand on Olivia's back. "You knew the rules years ago. Don't try crying foul to us now and hoping things will change."

Her slender shoulders rose and fell, then her strawberry-blond hair shimmied as she raised up her chin and said, "I meant it's unfair to Grandpa, taking away *his* car."

"Yeah, well, your grandpa violated a few rules himself." Ed glanced at Sadie and winked. "Like refusing to yield the right-of-way…to a four-story building."

"Following too closely—" Sadie crossed her arms "—behind a four-story building."

"And don't forget the worst one of all." Ryan swung around to face them, one sudsy finger thrust up in the air. "Denting up a classic, mint-condition Caddie."

The room went so still, Sadie could hear the soap bubbles drip from her son's hand onto the creased leather of his athletic shoes.

"On a four-story building," Ryan rushed to add.

Sadie laughed at her son's pathetic joke and shook her head.

Olivia took the leftovers to the refrigerator.

"Shame about that car, though," Ryan grumbled, turning back to his work.

"No kidding." Even with her head in the refrigerator, the pout came out loud and clear in Olivia's voice. "You know, he promised me I could have it someday."

"No way!" Ryan flicked bubbles in his sister's general direction. "That baby is mine. You wouldn't have a clue how to take care of it."

"That's what mechanics are for." She batted her eyes above the open fridge door. "All I have to do is drive it around and look great."

"You are not insured to drive that car, young lady." Ed labored to get his reading glasses balanced back in place again.

"*Someday.* I said someday."

Without moving his head an inch, Ed delicately picked up the paper again as he said, "Let's hope it's *someday* in the far, far future."

"Oh, Daddy, you have to stop thinking of me as a child." Olivia slammed the refrigerator door.

The sound made Ed startle, which sent the glasses tumbling into his lap. "I say someday in the far future because neither of you will get that car until Grandpa Moonie dies."

Die?

Her daddy? Sadie blinked. Why had Ed brought up such a ridiculous notion?

Olivia huffed out of the room.

"I give up." Ed snatched up the glasses and tossed them onto the table along with the remnants of the unread paper. "Think I'll head back down to the store."

Sadie swallowed hard, and suddenly, without even realizing she'd intended to say anything at all, she blurted out, "I wish I knew how Daddy was doing at Hannah's."

Ed stood, his iced-tea glass in hand, and stretched. "Then go over and see."

"And have her think I'm spying on her?" Sadie's hand went to her throat. "Never!"

Ed went to the sink. "You wouldn't be spying on her."

"Yes, she would," Ryan said, taking his father's empty glass and dousing it in the sink.

"She would be checking in on him." Ed spoke slowly, distinctly, the way they used to spell words around the kids when they were trying to keep a secret. "It's not the same thing."

"Speaking for those of us who have had Mom—" Ryan pulled his hands from the water, suds flying as he made quotation marks in the air "—'check in' on us when we weren't doing anything but practicing a guitar piece with Amy, I say it stinks of spying."

"Since you were 'practicing'—" Ed's large blunt fingers mimicked his son's gesture "—with Amy on the front porch, with the light off, it's fair to say that when your Mom checked on you, she had a good reason."

"And if I checked on Daddy, I would have a reason," Sadie told her son. Then she turned to Ed, her forehead scrunched down tight. "What would be my reason?"

"Well…you could…or maybe…" He stroked his chin, the lines around his eyes creasing deeply before his whole face lit and he said, "You know how your daddy loves chocolate-covered cherries?"

"Yes."

"And how Hannah never has any sweets around because she's always on a diet?"

"That's true, she is. Ever since she married Payt, she's always on a diet. In fact, she's completely banned all candy from her home. *Banned* it. That skinny little—" Sadie wrangled to find the right description "—candy banner."

"Well, we just got a fresh shipment in at the store today."

"Pretty lame, Mom." Ryan pulled the plug, and the water rushed down the drain in big gulps.

"Lame is in the eye of the beholder, son. My daddy likes chocolate-covered cherries, and there he is, stuck in a house with a woman who hasn't let sugar-laden fatty snacks cross her lips or her threshold for five years." She tried to look sincere, though not overmuch, as she didn't want to give her son the impression she didn't understand how thin a justification she'd chosen. "Can you imagine how that makes him feel?"

Ryan used the wad-the-tea-towel-up-in-a-ball method of drying his hands. Using that same level of attentiveness, he deadpanned, "If I say yes, can I go to my room?"

"Go." Ed waved his son off. "And speaking of that, I think it's time I headed out, as well."

"Yes, you should go. I have to go, too. I'm a woman on a mission."

"A spy mission," Ryan called out from the hallway.

"A family mission," Ed corrected, taking Sadie by the shoulders. "That is, it will be a family mission if you stop by and get April."

Sadie winced. As if things hadn't already been stretched to the limits between the sisters, to then have two of them show up on the third's doorstep armed with nothing more than a box of chocolate-covered flimsy excuses? "I don't think April and Daddy are talking yet."

"All the more reason to do it."

Sadie wanted to see her father. She wanted to see how Hannah and he were getting along. She wanted to know just what exactly happened between April and Moonie.

In the distance Ryan's bedroom door slammed shut.

She wanted to keep the channels of communication open between her sisters and father.

Ed already had his lab coat in his hand, ready to go back to the store.

But most of all she wanted not to have to spend yet another night feeling lost and alone in her own home.

"Okay, I'll do it. But don't lock up the store until you hear from me, you got that, Ed?"

"Okay, but why?" he asked as he ushered her out their front door.

"Because if I drag April over to Hannah's house to see Daddy unannounced, we may need emergency medical supplies before the evening is through."

✂ *Chapter Nine* ✂

"You're sure Ed suggested this?" April waited in Hannah's driveway, her arms folded.

"Yes." Sadie withdrew from the back seat of her sister's tiny car the biggest box of chocolate-covered cherries that they stocked at the store. "For the last time, Ed came up with the whole idea."

"He used to be such a reasonable man." April shook her head. Her ponytail bobbed like a wagging finger to underscore her disbelief. "What happened?"

The car door fell shut. Sadie headed up the walk without a backward glance. "You didn't have to come with me, you know."

April, who had not spoken to Moonie since the day of his great escape, kept at Sadie's heels. "Like I told you, I only came tonight out of loving compassion for Hannah and the desire to show support for and solidarity with her, as the one now responsible for the care of Daddy."

"Uh-huh." Sadie shot a look over her shoulder. "And?"

"And?" April blinked, her face pained like an innocent accused of high treason.

Sadie wasn't buying it. She prodded again, "And?"

April opened her mouth, closed it, then winced. Then, her eyes alight, she indulged in a delightedly wicked grin. "*And* because, if Daddy has got up to anything untoward or audacious, I want to see it with my own two eyes and not give that baby sister of ours a chance to put her goody-two-shoes spin on things."

"She can spin until she falls down drunk with dizziness, that won't change the reality. We know Daddy can make life very difficult. I mean, after what he pulled at your house."

"Nice try, but you won't get any information out of me that way."

"Fine." With a gentle but well-placed shove, Sadie propelled her older sister onto the long, narrow porch. "Just ring the doorbell."

"Me?" April's eyes grew wide. "Uh-uh. I refuse to leave my fingerprints at the scene of a crime."

"Which crime?" Sadie had to smile. "Us dropping in unannounced or Hannah strangling us for doing it?"

"Oh, she won't strangle us."

"No?"

"Too easy to break a nail that way." April crinkled up her nose. "She might, however, snatch those chocolates from your hands and crack them over your head."

"The crime then being, what? Assault with a delicious weapon?"

"Don't laugh." April wagged one finger. "It could happen. Good thing you didn't bring Daddy a sub sandwich. They'd have her for assault with a deli weapon."

Sadie rolled her eyes but recovered from her aversion to the awful pun quickly enough to add, grinning, "Or a crocheted scarf—assault with a doily weapon."

"Stop! I give up. I'll ring the bell." April depressed the lit button beside the wooden door with the leaded-glass panel in the center.

"Or a stuffed bear—assault with a teddy weapon."

"Quit joking, will you? If Hannah opens the door and finds us snickering together, she'll immediately assume we've cut her out of some family secret."

"We'll just tell her to be thankful we didn't show up with a bicycle."

April grimaced, then bit her lower lip. "Dare I ask?"

"Assault with a pedally weapon."

April groaned, but that didn't hide the fact that she did laugh at the horrible bit of wordplay. "Okay, now stop, I mean it. Someone's coming, and we have to straighten up and stop—"

"Hello, ladies!" Payt flung the door open.

"—clowning around," April managed to conclude despite her mouth hanging open in naked awe.

"How lovely of you to pay us a call." Their brother-in-law stepped out onto the porch and greeted them with effortless and genteel aplomb. Not something one normally finds in a fair-haired, handsome doctor dressed in purple scrubs, green high-top sneakers and sporting a big red rubber ball on his nose.

"We interrupting something, sugar?" Sadie went on tiptoe trying to peer through the quickly closing doorway.

"Just preparing for the next phase of my career." Payt held his arms wide.

April gave him a slow once-over. "Quitting medicine to go to clown college?"

"Not at all." He pulled off the bulbous nose, moved to the steps and waved to a passing neighbor, all with a sense of cool so liquid they could have bottled it. "Interviewing with a practice in Nashville that embraces the latest concept of healing humor."

"That's hardly the latest concept, Payton." April turned and tagged along after him right back down the walk they had just come up not five minutes earlier. "It does say in Proverbs that 'laughter doeth good like a medicine.'"

"Wait a minute!" Sadie did not budge from the porch. "Did you say Nashville?"

"Yup. Tennessee. Actually, just outside Nashville. Murfrees-boro," he said casually, all Southern accent and subtle slyness. His deepset eyes blinked slowly, and though he did not smile outright, he wore an expression of affable enthusiasm. "Ever hear of it?"

"Well, of course." Sadie had visited there, in fact. "But—"

"I have a map in the car. Let me show you where it is." With that he hurried away, and before either April or Sadie could say another word, had stuck his whole upper body into the passenger side of his new—well, new to him—shiny blue Lexus.

"What happened to staying close by?" April leaned in, ducking and weaving to get the best vantage point to continue the conversation.

"Just a…" He whipped around and almost collided skulls with doe-eyed April. Gently, he took her by the shoulders and set her back a couple steps. "Just a four-hour drive. Maybe more if you go scenic."

"More?" April asked.

He produced a stack of road maps and began shuffling through them. "You should, you know."

"Should what?" Sadie demanded. Something did not feel right about this whole thing.

"Go scenic. It's a gorgeous drive. Lots to see. Ever been to Cave City?"

"Payton Bartlett, what are you trying to—"

"Four *hours?*" April accepted each map after Payt examined the front covers then discarded them.

"Okay, you got me. Might be more like five. But that's still closer than the other group that showed interest in bringing me on—in Chicago."

"Chicago?" The maps crackled, sliding from April's hands into her open arms.

"Can't find the map of Tennessee. I know I had one, because Moonie asked to see it and... Wait!" He interrupted himself a little too abruptly and began an almost frantic search back through the folded rectangles with pictures of states on the cover. "I *do* have a map of Illinois, if you want to see where that other practice is located."

"We didn't come to admire your map collection, Payt." Sadie cradled the candy box over her chest, her own sacred shield of chocolate to fend off whatever distraction her brother-in-law would next fling her way. "We came to see our family."

April scowled. "If you go to Chicago, we'll never see Hannah."

"Hey, hop on a plane." Payt tossed the maps into the car then clapped his hands together. "There before you know it."

"B-but I don't fly well, Payt. And Sadie would have to arrange for four tickets for the family, and then we have to think about Daddy."

"Oh, don't give your daddy another thought," he said, and far too fast for Sadie's liking moved again to another subject. "In fact, it's entirely premature to worry about us moving away. All speculation at this point. Nothing set in stone."

"Are you sure about that?" Sadie narrowed her eyes. "Because this conversation is making me feel like I have rocks in my head."

"Always the kidder, eh, Sadie? Hey, are those chocolates?"

"Yes, we brought them over for—"

"Terrific." He slid the box from Sadie's grasp and planted a quick kiss on her cheek. "Really thoughtful, really."

"I didn't bring them for you. I brought them for Daddy."

"And I'll see that he gets them." The words had hardly left his lips before he'd popped open April's car door, waved to another neighbor, then swept his free hand toward the waiting front seat. "It sure was great to see you two. Come back again when you can stay longer."

"We haven't stayed at all." Sadie shut the door. She grabbed the chocolates from Payt and smacked him lightly across the arm with them, demanding, "What's going on? Where's Hannah? Where's Daddy?"

"I'm right here." Hannah stood in the doorway, the usually flawless waves of her auburn hair caught up in a slapdash topknot that had already begun to slide to the right side of her head. "Daddy…isn't."

April moved slowly to the front of her car. "Daddy isn't what?"

Sadie didn't have to ask. She'd sensed it from the moment Payt had gone into his routine.

In two bounding steps Payt reached his wife and, giving her a peck on the cheek, said, "Sorry, sweetie. I tried. I'll go inside and start making calls to try to track Moonie down and let you and your sisters, um, discuss the situation."

"Situation?" Sadie plunked the boxed candy onto the car's hood, then crooked her finger, motioning Hannah to leave the sanctuary of her front porch. "Why don't you come closer, little sister, and tell us all about it."

"I'm fine where I am, thank you very much."

"Okey-dokey, then we'll just stand in your driveway and shout the family's business back and forth at the top of our lungs for all of Wileyville to hear. Lollie Muldoon lives in this neck of the woods, doesn't she?"

That did the trick. Hannah shot off the front porch and dragged her sisters, each by one arm, under the nearest shade tree faster than someone could say, "What would the neighbors think?" "Before either of you say a word, I want it known that I did everything imaginable to make Daddy comfortable in my home."

"Nobody suggested otherwise," Sadie said.

"I made concessions to him, compromises in every single facet of my life—and didn't mind doing it."

"Preaching to the choir, little sister." April held her hands up in surrender. "I slept, ate and scratched my nose on 'Moonie time' the whole while he stayed with me."

"I ran him on a dozen little errands a day." Hannah's hand trembled as she fiddled with her hair.

"Did he make you go to the post office and scan the FBI's 'Most Wanted' photos?" April turned to Sadie. "We did that twice a week. I never could get him to say if he expected to apprehend one of those people on the wall or if he thought he might be among them."

Hannah closed her eyes, sighing. "I changed all the light-bulbs in freestanding lamps to sixty watts because he thought anything higher wasted money and—"

"'Might well set off a rogue electrical fire that'd spread through the place like that.'" April snapped her fingers. "He quoted all the statistics about every conceivable catastrophe just waiting to happen in the common American household to me, too."

"'Old insurance salesmen never die, they just become a pain in the actuary,'" Sadie muttered her father's favorite lousy joke about his lifelong profession and propensity toward spouting anxiety-inducing statistics.

April's shapeless shirt bunched up around her shoulders as she laced her arms over her chest and patted her foot on the soft dirt beneath them. "Did he try to make you vacuum out your dryer vent hose, too?"

"Try? I did it!" Hannah stuck the tip of her tongue out of the corner of her mouth and mimed poking the vacuum attachment into whatever dangerous nook or cranny her father pointed out. "Gladly. Whatever it took to please him."

"Pleasing Daddy?" Sadie rolled her eyes. "Who in her right mind would even attempt it? Placating him, maybe. Or perplexing him long enough that he forgets whatever had him on a tear to begin with, but what could any of us do to really please the old man?"

"Sadie." Hannah clamped her hands on her slender hips, her expression positively grim. "I *cooked* for him."

Sadie feigned a tiny gasp, then nudged her younger sister's bent arm with her elbow. "I don't know who to feel more sorry for over that, sugar, you or Daddy."

"Pity poor Payt on that score. He had to eat the outcome *and* pretend it wasn't absolutely awful."

"From what I saw of his performing skills a few minutes ago, he's slick enough to pull that off without straining any major muscle groups." Sadie smiled.

"We're all agreed, Payt's a regular dreamboat." April raised her head, her gaze on the lovely home Hannah shared with her adorable doctor hubby. She twisted one finger in her long, straight ponytail and heaved a sigh. "But let's not forget about Daddy."

"I refuse to accept the blame for his erratic behavior."

"Blame? Who said anything about blame?"

"I didn't do anything wrong. It's not my fault. Let's get that clear from the start."

"Fine. You didn't do anything wrong, Hannah. I think we can all concede *that* from the onset. Nothing you did could possibly be construed as at fault in any way. You are one hundred percent beyond reproach. Without culpability." Sadie really had to work on her tendency to go a bit overboard on the old sarcasm. But she didn't want to spend the next ten minutes dancing around trying to reassure her sister that they understood that she had done nothing to cause their father to pull another silly stunt. "Now, just tell us what happened."

"I scared Daddy off."

April's jaw set. She shifted her feet in the dirt. "You didn't do anything, but you scared Daddy off?"

"Maybe it was her cooking," Sadie said out of the corner of her mouth.

"Ha-ha, you two. Maybe you should borrow Payt's clown nose and take your comedy act on the road." Hannah's eyes narrowed to slits. "This is not funny. I'm telling you, I scared Daddy away."

"Oh, honey, I think maybe you're being too hard on yourself." Being too hard on yourself—and on those you loved—was an infamous Shelnutt trait, after all. Sadie stroked her sister's tensed-up back. "What on earth could any of us mere mortals do to scare away the likes of Moonie Shelnutt?"

Hannah took a deep breath, like someone about to bungee jump off a ten-story platform with eleven stories worth of rope, then said, quite softly, "I asked him about Mom."

"You *what?*" Sadie's hand clenched instantly into a fist against her sister's spine.

"Oh, no." April stepped backward. "No."

"Why, Hannah?" Sadie's mind was spinning. In a family where so little of any consequence ever seemed spoken, asking about Mom remained the ultimate taboo. No one spoke of her, not even fearless Aunt Phiz. Well, Aunt Phiz had spoken of her once and Moonie promptly sent her away and they didn't see her again for a very long time. That's how powerful a prohibition it was. "Why would you do that?"

"*Why?* Because she's our mother. Because we don't know one single thing about her. Because I am facing some serious fertility issues, and I don't have even a hint of medical history to give to the doctors to help them help me. How about that for why?"

"How about respecting Daddy's feelings on this?" April asked quietly.

"What about our feelings? I think about Mom all the time, y'all. I wonder why she left and if she ever thinks of us. Don't tell me you two don't have any questions about her, that you don't harbor a bittersweet fantasy of maybe even finding her and—"

"*Finding* her?" The words pushed at Sadie. Her knees went weak. She all but staggered at the sheer force of them coming at her. "You didn't mention that kind of wild impossible notion to Daddy, did you?"

"I…I don't know." Hannah cleared her throat. "Maybe. Would it be so wrong if I did?"

"You can ask Daddy for money. You can ask Daddy for advice. You could even ask Daddy to donate a vital organ, and he'd do it without needing to know why." The summer breeze fanned Sadie's face, but that did nothing to cool her passion as she gritted her teeth, took her younger sister by the shoulders and looked her square in the eye. "But you cannot ask him, after all these years, to just open himself up and talk to you about the woman who ran off and left him with three tiny children to raise all on his own."

"But that's not fair."

"Fair has nothing to do with it. I gave up on life being fair a long time ago." Sadie's cheeks stung. "It just *is*, Hannah."

"But if he'd only—"

"'If only' are two of the most destructive words known to man, Hannah." Sadie knew whereof she spoke on that. She had wasted the better part of this last year lost in 'if only,' and it still dogged her so closely that she didn't dare let her sister speak another word about it. "You cannot force Daddy to feel differently about this just because you expect it of him. And you should know by now you are never going to make him act the way you think he should."

"But she's our mother, and he alone can tell us about her."

"For all he has done and all his struggles and sacrifices on our behalf, if he chooses never to speak of our mother again, we have to respect that choice," Sadie insisted. "Right, April? Tell her."

April hung her head.

"April?" Sadie tugged at the hem of her sister's church-camp T-shirt. "Tell her."

"I'm afraid I can't, Sadie." She met Sadie's gaze, her eyes anxious and filled with unspoken aching. "Because while he stayed with me, I did the same thing."

"You *what?*"

"See? It wasn't just me," Hannah said. "April understands how I feel. April understands."

"I understand that of the three of us, I am the lone one who has any memories at all of Mama," April said softly. "It's been so long, and I've tried to preserve them, but they've begun to fade and get all jumbled up. I wanted Daddy to come stay with me because I had hoped…"

Hannah placed her hand on April's arm. "To get your answers?"

April looked from Sadie to Hannah to Sadie again, her eyes moist. "You don't know how hard it is to keep it all inside."

"Did you get your answers?" Sadie asked, her voice clipped but not void of compassion. When April did not respond, Sadie looked to the ground and sighed. "You could always talk to us, sugar."

"And tell you what? A bunch of hazy impressions about people and places I can't rightly recall? That would be cruel to you two."

Hannah tucked a stray hair in place and in doing so set off a cascade of red waves on the other side of her head. "Because it would be so awful for us to hear?"

"Because it might be wrong. I might be telling you something as fact that was just a dream or moment where I confused Mama with Aunt Phiz—the way I confused the park here in Wileyville with one I think I went to before Mama left."

Sadie could understand that. It did not comfort her, but she had learned to deal with things that could only be allowed, not embraced, this past year. Sadly, she realized Hannah, who liked everything tied up in neat little bundles, would never accept the way things had to be.

"No." April sniffled and drew her shoulders up. "Uh-uh. Talking to you two about that is a pointless exercise. Daddy's the only living person who could confirm for me what was real and what I'd just *wanted* to be real about Mama."

"April, you don't have to give us details. I just want to know if you found some measure of peace," Sadie said. All this would be worth it if someone in their family at least got that. "So did you get your answers?"

"I got…"

Hannah hunched forward, the fading sunlight through the trees obscuring her expression.

Sadie inched closer, though whether out of an instinct to protect April or to try to better read even the smallest nuance in her words and body language, Sadie didn't know.

April's hands slapped against her sides. She hung her head. "I got left in the dust when Daddy hopped on the lawn mower and ran away from me."

Hannah shut her eyes. "I know that feeling."

"He didn't take off on your lawn mower, too, did he?" Suddenly Sadie was Miss Pragmatic, aware that she had no idea of the aftermath of Hannah's self-professed scaring off of Moonie Shelnutt.

"I only wish he had. We'd have caught up with him pretty quick, since we have an old walk-behind electric mower." Hannah pantomimed pushing the machine, then raised her open hands to her sides. "No, apparently he talked a friend into giving him a lift while Payt and I were at work."

"Do you know who?"

"How could we know for sure? Daddy only knows three-quarters of all the people in town. Could've been his café cronies, or his insurance-roundtable pals or even one of the willing widows at the seniors circle at church."

Just then Payt appeared at the door, the phone practically glued to his ear, and shouted, "Found him!"

Hannah spun around. "Where is he?"

"Sitting on Sadie's front porch," came the reply through a relaxed and ready smile.

"My...?" Sadie tried to make sense of it all.

Her sisters didn't seem burdened with that problem.

"Well." Hannah laced her arms over her chest.

"I couldn't have said it better myself, little sister." April cocked her hip and mirrored Hannah's pose. "Well."

Being totally devoid of anything remotely appropriate, witty or wise to say about this unexpected turn of events, Sadie managed a weak smile and asked, "Well, *what?*"

"Well, it looks like the decision worthy of King Solomon has been decided and you have been chosen." April gave a quick nod of her head as if to sanction her own decree. Her ponytail followed suit half a second behind.

"Yep." Hannah sighed and, in a tone that wasn't quite smug and wasn't quite sympathetic, summed it all up, "Looks like

Daddy has chosen his favorite home away from home, and—
no surprise—it's Sadie's."

Sadie didn't know whether to celebrate or panic.

"Let's just hope she can do a better job keeping a handle on
the old man than either of us did," April added.

Panic, Sadie decided on the spot. Definitely panic.

❧ Chapter Ten ❧

"Sadie, you know how I hate graveyards." Moonie picked his way along behind her. Now and again he'd prod the path with the cane he had used ever since his car accident. The doctor hadn't found any specific injury beyond some bruises, but the old fellow claimed the whole thing left him "a bit shaky," and so they'd gotten him the antique walking stick to help steady his way.

Sadie suspected her daddy just liked using the polished wooden staff with the brass dog's-head handle because of the instant attention it garnered him. Always, wherever he went, people peppered him with questions. Was he all right? What had happened? What could they do for him?

Funny, Sadie thought, in all these months she had felt emotionally and spiritually "a bit shaky," none of those folks had rallied around her. The only questions she had been asked were: *Why don't you snap out of it? Can you do this for me? When's dinner?*

Not that she blamed anyone. Without any outward manifestation like Moonie's cane, everyone probably assumed she was just fine. And that's exactly what she would have told everyone if they had asked if they could do anything for her, that she was fine. Maybe in this instance she should act a bit more like her daddy, and not be afraid to solicit a little support.

One eye squinting, Moonie poked his cane into a patch of thick grass and took another step.

"What's the matter? You afraid the Lord wants to get a hold of your charming self so badly that if you make one false move, the very ground might open up and swallow you alive?"

"'Course not." He didn't sound convinced. "What possessed you to take a job in a place like this anyway?"

I must've taken total leave of my senses. Sadie stifled her first impulsive response and took a moment to riffle back through the set of ill-conceived choices and out-of-control consequences that had nudged her reluctantly to this spot. Which event, if any, would illustrate it all to a man who first and foremost embraced the concept of life-affirming, joy-seeking self-determination?

I wanted to make my family sorry they ignored me? Too pathetic, even to tell her own father.

Everybody told me I'd be great in the job and I didn't want to let them down? There was a one-way ticket to live-for-your-own-self lectureville.

"Why? Why *did* I take this job?" She had to have a good reason.

Wrapped in a hug of her own tightly woven arms, she took a moment to survey the serene setting.

Pale headstones, their words all but worn away, broken and brackish with age, jutted upward, often at odd angles from the land along the original wrought-iron fence. The newer markers—gray, pink or black granite polished to a mirror finish—filled row after row in the neatly kept rectangles framed by gravel lanes. Sweet yet somber figures of angels or lambs, usually denoting the death of a child, dotted the landscape. And crosses. In Barrett and Bartlett Memorial Gardens, every third grave site claimed a cross for its monument.

As much as the shops and offices of the downtown to their east, as much as the homes and churches and schools fanned out over blocks in every direction from them, this tiny preserve of land told the story of Wileyville and its people. Sadie tipped her head to one side and exhaled, long and slow. In a small way, it told the story of all of God's children.

Everyone born to this earth came to the same end. *Whether we live by grace or by greed, with exuberance or apathy, whether we treat others with respect or revile them, we all hurtle toward this same conclusion,* Sadie reflected. *It's all too brief, and in time all we achieved and owned will become someone else's treasure, someone else's burden.*

Knowing that it would not all end here, Sadie found solace in the awareness that one day all earthly troubles would fall away.

From where they now stood, along the far western edge, where the presold plots butted up against the dwindling land set aside for what was once called the Paupers' Field, Sadie could hear the laughter of children on the swings.

A young mother clapped her hands and urged, "Hold on. Go higher. Don't give up. You can do it."

And, though Sadie could not always make herself trust it, this testament to the possibilities life held served as a reminder that no matter what might weigh her down, she had help and she had hope. Even in the midst of her confusion and turmoil, she had hope.

You can do it. Don't give up. Sadie lifted her face into the warm summer sun and closed her eyes. She breathed deep and caught the scent of the roses that grew in leggy, tangled masses along the cinderblock foundation at the back of her office.

She hadn't expected it, but working in the narrow space between a children's playground and the dearly departed had
brought her a peace that she hadn't known for quite a while.
A sense of being woven into the pattern of God's big tapestry
instead of a loose thread clinging to the fringe.

She *liked* it here.

How could she explain that to a man who hated the very
notion of this place? And why should she have to? Wasn't she,
after all, Moonie Shelnutt's daughter? Hadn't he lived his life
providing her with the exact example she needed for a moment
such as this?

"I work here, Daddy, because I want to." She motioned to
the spot she'd set out to examine and, taking her father by one
arm, started to walk toward it. "If you personally dislike
spending time in the cemetery, well, maybe you should have
thought of that before you ran off to the daughter who *works
in one*."

He matched her pace with only a trace of the hobble that
had slowed him down earlier. "Well, at least you got that
right."

"What?" She stopped in the section of land set aside for the
burial of the town's indigent citizens.

"I aimed to run *to* something, not *away* from anything." He
cast his gaze downward. His muted gray hat hid his expression,
but the shake of his head revealed his melancholy. "Your sisters don't seem to grasp the differentiation."

"That's because the way you did it hurt their feelings."

His head went still. His body tensed and the knuckles gripping the cane went white.

"Nobody, least of all a Shelnutt, feels up to first-rate differentiation when they are sitting on top of a big old mound of
wounded feelings." Sadie looped her arm around his slumped
shoulders and gave them a squeeze. "They'll get over it."

"Didn't intend to hurt anybody, Sadie-girl." His bushy eye-brows hunkered down over his fiery eyes. Gruffness, not re-morse, gave energy to his words. "You know that, right?"

"I know what I see, Daddy." She dropped her arm to her side and turned to begin searching for what she came after.

"What do you see? Because I sure can't find anything wrong in what I did."

Sadie tensed, her gaze still on the grounds around them. She had wondered if she should be more Moonie-like. Well, here was her chance. Her daddy would not hold back, and at a time like this, maybe she shouldn't, either.

"What I saw, Daddy, in April *and* in Hannah, was…was…a feeling that they had somehow failed you. That nothing they did was good enough." *Was she talking about her sisters or herself?* Sadie gripped her hands together and fixed the focus back where it belonged, on her father's actions. "What I saw makes me wonder if you ever seriously think about your exploits before you start off on one. Do you ever take a good long, sobering look at your family and ask yourself if the momentary gratification of whatever stunt you plan to pull is worth the consequences those who love you have to suffer?"

"Suffer?" The color drained from his face. "Oh, Sadie, I never…all my days I tried to create just the opposite effect. I'd give my life—I have given it—to keep you girls from ever hav-ing to really, truly suffer."

Sadie felt like a perfect heel. "I'm sorry. I had no call to talk to you like that."

"If that's what you believe, you had every call—"

"I *don't* believe it, not the suffering part. 'Suffer' is not a word I should have used. 'Insufferable,' maybe, but not 'suffer.'"

"Really?" He peered up at her from under the rim of his trusty old hat. "You mean that?"

"I sure do—especially that part about you being insufferable."
He chuckled weakly.

Sadie laid her hand on his arm, and for the first time she
could ever recall, she did not feel warmth and strength radiat-
ing from her daddy. It startled her, but she didn't dare let on.
So she swallowed hard, to chase away any sound of fear or anx-
iety, and whispered, "You'd never cause any of your girls to suffer. You couldn't."

He rested his hand on hers so lightly that she had to look
to make sure he actually did it. "I hope you always feel that
way, Sadie."

They stood there for only a moment before the old fire lit
his face and he blustered, "So now that you've dragged me into
the middle of the last place on earth I ever planned to go, and
I mean that literally, what are we looking for?"

"A grave."

"There's one now." He pointed with his cane at the nearest
tombstone. "And another." He indicated the next stone over.
"And another and another. Can't swing a cat without hitting a
grave out here, girl." He waggled his cane left and right, then
leaned it against his supposedly injured leg and smugly slapped
his hands together. "There. Seems our work is done. Let's get
out of this place."

"Very funny. But I'm not looking for just any grave. I'm
looking for a fresh one."

"Fresh grave? Anyone tell you that this job has turned you
positively ghoulish, girl?"

"I'm not looking to exhume a body, Daddy, though I have a
sneaky inclination we just might dig up a little dirt."

"Now you got my interest."

"Yeah, mine, too." She rubbed her temple. "Going back
through the records yesterday, I found some paperwork on
Melvin Green."

"Wait. I know that name. The last holdout living in the Paddock Hotel, right?"

"Uh-huh. He had a contract, and they couldn't tear the place down until he moved out."

"Or moved on." Moonie pointed skyward with his cane, his face a mix of reverence and humor. "To that great men's dormitory hotel in the sky."

"Which he did four-and-a-half months ago."

"Nothing suspicious in that, I hope?"

"No, no. Not unless you find it suspicious that a crotchety old man who smoked for eight decades and lived on a diet of sardines and candy bars would die quietly in his sleep at the age of ninety-eight."

"Sardines and candy bars?" He clucked his tongue. "The poor lonely old soul."

"I know. When they scoured the place after he passed, looking for anything that might give the name of his next of kin, a will or at least some indication of his financial situation, that's all they found. No bankbook. No legal documents."

"If he had insurance, I sure didn't sell it to him."

"He didn't have so much as an address book or a birthday or Christmas card tucked in a drawer that might have provided a clue about his friends and family."

"Then he died isolated and utterly alone." Her father's mouth set in a grim line, his shoulders drooped. He clutched his cane. "Ain't right for a human being to end up that way, unnoticed and unloved. Surely he had someone, somewhere—"

"No one found any indication of it—just a cabinet full of cigarettes, candy wrappers and sardine tins. That's why he ended up buried in the county lot for the destitute."

Moonie jerked his chin up, his jaw tight. "So where's this poor, forgotten man's grave?"

"I don't know. There should be a temporary marker out here, but I can't find it."

"Maybe the groundskeeper knocked it over and forgot to re-place it, or maybe some ill-behaved kids came round to snatch it for a souvenir."

Sadie sighed. "I guess. I just think there ought to be some evidence of a grave that's less than six months old, that's all."

"Could someone have come up with the funds, you know, last-minute-like, and afforded the lonely old boy some swank-ier digs?" Solomon suggested.

"Oh, Daddy, *digs?*"

He chuckled. "If we can't laugh a little at what scares the devil out of us, then we're too scared to enjoy life."

Scared? She never envisioned her father as scared of dying. Or maybe something else about Melvin's passing had Daddy on edge. "You feel sorry for Mr. Green, don't you, Daddy?"

"Ain't right. A life shouldn't end up that way."

"Well, maybe he didn't. Maybe you figured it out. Someone came forward and paid for a proper burial for the man, and the data didn't get filed right. Anything's possible, given the state the records are in."

"Bad, huh?"

"A total wreck."

He laughed. "I'd say that surprises me, but having worked with Wileyville officials most of my life, I've grown to expect the unexpected."

"Little of the ol' pot calling the kettle black again, there, huh, Daddy?"

"Difference is, folks voted them into power on the promise they'd act better than they did. Me, I never had no power and never promised anyone I'd be anything other than myself." He winked. "Don't worry yourself overmuch, Sadie-girl, you'll sort it all out in no time."

"Sort what out? You acting like yourself, or the mess the last administration left in my office?" Either way, she found his confidence in her quite touching.

He rasped out a soft chuckle. "Let's go see if we can't locate Melvin's final resting place."

"You don't have to do this, you know, Daddy. Knowing how much you dislike cemeteries, it doesn't seem right to ask you to traipse all over one looking for a stranger's grave."

"No, having heard the story, I feel I owe it to Melvin Green. And I want to help you, Sadie. When I've gone on, I don't want you to have any added reasons to think of me as a man who put his own choices and reservations above the best interests of his daughters."

"Daddy…why would you say such a thing?"

He searched her face but gave no answer.

The summer breeze lifted the hair off the back of her neck. She shivered. "Oh, Daddy, I'd never feel that way."

"I hope not, sweetheart." In a few shuffling steps he put his back to her, then whispered, "But what about your sisters?"

"I can't speak for them. In fact, the way we left things, I can't even speak *to* them. Or they to me."

"Did you three quarrel?"

Quarrel? No, not out and out. But then they never did. Silence was their system and that's how they had left things after Hannah had pointed out that Daddy had ended up with his favored daughter.

She patted his back and moved ahead of him, down along a row of newer markers. "Don't worry about it."

"But I do worry. You girls… I went through so much to keep you together…."

"It's nothing you can do anything about, Daddy." She dismissed the subject with a wave of her hand, her focus on the ground stretching to the far side of the site.

"More than once I've wondered…did I do the right thing? Should I have—" His voice broke. He coughed. "Sadie-girl, I'm afraid."

"Daddy?" She whipped around.

He held his hand up to stop her coming to help him. "I'm afraid I've done something very wrong for all the right reasons. And now I have to ask myself if I should do something more, something I swore I'd never do, to make sure you girls always stay…to…to…"

He stared straight ahead. He reached out his hand to nothing, staggered, then stumbled. His knees crumpled and he went down.

"Daddy!" She rushed to his side just in time to catch him by the arm. "What's wrong?"

"I'm fine. Fine." He put his cane between them.

"You're *not* fine. Let me help you." She tried to push aside the sturdy walking stick, but he resisted with astounding strength. Maybe Sadie was more like her father than she ever knew.

"I am fine, I tell you." He blinked rapidly, then lowered his head. When he raised it again, anger flashed in his eyes. "Fine as I can be given you've hauled me into a graveyard, child. You know how I hate them."

Right now Sadie didn't know anything except that she wanted her daddy to act like his normal, ornery, insufferable self. So she set the example by making the kind of impatient, offhanded remark she would have made if she had just not witnessed what felt to her like the very end of her world. "Daddy, we already had this conversation."

He looked around them as if he'd just now arrived on the scene, and said with a trembling, quiet voice, "I haven't been in a cemetery since…well, a good long while."

"Not in my lifetime." She tried to sound light despite the suffocating apprehension rising from the pit of her stomach.

"Thirty-five years," he said softly.

"Thirty-nine," she corrected him. "Hannah is thirty-five, Daddy."

"Hannah?" He blinked.

"It's Sadie, Daddy. I'm Sadie."

He gripped her hand. He nodded his head in a way that showed he understood, but his eyes remained unfocused and distant.

Sadie couldn't think.

She couldn't distinguish anything but Moonie's gray face.

Her ears filled with his labored breathing.

Still, she must have had a well of great reserve within, as she found the power to lift her father to his feet and say in a calm, comforting tone, "I think maybe we'd better get to the hospital."

"Do you?"

"Yes, I do. Can you walk?"

"I can walk." He leaned on her and let his cane fall to the ground. "If *you* want me to walk, I can."

"Okay, nice and slow then. Steady, steady." They eked along, one uncertain step after another. "Just keep walking."

"I can do anything for you," he muttered again.

Anything?

"Step, Daddy, keep moving."

How about never, ever growing old? Never getting sick or feeble?

"Lean on me," she said. "Just a little ways more."

Never thinking I'm too old to need my daddy and never scaring me like this ever again?

She scanned their surroundings furiously, hoping to spot someone she could call to for assistance. But no one else ever hung around the graveyard on a bright summer day. She got them both to her car and opened the door. "I'm going to have to drive you, Daddy. It's just a quick trip to the emergency room. Can you sit up in the car?"

"Anything." He dropped into the passenger seat, and when Sadie bent down to tuck his feet inside the car, he touched her cheek. "I'd fly if you asked me to."

"Well, I plan to drive fast, but we'll try not to let it go that far."

"I only wish I could have made you trust in that more."

Before she could formulate some answer to the odd comment, her father spoke again, his eyes teary.

"I only wonder what might have been if you had understood how much I loved you, dear."

"I do understand that. But right now I need for you to sit still and hang on."

"For you, I'd do anything." He smiled, settled down into the seat, laid his head back and shut his eyes. "Anything for you...Teresa."

✎ Chapter Eleven ✎

April rushed past the windowless blue-on-blue waiting room. Before Sadie could call out to her, her hiking boots scuffed on the old tile floor and did a thundering turnabout. Seconds later, she stood in the doorway, her hair clinging to her damp forehead and her cheeks flushed. "What happened?"

Hannah, seated in the corner, barely looked up from the tattered magazine in her hands. "Sadie broke Daddy."

The fluorescent lights overhead buzzed.

Sadie gritted her teeth. "I did not *break* Daddy."

"Oh, really?" The pages flipped closed in Hannah's lap. She laced her arms over her chest, and when she spoke she looked all of five, fretting and frightened. "He left my house in perfect health, and I can present the testimony of a live-in doctor to prove it. But give Daddy one day in Sadie's care, and what happens?"

"I don't know," April said, trying to catch her breath. "That's what I'm trying to find out. What happened?"

"We got calls to rush to the hospital, that's what. The *hospi-*

tal—and me working the desk in Payt's office just down the street. She could just have easily brought him there for care."

"No offense to Payt's skills as a doctor—or yours as a receptionist—" Okay, it was a snotty thing to say but sometimes Hannah just brought out the…the…the *sibling* in her. "But Daddy didn't need to go to a pediatrician's office. He needed a hospital. It's not like it took more than a minute longer to get over here."

Small though it was, Wileyville, being the county seat, did have a regional health center on the edge of town. In truth it got more business from people in the more rural outlying areas, while the locals tended to drive the seventy miles to the nearest sizable town for medical attention. But today Sadie had whispered praises to the Lord for every second the proximity of the medical center shaved off the trip to the E.R.

"What's his condition?" April wrung her hands, and a tiny bit of potting soil trickled between her fingers. Obviously she'd run over straight from work without even stopping to clean up. "Grave? Because I swear that Olivia said on the phone he was grave."

Sadie shut her eyes. For an instant she thought to blame her seventeen-year-old's cell phone for the miscommunication, but in her heart she recognized that even in a dire circumstance Olivia only half listened to whatever Sadie tried to tell the girl.

"He *fell* in a grave," Hannah supplied, which at least gave Sadie some hope that Olivia's lack of attentiveness might well be genetic instead of a personal slight.

"He did not fall in a grave." Sadie's heels clicked over the short distance from the bank of chrome-and-vinyl seats to the doorway. She took April's arm to bring her inside. "He sat on a grave."

April pushed her hair away from her eyes. "Why would he do that?"

"Because Sadie dragged him to work with her, that's why."

Hannah had that same impassioned tone she'd had at thirteen when she'd misheard Sadie and April and thought they were going to put a bag of cats in the oven. Even after they had shown her the *baguettes* of bread for dinner, Hannah had taken a while to calm down and get the incident clear in her thoughts. When Sadie's noble-spirited, willing-to-take-on-the-world-for-a-just-cause sister got going, neither fine points nor facts got in the way of her having her say.

"Knowing his intense aversion to the place, the woman who had the nerve to lecture *us* on not forcing him to do anything against his will hauled Daddy into the cemetery and made him walk around with her." Hannah's lower lip quivered. "No wonder he had a stroke."

"A stroke!" April sank down to sit on the edge of a sofa cushion.

"A transient ischemic attack," Sadie said with measured precision, wanting to make sure she got every word right.

April flattened her hand over her heart. "In English?"

"A *stroke*." Hannah crossed her legs, then her arms, then she shifted on the vinyl seat, literally giving Sadie the cold shoulder.

"A teeny-weeny, itty-bitty, minor, paltry, ministroke." Sadie held her thumb and forefinger a hairbreadth apart. Looking at the meaningless gesture, she had to admit it did not ease her angst one teeny-weeny, itty-bitty paltry bit.

"A ministroke, which could be a precursor to a big fat massive stroke," Hannah muttered.

"Have you called the church?" April looked around as if she expected to find a phone nearby. "Did anyone notify the prayer chain?"

"Done and done." Hannah's expression softened. "We've been doing our share of praying here, too."

"And?" April prodded.

"And Daddy's going to be okay." Sadie raised her chin and leaned back against the doorframe.

"Thank you, Jesus," April whispered, the heel of her hand pressed to her forehead. "Thank you."

"God heard our prayers." Hannah reached out at last and grasped their eldest sister on the knee. "He always does, you know. He hears. Even if some of us don't seem to think we have anything to say to Him."

Sadie twisted her upper body so she could look down the long, silent hallway.

A moment passed and then another.

Finally April cleared her throat and scraped her boots lightly along the floor beneath the seat. "So a transient, uh, what?"

"Transient ischemic attack." Sadie still could not turn to face her sisters.

"TIA. See, it's so common it has its own nice, tidy abbreviation." Hannah dropped the antagonism and shifted into hyperperky reassurance mode.

Sadie wasn't sure she'd call it an improvement.

"Payt says some people have them and don't even know it."

"What caused it?" April asked.

Hannah put her hand on Sadie's arm. "Sadie?"

"I *did not*." She whipped around to confront her accuser. "And let it be known here and now that I refuse to allow anyone to reduce this to a lot of senseless finger-pointing!"

Hannah harrumphed.

April pursed her lips. The faintest light of humor shone deep, deep in her worried gaze.

Sadie followed the dip in her sisters' line of vision to the finger she had been jabbing repeatedly into the air as she preached against finger-pointing. She closed her fist, then tucked her hand behind her back.

Hannah curled her legs up under her in the seat and smoothed back her hair. "As I was going to say... Sadie, since we're all here now, why don't you tell us what happened in the cemetery."

"Well, it all happened so fast. One minute we were discussing Melvin Green—"

"Whoa." April held up a hand, her expression intense as a crime-scene investigator combing for even the most seemingly insignificant of clues. "Melvin Green? That some friend of Daddy's?"

"Far as I can tell he wasn't a friend of anybody's," Sadie said. "The only reason I brought him up was because the thought of that man dying unloved and forgotten really seemed to agitate Daddy."

"So that's when you first noticed the onset of the attack?" April scooched closer.

"Yes. Well before that he said some things about..." What had he said? The panic of the moment had blanked much of it from her mind. "He said he hoped we never thought he'd put his own motivations above ours and that he wished you two could understand he wasn't running from you but *to* something."

Hannah's head snapped up. "To what?"

"I don't know but...I think...no, I'm almost certain that it involved Mama."

"Mama?" April whispered.

"Why?" Hannah closed in, leaning in Sadie's direction as far as possible without actually tumbling forward out of her seat. "Why do you think that? Did he say something specific?"

"No, he rambled on about whether he made the right choices and sounded like he had some regrets...but it was all so vague."

April swept her hand back over her forehead to push the stray hairs from her face. The brown strands that clung to her trembling fingers looked darker than usual, but Sadie didn't know if that was because of sweat or potting soil. "Then why do you think it's about Mama?"

"Because." Sadie hated to say it aloud.

Saying it seemed, somehow, both a betrayal and a confirmation of her father's weakness. If he were here and had any cognizance of his words, would he have told his daughters what he'd said? Would he want them to know? Silence was the hallmark of this small sisterhood, after all, and they had learned that from none other than the man they now wanted Sadie to expose.

And yet that same man had admonished her to start something. *Someone has to start, Sadie. Whatever you're doing isn't working—surely you can see that? If you won't do it for yourself, someone has to start—start talking the truth, start looking at things in a new light, start reaching out.*

Someone had to start to change things between the three of them, and it might as well be her and it might as well be now. "Because as Daddy was fading in and out of coherence, he talked about doing anything for me."

"No surprise there," Hannah muttered.

"No, you don't understand. Then he said, 'I'd do anything for you…Teresa.'"

At the mention of their mother's name, April and Hannah exchanged wary glances.

"Did he…" Hannah finally ventured. "Did he say any more?"

Sadie shook her head. "But clearly he spoke like a man filled with regrets. He loved her, y'all. After all these years, I think he still does. It must have nearly killed him when she ran away."

Sadie braced herself for an outburst from Hannah about what their mother's leaving had done to them, but it did not come. Only silence and sorrow filled the space between them.

April sniffled, raised the back of her hand to brush the tip of her nose, then froze midgesture. She opened her hand to show the streaks of dirt on her knuckles. "Look at me, I'm a mess."

"No more than the rest of us," Hannah joked as she pulled a tissue from her purse and handed it to her sister. "Sadie and I just wear our mess in different ways."

"When did you get so wise?" Sadie asked, venturing a tiny smile.

"Well I should be wise." Hannah held her head high. "As should you. It's our birthright, isn't it?"

"What birthright?" April blew her nose.

"As Solomon's daughters!" Hannah laughed, a warm though not hearty laugh. "That experience alone should make us wise beyond our years."

"You'd think, but so far all it's made me is *old* beyond my years," Sadie muttered. Then she managed a half smile and added, "Can you imagine how young we'd all look if we'd had a regulation, standard-issue, no-nonsense father?"

Hannah scoffed. "We might have looked younger, but it would have bored us to death."

"I tell you, Hannah, this wisdom thing you've got going all of a sudden, it's starting to scare me." Sadie laughed.

"Maybe I'll put it and my three years as a journalism major to good use and start an advice column in the paper." Hannah struck a regal pose that might do for a publicity photo, her hand sweeping out as if she were reading a headline. "Dear Hannah."

"You should." Sadie nudged her sister's knee. "You should do more with your writing."

Hannah shook her head. "With work and now trying to start a family one way or another…I wouldn't have the time."

"You never know," Sadie said, softly but with all the authority of a person who understood that sometimes opportunities to do a life's work found you, not the other way around.

They fell into silence for a time.

Finally April looked around and asked, "Where are my brothers-in-law?"

"Payt had to stay at work. He'll be here as soon as he can."

"Same with Ed?" April asked.

"No. Actually, Ed... Ed was taking a golf lesson."

"You're kidding? Why?"

Should she tell them the long, convoluted story about Carmen Gomez coming back from her trip full of ideas that she'd gotten from other sales reps from around the country? About how the girl they called "Go-Go" had gone and mentioned Downtown Drug to someone in acquisitions for a national chain of pharmacies and they wanted to fly Ed out to a resort to talk? Did her sisters really need to know that when Sadie had needed her husband, he was out on the eleventh hole of the golf course taking lessons so he wouldn't look like a country bumpkin when he met with the big boys who might just offer to buy his business?

Sadie looked up at the white acoustical tiles in the ceiling, folded her arms and said, "Ed had a...meeting. He won't be long."

Her sisters nodded.

No one said anything more for a few minutes until April tossed the tissue she'd used to tidy up with into the trash can and said, "Well one good thing will come of all this."

"What's that?" Sadie asked a bit too brightly.

"The doctors will probably take away Dad's driver's license for us."

Hannah shook her head. "Give me one reason how that would stop him if he really wanted to get behind the wheel."

"No license, no insurance," April said.

"Ladies and gentlemen, we have a winner." Sadie clapped a couple of times, then dropped her hands to her sides. "It doesn't feel much like winning, does it?"

"It feels like a dirty rotten trick for age to have pulled on someone who's still so young at heart," Hannah muttered.

This time Sadie and April nodded their agreement, and again the room went still.

After a few minutes, Hannah picked up a magazine, flipped through a few pages, then slapped it back onto the table. "It's the quiet that gets on my nerves."

Sadie couldn't have agreed more with Hannah on that. The not knowing gnawed at her already frayed nerves, but the *quiet*...

The quiet crept into Sadie's consciousness around every guard and gate into the center of her soul, and with it brought reminders. One floor up in this very building she had waited first for the doctor to bring her test results, then for Ed to come and get her. It had been quiet then, and with the heartbreaking news that she had lost her last chance to have another child, Sadie had carried a bit of that quiet away with her.

From that point on the quiet had permeated her existence, often drowning out the sounds that had once meant so much to her. The daily yakking about nothing in particular with Olivia. Joking around with her son. Breezy phone chats with one sister or another. Long, meaningful conversations with Ed. And prayer.

Earnest, humble, personal and profound prayer had given way to this thing that was not quite silence and not near noise. Quiet.

Sadie shuddered. "I know. I wish somebody—anybody—would come talk to us."

Hannah craned her neck to peer past Sadie's shoulder. "I think you're about to get your wish, big sister."

"Mrs. Pickett—Sadie—I came as soon as I heard about your father!"

Only thing that traveled faster than juicy news in a small town was a politician looking for an angle to make that news work for him.

"Mayor Furst! Whatever brings you here?"

Photo op?

Naw, not a local reporter in sight.

Chance to get a jump on the next election by showing active concern for an elderly citizen?

Not likely. Of all the folks in the seniors crowd, the man a politician would least like to have his name linked to would be a loose cannon like Moonie Shelnutt.

Trying to ingratiate himself to the medical community in order to garner volunteer first-aid workers for the Bass-travaganza?

Possible, but…

"Sadie, Sadie, do you need to even ask? Worry over Moonie brings me here, of course. Word is, he took a tumble in our Memorial Gardens?"

Ah, fear of a lawsuit.

Always a popular means of prying the powers-that-be out of their ivory towers to mingle with the voter base.

"He had a…" She didn't have the energy go into details for yet another person who, she realized, wouldn't fully listen to or care about what she said. "He had a medical thing. It could have happened anywhere. He didn't fall in a grave or trip on a tombstone or get stung by a bee cruising the flower arrangements—or whatever's the current gossip."

"Good. Good to know." He nodded slowly, then stroked his jawline. "How's he faring?"

"The doctor hasn't told us anything for a while, but Daddy was walking and talking just fine—" if "just fine" meant soaking up every last drop of attention from the staff and asking if they thought he'd now qualify for an electric wheelchair to tool around town in "—when they took him off for an EEG."

"That's terrific. Just terrific." The mayor glanced up and down the hallway, all the while giving her what he must have intended as a sympathetic pat on the shoulder.

Sadie pulled her head back to avoid another distracted *whap* to the side of her head and said, "Well, if that's all you wanted…"

"All? Did I say that was all?"

"I just assumed."

"Never assume, Sadie Pickett. You're a public personage now, you don't have that kind of luxury."

"I don't think being the cemetery lady makes me a public personage."

"You think we can step into one of these empty rooms and have a talk?"

"I really hate to leave…"

"Won't take a minute."

"But if the doctor comes back…"

"Your sisters are here, and your wonderful husband and…" He made a quick check of the waiting room, scowled, then blustered, "Your sisters are here, they can come get you if you're needed."

"Ed's coming over as soon as he finishes an important…thing," Sadie volunteered too eagerly. "Ryan's manning the phone at home and Olivia is hurrying back from a shopping trip in Lexington."

"You're lucky to have them," he muttered, taking Sadie by the elbow. "Let's step across the hall."

Sadie yanked her arm free. "Perhaps you should tell me why first. Am I in some kind of trouble with the city government?"

"Trouble? No, no trouble. If it's one thing we pride ourselves on in Wileyville, it's that we have no trouble here. An absolute absence of trouble is how I'd describe the political scene in this town. In fact, some folks find it troubling how very little trouble we tend to have. Makes them wonder what their elected officials are paid to do—since it's certainly *not* to deal with a bunch of trouble."

He finally took a deep breath.

Sadie did the same, then asked, "So why do you need to talk to me?"

"Something I heard about your work has me troubled."

"My work? Has someone complained about the way I do my job?"

"No, no, no. I've just had some concerned feedback about the way you are doing your job."

Sadie rubbed her temple and wondered if there was such a thing as a mayor-to-English translation booklet.

"Walk with me a moment, Sadie, and I'll tell you what I see." Before she could ask for a clarification, he had slipped his arm around her shoulders and began steering her down the hallway. "I see a dedicated public servant. A conscientious employee. Someone unafraid to put in long hours, to tackle the thankless jobs, to go the extra mile. I wish everybody on the city payroll had that brand of commitment."

"And?"

"And I want you to knock it off."

She halted halfway down the hallway. "But you just said—"

"Sadie." His arm slid away and he took her by the shoulders. "You're doing too much. You've taken a handful of responsibilities that took your predecessors a couple days a week to keep on top of and turned it into a...well, for want of a better word, a *job*."

"But I thought—"

"You know what they say, Sadie—when you work for the government, you don't get paid to think."

"Who says that?"

"Most people would love to draw your pay for just showing up a few afternoons a week and doing some filing. Maybe sitting at the guest book and donation table on Memorial Day."

"Full-time pay for part-time work doesn't seem like the best use of taxpayer money, Mr. Mayor."

"Who said you don't work full-time? You're on call 24/7. That's why the city supplies you with a cell phone, you know."

Sadie blinked, wondering if she should tell the mayor that the sleek little phone with all the tiny buttons and gadgets stayed in a drawer in her office most of the time.

Before she could decide to say anything, Mayor Furst charged on ahead. "Don't make too big a deal out of all of this. Do your job, sure, but don't let it get out of hand. Relax. Enjoy. Have fun."

"Have fun?" *Being the cemetery lady?* "Relax?" *While waiting for news about her father in the hospital?* "Enjoy? Mayor Furst, I don't think you—"

"Now what did I say about thinking, Sadie?"

She sighed. "Not to do it too much."

"That's right. Now I won't intrude any longer. Your family needs you."

Right, her family needed her. Well obviously her kids didn't need her, or they'd be here, and her husband hardly needed her, at least not right now, not unless she could teach him the intricacies of the long putt or act as a caddie. But her sisters...

She peered into the room to find April and Hannah chatting away.

Sadie sighed.

The doors on the elevator behind her whooshed open, and Mayor Furst got on, probably pleased as punch for the small but captive audience. Someone got off the elevator, and the doors rolled to a close again, but before Sadie could turn to see who it was, a commotion from around the corner demanded her attention.

Moments before he actually came into view, Moonie made his presence known. He was all right! He had to be, given the way he was shouting and laughing and giving the nurse directions on how to steer the wheelchair.

He was okay for now, but that didn't mean he was out of the woods. He would require help. Maybe her employer didn't need her. Maybe her family didn't need her. But one thing Sadie could always count on, her father most definitely needed her.

The nurse wheeled the old man around the corner just as Sadie felt a familiar reassuring hand on her shoulder.

Moonie's face lit up.

Sadie grinned.

In his most booming voice, her daddy spread his arms wide and shouted to the woman standing at Sadie's back, "Martha Tatum Fitts McCrackin! Good to see you, girl! Are you ready to take this old man home?"

⊸ Chapter Twelve ⊸

"And they lived happily ever after." The back cover of the storybook in Sadie's lap fell shut. There. Sadie had fulfilled her obligation to share her favorite children's book as part of the Leaders Are Readers program. She hadn't left the house since Daddy had gone to live with Mary Tate and Royal. It had been made clear that no one needed her, so why bother? If she hadn't made the commitment to participate in this program for the library, she'd still be home now in her chair.

A dozen young children leaped up from the blankets spread out by their parents in a shady spot in the park. With mothers and caregivers watching over them, some raced off, calling dibs on the swings or to be first on the slide. Some called out for the others to join them in one game or another.

One towheaded boy in red overalls and sneakers with laces that wouldn't stay laced chose to unleash his pent-up energy by running in circles with his arms outstretched, making sputtering-engine noises.

Sadie rested her chin in her hand.

You could use these kids as a metaphor for the types of people in this life; achievers who set their sights on their goals and went after them, leaders who naturally attracted others and seemed to intuit how to keep them working together and...

She turned in time to spot the towheaded boy trip over a tree root, careen out of control, then stumble backward and plop down on his behind. He sat a moment, wearing that stunned expression somewhere between an end-of-the-world wail and an oh-well-let's-chase-a-bug shrug. Finally, he let out one last engine sputter and flopped backward to lie in the grass looking up at the sky.

If these kids were a metaphor for human archetypes, then Sadie was definitely of the spinning, sputtering, plopping and flopping variety.

In fact, it looked so good, she decided to try it. Not that anyone cared about what she did, anyway.

The grass crunched softly when her head lay back on it. A few wayward blades grazed her neck but did not tickle her. In fact, she felt nothing. Absolutely nothing but...

Blue sky and the mosaic of leaves overhead blurred. She shut her eyes to try to hold the warm moisture back.

It did not work.

"You know, Mrs. Pickett, you keep that up, you're going to get tears in your ears."

Air rushed against the back of Sadie's throat, then into her lungs so suddenly she had to sit up and cough to keep it from overwhelming her. When she could speak at last, she placed her hand on her hot cheek and looked deep into the dark, sensitive eyes of Claudette Addams and said, "And here I clean forgot my earplugs."

Brilliant. Found sprawled out in the grass, did Sadie come up with some clever reason to explain it away? Had she had the quick-wittedness to point out that from that position the sun made her eyes sting, thus excusing the tears? No, she'd sat up and babbled something about earplugs to the wife of the town's newest minister.

Mrs. Addams had arrived last winter with her husband and two sons, and since her husband had taken the pulpit to lead the fourth largest congregation in town, promptly joined the Council for Christian Women.

Sadie knew nothing else about the woman except what her eyes told her.

She wore coral lipstick. So few woman could. But playing against the rich mahogany of Mrs. Addams's complexion and the flawless white of her teeth, it couldn't have looked more right. And she always dressed as if she had just come from or was just about to head off to sit in the front row at Sunday service. Today, the sherbet color of her linen suit looked like something fresh out of a watercolor painting. Not a hair on her head was out of place. Down to her pearl earrings, everything about the woman communicated serene dignity.

Sadie sniffled. She swiped her knuckle over her damp cheek. She lifted her chin and mustered a weak smile to show her own depth of poise. She opened her mouth to say something she hoped would come out witty and wise and wonderful, and promptly hiccuped.

Mrs. Addams reached into her purse and pulled out a stark white tissue. The large diamond of her wedding set winked in the sunlight as she held her hand out to Sadie and asked, "Are you all right?"

"Yes. Perfectly all right." Sadie accepted the tissue, then dragged it under her damp lashes with a casual chuckle meant to show that she did this kind of thing all the time. Well not *all* the time...and not *this* kind of thing. "Of course, I...I...don't usually lie around in the park like this."

A light shone from the depths of the other woman's eyes as she laid her hand on Sadie's arm and said, "I know."

"I was just…" The warmth of that touch could have cut through icy bone. Just that fast, in no more than an instant, the tender gesture sank beneath Sadie's threadbare facade and went straight to the center of her pain. She drew a shuddering breath. "…having a moment."

A moment? A momentary lapse of all good sense was more like it. Sadie could only hope that a minister's wife would simply assume she'd meant a moment of prayer. How could a woman so spiritually advanced, so socially adept, so successful in her home and so outwardly pulled together, understand Sadie choosing the middle of a public park to throw herself a pathetic little pity party?

But when Claudette Addams leaned so close that Sadie could smell the lilac scent of her perfume and whispered, "Trust me, I've had *days* like that myself," Sadie believed her.

"Why don't we get up off this grass and…are you heading to your office now?"

"Office?" The small building loomed large in her perception, as it had when Sadie had first arrived in the park to participate in the citywide Leaders Are Readers program today. She scrambled to her feet with a little help from Mrs. Addams, and pretended to brush unseen grass from her clothes. "Oh, no. No reason to go into the office today."

Or any day, according to the man who'd approved her appointment to the job.

"Then are you free for lunch?"

"Lunch?" Someone wanted to have lunch with Sadie? Did the woman not have a clue? Sadie was inept, insignificant, invisible. Did Claudette Addams have any idea how hard it would be to have lunch with an invisible companion?

"Yes, lunch," the other woman said softly.

"I would love to, but it's sort of a crazy day." *And I'm sort of a crazy lady.* "Things to do, places to…do them. You know how it is."

"Oh, of course. You're probably on your way to see your husband or your sisters—they all work downtown, don't they?"

"My…? Um, yes. Actually, Ed, April, Hannah *and* her husband all work within a stone's throw of here." *And me fresh out of stones.* "But they're much too busy for me to bother them right now. I was just…" She made a half-hearted motion in the general direction of the opposite end of town, and without any idea of what else to say, concluded, "…you know."

"Going down to the dance school to see the woman who cares for your father?"

"The Royal Academy," Sadie corrected. "It's more of a multipurpose school of charm and, um, movement."

Sadie swept her arms out, hoping to look like gracefulness incarnate, lost her balance and almost pitched forward onto her nose. She cleared her throat, shrugged and twisted her fingers together. "You can take a class in pretty much anything from poise to Pilates to pumping iron to preparing for the annual cotillion."

"The Royal Academy," the other woman repeated. "That's run by your friend, then, Mary McCrackin, isn't it?"

"Mary Tate McCrackin, yes." *What was this? A setup for This Is Your Life? Would this woman she hardly knew suddenly cry out "And do you recall this voice from grade school?"*

"Charming lady. I recall Mrs. McCrackin from the last meeting of the Council of Christian Women."

You mean the one where Moonie almost plowed you and the others down with the lawn mower? "Oh, of course."

"I had hoped to see her at the next meeting." She clasped her hands together and cocked her head, her eyes no longer so sympathetic. "But so far, unless I'm wrong, you've failed to schedule another meeting."

"No, you're not wrong." I have failed. *I failed as council president just like I fail at everything. So good of you to come all the way over to the park to point it out to me.*

"Then I didn't miss this new council's second meeting. Because you haven't—"

"Scheduled one. Yes, we established that. I have fallen down on the job." Sadie spread her hands as she glanced down at the spot where Mrs. Addams had found her, and still trying to make light of it all said, "You can see that's sort of a pattern with me. Falling down."

Mrs. Addams frowned. "If it's a pattern with you, then why were you put in a leadership role over the council?"

"Because…" Sadie rubbed her hands together, her shoulders hunched. "I was…the only regular member who didn't show up the day they nominated officers." She cleared her throat. "It was a joke…the whole falling down…the pattern…that was a joke because you found me…"

"Then you weren't elected president by default for not showing up?"

"No, actually, sadly, that is true. That did happen."

"Well, if they elected you, then surely they trusted you to carry out your duties?"

"Um…" Sadie drew out the single syllable into a soft hum as she nodded, then raised her hands in surrender. "One would think."

"And do you plan to?"

"Think?" According to the mayor, that wasn't part of her job description.

"Carry out your job. What do you plan to do about a second meeting of the council?"

"Well I don't know. I mean, what could I do to top that first one?" Sadie laughed nervously. "'Course, if I give my daddy enough time, I'm sure he could come up with something. Maybe come riding by on a circus elephant or as a one-man band."

The woman exhaled, shut her eyes and visibly composed herself before meeting Sadie's gaze again and asking warmly, "How is your father? Is he feeling better?"

There were no secrets in a small town. Everyone knew about Moonie's health crisis. They also all knew that while he had only lasted a day in Sadie's care, the old goat was thriving under Mary Tate and Royal's ministrations.

Sadie gritted her teeth. "My daddy is just...peachy."

"Peachy? You sure? It's none of my business, but that sounds more like sour grapes to me."

"You're right."

"Oh?"

"It is none of your business."

At last Claudette Addams's smile blossomed into a full-blown grin. "There. I knew if I asked enough questions, I'd finally get an honest answer out of you."

"Honest?" Was the women implying that Sadie had been trying to hide something? She was—trying to hide something—but who did Claudette Addams think she was to throw it in Sadie's face like that? Sadie put her hands on her hips. "You want honest?"

Mrs. Addams did not back down an inch. "Seems a fitting way to go between Christian sisters, wouldn't you say?"

"Careful what you ask for, Mrs. Addams. I am known to be quite hard on my sisters."

"Well, bring it on, I can take it as long as it's honest. And call me Claudette."

"And I'm Sadie. Now, okay, Claudette, how's this for honest? My own father has chosen to live with my best friend rather than rely on me or my sisters. Said sisters are at the moment not speaking to me because they think *I* think I'm the only one of us competent enough to look after Daddy, despite the fact that I almost killed him. My husband, who never has a moment of spare time for me or the family, suddenly has all the time in the world to take up golf under the sweet tutelage of a young, pretty, vivacious, go-getter, a young cosmetics sales rep—"

Claudette raised a finger to interject, "You said *young* twice."

"I know. She's *that* young." Sadie drew a deep breath. "And if that weren't enough, the job I thought would revitalize me has turned out to be a farce, my spiritual life isn't much better *and* my children are teenagers! And that, Mrs. Addams, is why calling a second meeting of a council that only elected me because they pretty much thought they could boss me around is not the first item on my personal agenda!"

Claudette let out a long, low whistle and laughed. "Just hearing all that makes *me* want to lie down in the grass and weep."

Sadie managed a wry smile. "Maybe if we both do it, we'll start a trend."

"Honey, if every woman who felt overwhelmed by her life joined in, the salt from our tears would kill every blade of grass in the park."

"Really?" Sadie blinked. "Do you think so? When I look at the women around me, they all seem so competent and confident and capable of anything. I feel like I'm the only one whose life is a runaway bus that just broke through the guardrail over a rock-strewn embankment."

"On fire."

"What?"

"You left out the part about feeling like that bus is on fire. Oh, and children bouncing on the back seat screaming, 'Faster, Mommy, make it go faster.'"

"You *do* know."

"Honey, believe it or not, that's one crowded bus." She raised her head and looked out toward the street. "In fact, I heard in a sermon once that if you think of everyone you meet as an uncertain, hurting individual, most of the time you'll be right."

"So you've felt that way?"

She nodded. "And you?"

Goose bumps rose on Sadie's arms. She clenched her jaw and moved her gaze slowly from the cemetery to the distant point of town where the pharmacy stood. "Sometimes I think I'm going to jump right out of my skin, you know?"

Claudette nodded again. "Uh-huh. Jump right out and run away."

"Yes! It's like when I was six and I broke my arm."

"Trying to jump out of your skin?"

"No, trying to jump off the garage with an umbrella for a parachute."

The other woman winced.

"It hurt bad at first. Then the pain subsided and I didn't give it much thought. Then I got this itch deep, real deep inside, way beyond where I could stick my fingers down into that ratty old cast to scratch. Nothing worked. Nothing satisfied that need to get at the itch. I thought it would drive me right out of my mind."

"But it didn't."

"Some people might argue with that, but I do thank you for saying it, especially given how you found me today."

The grass swished around their ankles.

"So you were saying you feel that way now? Like you can't satisfy some need in yourself?"

"I don't know what to do, how to help, how to cope, how to give the things that used to come so naturally to me."

"You feel all hemmed in."

"I do." Sadie pushed her hair back and lifted her face to the breeze, her eyes narrowed. "Hemmed in and cast adrift all at the same time. Does that make any sense?"

Claudette stood there a moment with her hand clenched in a loose fist, then took a deep breath and let it out. "It does to someone who's felt it."

"Not you," Sadie whispered, though she already knew the answer.

"Yes, *me*."

"But you look so pulled together, and your family...your sons are just precious, and your husband is a *minister*."

"Ministers and their families and their wives are not exempt from the harshness of this world, Sadie. Including family trials and insecurities about young, pretty, vivacious, *young* go-getters."

"Really?"

"Really."

"The worst part about that is that I trust Ed. I don't think I have reason to worry that he will stray from his vows."

"I know. Makes it worse, doesn't it? Makes you feel like a shrew for even bringing it up to him."

"A shrew. Exactly, a jealous shrew."

"But that's not what's at the root of what brought you literally to the ground today, is it?"

Sadie shook her head. She turned, her hands folded together, to watch the kids on the playground for a moment. "I had a miscarriage a little over seven months ago."

"Seven months? Then you're coming up on the due date anytime now."

"Yes." Her cool fingertips pressed against the hollow of her throat. "It...it just passed. How did you think of that? No one, not even Ed, remembered about it."

"I've marked a couple of those not-to-be-birthdays in my life, as well."

Sadie reached out and laid her hand on the other woman's wrist. "I'm so sorry."

"It's all right. I have my sons and they are the light of my life."

"But?"

"I still wonder sometimes what might have been."

"Do you still have that itch?"

"No. I have 'the peace that passeth understanding.'"

"I guess that comes in time," Sadie murmured.

"Not always. Sometimes *time* needs a little help."

Sadie threw her hand up. "Spare me the come-to-Jesus-talking-to about how if I laid my troubles on the Lord and truly trusted in Him, I'd be all better by now."

"I wasn't going to question your faith. I was going to ask if you'd consulted a doctor," Claudette told her.

"A doctor?" Sadie shook her head. "And have him tell me to face the fact that after a certain age some women just aren't going to be able to become mothers again and isn't it time I accepted that reality and moved on?"

"Is that what your doctor told you?"

Sadie nodded.

"Then the man's right. It is time you moved on—to another doctor."

"I...I just can't. And I don't see the point of it, really. We didn't plan the baby that I lost. So it's not like we need fertility counseling or anything. I just don't see what a doctor can do."

"Did you have...trouble after your other children were born?"

"Not bad. I mean, that whole year after a baby is born is so hectic and you're so tired. How could a person judge really if they were sick or sad or just worn to a frazzle?"

"In other words, yes. You did have postpartum issues in the past."

Sadie looked away. "That hardly applies this time, though, does it? I *lost* the baby."

"But your body still—"

"Don't, please." She held her hand up. She'd said more than she wanted to and heard more than she could deal with under the circumstances. "I don't want to talk about this, not here, not now."

"When you're ready to talk—and to hear—more, I hope you feel you can call me."

She did feel that she could, but it felt so strange to say that aloud.

"Do you really believe that about the itch? That it's a sign of healing?"

"It's a sign of feeling something, isn't it?"

Sadie drew the fresh-smelling air into her lungs and let it out with a smile. "I guess it is."

"So what are you waiting for, Sadie? Maybe it's time you scratched that itch, girl. Scratch that itch."

"You know, Claudette, maybe I will!"

◆ Chapter Thirteen ◆

"Are there going to be fireworks in the park tonight?"

Ryan tucked the last of six sparklers into the red, white and blue bandanna he'd tied around a beat-up old cowboy hat while he waited for Sadie to pour milk onto his cereal.

"Oh, grow up!" Olivia, leaning against the refrigerator, didn't even bother to cover the mouthpiece of the phone when she snapped at her younger brother. "When have there ever been fireworks in the park on the Fourth of July?"

"Never. But maybe this year it will be different." Ryan pushed his hat down low on his head, then nudged his sister out of the way so he could put the milk container back in the fridge.

Olivia nudged him back.

"Things change." Ryan leaned close enough to make himself heard by whatever friend his sister had on the other end of the line and said, "Mom's in charge this year."

In charge. Sadie smiled. She liked the sound of that. And it fit since she'd taken Claudette's advice, at least professionally, and stood up for herself at work by posting office hours and faxing the mayor a revised job description that included her goals for the coming year.

So far, the man hadn't sought her out to take her to task over it. He hadn't called her with a rousing "you go, girl," either, but at this point Sadie gladly accepted his silence as the ultimate triumph.

"Get real, Ryan." Olivia turned her back and flicked her strawberry-blond hair over her shoulder. "Mom doesn't have anything to do with fireworks."

Ryan plunked the bowl onto the table, swiped his hand along the fringe of red hair touching his collar and mimicked, "Mom doesn't have anything to do with the fireworks."

"Stop it, both of you." The triumph of silence was something she hadn't quite accomplished with her children.

"Regardless of how we might feel about an opinion expressed in this house, we respect the person expressing it. Ryan, you're smart enough not to have to stoop to mocking and sarcasm to get your point across."

"Yes, ma'am." He ducked his head, pulled out a chair and swung his leg over the back of it to take his seat at the table.

"You may be overestimating by calling him smart, Mom. He hardly seems trainable in basic skills like how to sit down like a human." The girl sneered and muttered something into the phone, then laughed.

Sadie crossed her arms. Silence might be asking for too much, but certainly she still had the power to maintain a little civility in her own home. "Olivia Amaryllis Pickett, have you ever considered how your brother might feel when you talk to him like you're a princess and he's a peon?"

Her daughter blinked. Her mouth hung open. A faint pink started to burn over the apples of her cheeks.

This was it. The moment where Olivia pitched a fit, and for the last seven or so months, Sadie had backed down. This was the moment Mary Tate had predicted, when Sadie had to risk Olivia not liking her, and trust that she would understand that Sadie did what she did out of love.

Olivia shook back her hair and started to say something.

But Sadie was too fast for her. "Because there are no princesses in *this* house."

Olivia glowered at her mother, then raised the phone and muttered, "You are not going to believe this—"

"Oh, I think she will believe." Sadie slid the phone from her daughter's hand, put it to her ear and told the party on the other line, "Olivia has chores to do. She'll call you later."

"Mom!" Fire flashed in Olivia's green eyes.

Sadie hung the phone back in its cradle. Now or never. she had to stand up and put things back into the proper order in her home, or she might forever lose the chance to give her daughter the gift of loving discipline.

"Like I said, Olivia. There are no princesses in this house." Sadie offered a magnanimous smile that warned she'd brook no argument. Then she laid her hand over her denim shirt with farm animals staging a patriotic parade across the front, and dipped her head most regally, adding, "But there most certainly is a queen."

"Mom, I was making plans to meet my friends tonight," she whined.

"Tonight is for family." She rubbed her daughter's back as she moved past to refill her own coffee cup. "I've got all the fixin's for a picnic after we go down to the parade."

"Fixin's? Go down to the parade?" She rolled her eyes but stopped short of the kind of theatrics that had become part and parcel of her repertoire for getting her own way. "Since when did you turn into Granny from a bad episode of *The Beverly Hillbillies?*"

Sadie took the absence of high drama as a sign she had made her first inroad into getting her old Olivia back again. It made her feel good and so she decided to respond in kind, raising her fingers as she counted off her reply. "In the first place, there are no bad episodes of *The Beverly Hillbillies*."

Ryan snickered.

Olivia shot him a daggered look.

"In the second place, *Granny?*" Sadie's mouth hung open a moment to show her utter amazement at the comparison. "Aunt Pearl, maybe, but *Granny?*"

"Tell her, Mom," Ryan said.

"Tell *me?* Mom, you already warned Ryan about being sarcastic, why are you letting him—"

"And third," Sadie all but shouted, cutting off the fracas before it could begin. "The queen has spoken. End of discussion."

Eyes narrowed to angry slits, Olivia studied her for a moment, then her shoulders slumped forward just a little and she shook her head. "You sure are in a black mood today."

"Actually—" Sadie paused to double-check her own emotions then continued "—for the first time in a long while, I'm not in any kind of mood at all. Not a black mood. Not a blue mood. Not a stuff-my-face-with-licorice-jelly-beans mood."

Olivia cocked her head, her lip thrust forward just enough to remind Sadie of how she used to pout as a five-year-old.

"Give it up, sugar." With a gently placed hand on her daughter's back, Sadie sighed and gave her best sublimely imperial smile. "You do not want to mess with the queen when she's *not* in a mood."

Olivia jerked away, her face set in a squinty-eyed scowl. "You're just being mean."

"Nope." Undeterred, Sadie put her arm around her child again and gave her a quick hug. "I'm being something I haven't been in a long while—the mom."

"Yeah!" Ryan clapped his hands. "It's about time!"

Olivia frowned at her younger brother, then at Sadie.

"That means we're going to start sticking to the rules around here." Sadie's smile did not falter.

Olivia raised her chin and challenged, "*All* of us?"

"All of us." She gave her daughter an extra squeeze. "Including me. I know it's been hard for you to have me so out of it these past months, but I'm better now. *Everything's* going to be better now."

"Better for who?" Olivia slipped away, her head down, and slunk off toward the door.

Sadie did not call after her. She had hoped for more, but understood that too much had gone undone and unsaid the last few months for her to repair it all with a promise.

Still, it warmed her heart in ways she couldn't describe when her surly teen stopped at the threshold, turned, and with only a fleeting glance to meet her mother's gaze whispered, "Welcome back, Mom."

And then she was gone.

"That went well." Sadie rubbed her hands together and grinned at her son.

"Yeah, I especially liked the part when she compared you to Granny Clampett."

"Moses."

"Don't go biblical on me now, Mom, I'm still eating cereal."

"Not *that* Moses. Granny's name was Daisy Moses, not Clampett."

"Okay, should I worry that you know so much about a fictional character or pretend it's cute?"

"Cute, unless I start mistaking myself for a fictional character, then…"

"You did call yourself the queen," he reminded her.

"That's not fiction." Sadie grabbed a wooden spoon from the countertop and waved it with a royal air.

Ryan stood, carrying the empty bowl freshly slurped of all the cereal. As he passed his mother, he dropped his sparkler-adorned hat onto her head and beamed down at her. "If you're the queen, you need a crown."

"Thank you very much." She gave a curtsy. "Now all I need is my prince to come galloping up on his white horse."

"See ya, Sadie!" Ed strolled into the kitchen…and right out the back door. His golf clubs rattled along behind him.

"So where are the fireworks going to be, Mom?" Ryan asked as he rinsed out his bowl. "Can we have some at home?"

"You want fireworks at home? Stick around," Sadie muttered. In a few quick steps she crossed the floor and stepped out onto the back porch.

"What?" Ryan moved to follow her.

"Never you mind." She waved for him to go on about his business, calling as an afterthought, "The city fireworks display starts at dark out at the fairgrounds. And be informed—we are going as a family."

She let the screen door fall shut with a decisive *whap* before an argument could arise—or maybe just in time to keep her son from hearing the potential argument brewing in the driveway. "I don't suppose you heard that, did you?"

"Heard what?" The bright morning sun washed Ed's thinning hair out to a soft gray rather than the distinguished salt-and-pepper it shone under the lights at the pharmacy.

"My pronouncement about spending this holiday as a family."

"Okay. Good plan." He opened the trunk of Moonie's yellow convertible, then turned to get his golf bag.

"If it's such a good plan then where do you think you're going?"

"To make a fool of myself." He held up a putter and grinned. "And before you get upset, it's an all-male outing. You have nothing to fear—Go-Go is a no-show."

"Clever. But this isn't about Go-Go. This is about priorities. We need to talk."

"The four most dreaded words in the female vocabulary." Ed crimped his forehead down, his eyes sparkling with undiluted good humor. "Sadie, honey, you know I'd be happy to talk to you. I love talking to you."

"You do?"

"Of course." He looped his arm around her waist and ducking under the brim of her cowboy hat–crown—planted a kiss on the side of her neck. "It's my second-most favorite thing we do together."

"Ed!" She feigned shock, then laid her hand on his cheek and shut her eyes.

He turned his head and kissed her palm.

Her pulse picked up. She loved this man.

He kissed the inside of her wrist.

And he loved her.

He always had, all these years. She knew that. But he'd neglected these sweet reminders for so long. Too long. No wonder she had begun to doubt the strength of the bond between them.

She took a long shuddering breath and held it. She knew what she wanted to hear. He could mend so many bridges if he'd only take her in his arms and tell her…

"I have three guys expecting to meet me at the course in half an hour. No time for talk now." He checked his watch, then moved around her so quickly that it knocked her crown forward over her eyes. "Can't it wait?"

If he had worded it any other way, she just might have backed down. She pushed her hat to the back of her head. Maybe.

"Wait? You want me to put my frustrations with the state of our marriage on hold because you're too busy to take the time to discuss it—again?"

He skimmed his thumb along the dirt-smudged edge of his nearly new putter. "Sadie, this is not the time."

"It's never the time, Ed." She snagged the club from his hand, knowing his attention would follow the object of his newest infatuation. "Because you never have any time, and when you do, you spend it on anything but me and the kids. Work first, now golf."

"All that work has supported this family. It's kept us fed and a roof over our heads." He took the putter back, gently but firmly. "And my taking up golf is just an extension of that."

"I know, I *know*. That's how business is done with these money types. You have to show the potential buyers for the pharmacy that you're not some small-town rube they can take advantage of. You have to play the game on their turf, literally." She echoed all the things he'd told her over and over again about the motivations for his actions. Hearing herself voice it didn't give her any more comfort than listening to him spilling out one justification after another. "But what about the home turf, Ed? What about *me*?"

"Why do you think I'm going through all this to sell the pharmacy?" He set his jaw.

"Oh, Ed, who are you fooling? You're never going to sell that pharmacy."

He did not argue with her, and he did not meet her gaze. He simply pitched the putter in with the rest of his clubs and raised his hand to close the trunk.

"Ed, listen…"

"Let it go, Sadie. This whole discussion will have to wait."

"But I'm so sick of waiting, Ed."

He slammed the trunk shut, then turned, his eyes tired but still caring and kind. "Sadie. My sweet, sweet Sadie, I—"

"Sadie! Thank heavens you're here!"

"We couldn't get you on the phone, so we just came on straight to your house."

April's and Hannah's words stumbled all over each other, and the sisters nearly did the same as they rushed up the driveway in a flurry of hand gestures, hiking boots and high heels. "Sadie, we have to do something and we have to do it *now!*"

"Would you two cool it for one minute?" Sadie made the universal sign for "stop right there."

They pulled up short and shut their mouths but she knew that wouldn't last after the initial shock of hearing her take control wore off.

Why did everyone in her family have to have such bad timing? She glanced at Ed, wishing she could ask him to finish his sentiment, but knew that the time for that had passed.

"You might as well go on," she said. "Looks like I don't have time for that talk, anyway."

"Actually, Ed might want to hang on a minute." Hannah had April by the arm and had begun advancing up the driveway again.

Both sisters started to chatter at once, only allowing snippets of their message to get through.

"Charm school? That's the last place..."

"The police aren't involved...yet."

"We'll never live it down, you know."

"What's with the hat?" April asked at last without missing a step or taking a breath.

"Forget the hat, April, this is no time to be nitpicking about—" Hannah stopped, studied her older sister, then scrunched up her whole face in distaste. "Please tell me you weren't planning on wearing that thing around town today, Sadie."

Sadie's hand automatically went to the front of her son's creation. Her fingers whisked upward over the rough surface of the five sparklers sticking up from the folded bandanna. She probably looked like a perfect nut.

But then, she was in her own home. If that's how she wanted to look, who were her sisters to come over and tell her to knock it off?

"I like my hat," she said a bit too loudly. "And since I'm guessing you didn't come over here because you both just earned your badges as Wileyville's foremost fashion police and heard I'd violated some holiday-headwear ordinance, I don't want to hear any more about it."

"Oh, don't you get snippy with us." April jerked her head up so hard her braid bounced against her back. "We didn't *want* to come over here on a holiday morning. We *had* to come over, you know."

"Yeah," Hannah added. "And that hat looks silly."

"Enough!" Ed sighed.

The sisters hushed instantly.

"Thank you, Ed." Sadie gave him a regal nod of her head. "For stepping in and defending my sense of style…and my hat."

He blinked, and from the look in his eyes Sadie realized this was the first time he'd actually given the thing a good long look.

"Okay." Ed cleared his throat. He looked at Hannah and April, then stole another glance at Sadie's sparklers before he shook his head and met the other women's gazes full on. "So tell us, what has your father done now? Hijacked the fireworks for tonight's celebration? Exerted his own independence by renting a horse and riding through town crying 'The Shelnutts are coming, the Shelnutts are coming?' What?"

The two sisters started to speak at once again, but before one of their stories emerged in full, Mary Tate roared up in her car.

"This is not good," Sadie whispered to her husband.

"Not good at all," Ed agreed.

And to confirm their worst fears, Mary Tate leaped out of her car waving a piece of notepaper in one hand and shouted, "At least he left a note this time!"

❧ *Chapter Fourteen* ❧

"'**M**y Precious Daughters,'" Ed read the note aloud because Sadie, Hannah and April couldn't agree which one of them should get their hands on it first. "'I hope you will forgive me when you find out what I've done.'"

April put her hand to her mouth.

Hannah covered her eyes.

"Well, speak-no-evil and see-no-evil have reported in, what say you, hear-no-evil?" Mary Tate, who'd taken a comfy seat on the hood of Moonie's yellow Caddie, whispered as she swung her foot out to prod Sadie with the toe of her silver-spangled tennis shoe.

"I say I wish I *could* stick my fingers in my ears and not have to listen to another word. If Daddy has done something that he feels calls for an apology, in advance, in *writing,* the last thing I expect to hear is a joyful noise."

"'It may not seem so, but I've always acted with the best interests of you girls in mind,'" Ed read on. "'I understand now that maybe I wasn't the best judge of what was in your best interests versus what served my broken heart.'"

April twisted her hand so that she could chew the tip of her nail.

Hannah separated her fingers to peer between them.

Sadie hung her head. As a parent, she understood more than her sisters that fine line that sometimes had to be drawn between what was right for your children and what was all you could afford to give of yourself. Daddy had always done his best, and they should have recognized that whatever pain they carried from their mother's leaving, he had carried twofold— for himself *and* for his children.

"'Please remember I love you,'" Ed continued softly. "'And for strength, may you draw on the Bible verses I chose for each of you when you were small.'"

"'Gird your loins.'" April laced her arms over her chest and squared her shoulders.

Sadie half smiled and looked up into the blue, blue sky. "'Wait on the Lord.'"

"'Peace, be strong.'" Hannah dropped her hand from her eyes. She raised her head.

"When you string them together like that, they actually do give good advice." Mary Tate held up her hands to frame the unseen phrases as she said, "'Gird your loins.' 'Wait on the Lord.' 'Peace, be strong.'"

"He signs it 'Love, Daddy,'" Ed concluded. He started to fold the letter in half.

"There's more." Mary Tate pointed to the bottom of the page.

Ed glanced down, then flipped the paper over, following the direction of the arrow on the bottom right-hand corner of the note.

"'P.S.'" Ed stopped and read on silently, then he lifted his gaze to Mary Tate.

She spoke with soothing confidence, her gaze remaining on the sisters as she pointed again to Ed. "I think that note will make a little more sense when you hear this part."

"'What I go to do, I should have done a long time ago.'" Ed stared at the page in his hand as if he wasn't quite sure if he should read on or not. Finally he fixed his gaze on Sadie and spoke the rest as he folded the paper and offered it to his sisters-in-law. "'I'll be gone a few days, but when I come back I will have whatever answers I can provide about your mother.'"

April's tightly crossed arms slid apart.

Hannah seized the note, read it for herself, then leaned on the fender of Moonie's convertible for support.

Without a moment more of hesitation, Sadie charged headlong toward her house to gather what she'd need. "I'm going after him."

"After your big speech to the kids about this being a day for the family?" Ed grabbed her by the arm. "Besides, you wouldn't even know where to go."

"It *is* a day for the family, Ed. For the family to pull together and support each other, to support me in this thing I have to do." It wasn't as if any of them had been all-fired anxious to cooperate with her plans, anyway. She imagined it wouldn't take any of them more than fifteen minutes to find alternative activities. "And I *do* have a pretty good idea where Daddy is headed."

"Where?" he asked.

"Tennessee."

"How'd you know that?" Hannah hurried up to stand beside her sister.

Sadie eased her arm from her husband's light hold. "The map Daddy took from Payt's car."

"Yes, the map!" Hannah spun around, heading for the passenger side of their father's car. "He took off from my house in his own car, remember?"

"So?" Mary Tate's gaze swerved from one Shelnutt sister to the next.

"So I'm going to check the glove compartment and see if he left the map in there. He might even have highlighted a route." Hannah scrambled into the passenger-side front seat and in moments had the not-so-neatly refolded map in hand. "Okay, he's marked 65 South ending in…"

"Alphina," April said solemnly.

"How'd you know that?" Mary Tate wore the expression of someone who'd come in late to a mystery movie and was trying desperately to catch up.

"It's where Hannah and Sadie were born. The last place we know Mama lived."

"But there is no Teresa Shelnutt residing in Alphina, Tennessee." The map collapsed in Hannah's hands. "I checked on the Internet years ago."

"Maybe she remarried?" Mary Tate suggested eagerly.

Sadie slashed one hand through the air. "Whatever happened, Daddy is heading for Alphina. And so am I."

"Well if you're going, I'm going." Hannah clutched the map to her chest.

April clucked her tongue and shook her head. "There's no sense in *two* of you going on what's probably a wild-goose chase."

"I've heard Moonie called a lot of things, but that's about the most apt ever—a wild goose." Ed laughed. When no one joined in his joke, he tapped his hand on the car trunk like a judge calling for order and said, "The note says he'll be back in a few days. Now why not wait and—"

"No." Sadie sounded surprisingly firm, even to her own ears. But calm. Collected. And…and…queenly. She lifted her head with her hand on her hat, and careful not to sound scolding or overwrought, stated her case. "We can't wait. Who knows what kind of mischief he's already gotten into? He's had a head start, too. Mary Tate, do you have any idea how long he's been gone?"

"I noticed the Academy van was missing first thing this morning, but I figured Royal had taken it to get something for your daddy—has anyone told you your daddy is a might particular about what he wants and when he wants it?"

Sadie snapped her fingers to keep anyone from going off on the tangent of things Moonie demanded as a houseguest and when all eyes turned to her, she asked her friend, "When did you find the note?"

"I tried to call you, maybe a half hour ago, then called your sisters instead and asked them to meet me here." Mary Tate tapped her temple as if that somehow helped her access the needed information. "Royal said he hadn't heard a peep from your daddy's room all morning, but the van was in the driveway at sunup when he—"

Sadie took her friend by the wrist in hopes of making the machinery of her mind slow down. "So Daddy left sometime after sunup and before a half hour ago?"

"He could be three hours down the road then." Hannah waved the map in her hand as though offering incriminating evidence in a trial.

"Three hours. That's not too long." Ed rested his hand on his wife's back.

"When it comes to getting up to something, it doesn't take that man long." Mary Tate slid off the hood of the car.

"Granted," Sadie pressed on. "But there's more to worry about than that. What if he has another stroke?"

"I never thought of that," April murmured.

"We can't risk him having another TIA and getting stranded, having a wreck or worse." Fear rose from the pit of Sadie's stomach, but she didn't let it overtake her. "How would we live with ourselves if we waited until something happened and he was out there for who knows how long?"

"Sadie's right." Hannah narrowed her eyes. "He could get into a lot of trouble alone. And even if he doesn't, I, personally, don't want to think he might get to Mama before we do and maybe scare her off. This can't wait."

"Right." Sadie nodded, already thinking ahead to how she could grab the picnic food, a few clothes and get on the road shortly. "I'm done waiting. I am ready to take action."

"Not without me." Hannah stepped up-front and center.

"Or me," April chimed in.

Sadie turned to her older sister. "You said this didn't make any sense."

"I said the two of *you* going didn't make sense. Now, me?" She pointed to her chest, which had a picture of Uncle Sam pointing outward on it. "That makes all the sense in the world."

Hannah, dressed in an apron-front summer dress that looked like a red-and-white tablecloth with watermelons embroidered here and there, tapped her high-heeled sandal on the concrete driveway. "How so?"

"Because I actually have some recollections of the town we lived in. Something I see might stir a memory. I say if two of us go, it should be Sadie and me."

The tapping stopped. Hannah's auburn hair shimmied with the tightly controlled shake of her head. "Oh, no. You two are not leaving me out of this."

"Sadie?" April turned to the middle sister to play the role she routinely played among all members of the family—the middleman and moderator.

Sadie threw her hands up. They'd lost enough time already. She didn't want to waste any more arguing. "I don't care who goes or why they go or what they expect to get out of it. I only have one question for the two of you."

"What?" Hannah's eyes grew somber.

April inched closer, her expression grave.

"How fast can you two pack?"

Mary Tate laughed. "When you decide not to wait around anymore, you get serious."

"Why not?" Hannah flew into her role as organizer. Where Sadie just seemed to have the one hat—and a rather silly one at that—the youngest Shelnutt sister seemed most comfortable when she was wearing many and orchestrating a dozen things at once. "Today is Friday and a holiday. That means Mary Tate will be around to man the phones in case Daddy calls to check in."

"Sure thing." Mary Tate nodded.

"Ed has extra holiday help on at the store, so he can handle any emergency that happens here at home." Hannah motioned to the man on the cell phone canceling his golf plans. "Payt's office is closed today. So if we go now, that gives tomorrow to deal with whatever we find, and then we can drive back Sunday and I won't miss a single day of work."

"What about me?" The hurt shone clearly on April's fresh-scrubbed face. "My store is covered for today, but I have to open it tomorrow. Saturday is my biggest day, salewise, and I don't have a husband or kids to cover it for me."

Hannah's foot went to tapping again. "You have two employees—"

"Who don't work weekends," April filled in.

Sadie didn't know why, but it seemed important that she make physical contact with her oldest sister, to prove to her that she was not alone. So she touched her elbow as she said, "Olivia can do it."

"Olivia?" Mary Tate flicked her wrist as though to flip her hair off her shoulder.

Ed shifted his weight. "She's helped April out at the store before."

"Yeah, before she become the princess of teenage hormones," Mary Tate grumbled. "Face it, Ed, honey, Olivia is—"

"Family," Sadie finished. "And family helps family."

April's eyes softened with hopeful light. "You think she'll do it?

"If the queen decrees it, you bet she will." Sadie adjusted her hat from the back.

"What?" It was unclear whether Hannah was actually confused or if she was just challenging Sadie's right to call herself the queen. A title that, in her own little world, Hannah would certainly feel belonged to her and her alone.

Foolish girl.

"Never mind." Sadie smiled to have her own personal joke. "I'll get Olivia to do it."

Mary Tate clapped her hands once decisively. "And I'll look in on her and help if she needs me. I owe you that much."

"Then it's settled." Sadie whisked the cowboy hat from her head and sent it sailing into the back seat of Moonie's beloved old Caddie. "This car is pulling out of here in one hour. If either of you want in on the goose chase, I suggest you be back here in fifty-nine minutes or less."

A little more than an hour later, after squalling, squabbling and squishing all their necessities into every available square inch of the classic car, they were off. Well, Ed told them they were "off" before that—when they had resorted to drawing straws to see who would take the first, second and third shift driving.

Sadie settled into the back seat with her long straw between her teeth and stewed.

Hannah, in the passenger's seat, played navigator.

And April, looking a bit too pleased with her short-straw-drawing self for Sadie's liking, took the wheel.

"Turn right here," Hannah shouted when they had almost reached Wileyville Road.

"If I turn right, I'll run into the back of the bank. What do you want me to do, create another crack to match the one Daddy made?"

"Not right as in *right,* right as in immediately." She stretched her arm out to point to the street they had just passed, on their left.

"Why would I do that? It's just a short jog through town to pick up the old highway that leads to 65." April took a right turn at the next street. "Your way sends us in the complete opposite direction of where we need to—"

The car rolled to a stop at the end of the block where streamers of red, white and blue crepe paper hung low across the intersection with the main road April had wanted to take.

"Let that be a lesson to you both. Listen to your navigator."

The booming cadence of a marching band carried from down the street where the judges' grandstand stood decorated to the hilt with banners and flags.

"The way I see it, we have two choices. You can try to back up the entire length of this block." Hannah glanced back over her shoulder. "Or we can sit here and wait until the parade passes by."

Wait until the parade passes by. On the very day when she had gone to such trouble to announce to everyone she loved that she was done waiting, Sadie could hardly sit there and let that choice be made on her behalf.

The conversation she'd had with her father over the Memorial Day parade rang through her thoughts.

"There's going to be a celebration in town, and I say why not be a party to it?"

"Daddy, everything in life can't be your own personal celebration."

"I'd have to ask you again, Sadie-girl, why not?"

"Why not?" Sadie echoed the question that had come back to her time and again since then.

"April, either back up or—"

"Or…" Sadie reached down to the floor to retrieve the hat she'd flung into the car earlier. "Maybe there is a third choice."

"What have you got on your mind, Sadie?" April asked.

"Forget her mind," Hannah snapped. "What has she got on her head?"

"Just hear me out," Sadie said.

The music rose as the high-school band stopped to do an intricate number involving flat twirling and frantic movements for the benefit of the dignitaries observing from the VIP seats.

As she detailed her idea to her sisters, Sadie glanced around them at the small but lively crowd clustered at the corner waving flags and holding balloons. Looking down the larger street in both directions, she could see the older folks sitting in their lawn chairs on the sidewalk. Children perched on the curb, ready should the next float or group throw small wrapped candies to the spectators. Though she could not see them from here, Sadie knew the food vendors she'd given permits to would be lined up at the front edge of the park. And the vendors who hadn't gotten the proper paperwork would set up in places like Downtown Drug's parking lot, along with the booths of civic, church and school groups raising money.

In other words, pretty much everyone in Wileyville or thereabouts was gathered at or near this crossroads today.

And that was just fine with Sadie.

"Well?" she asked her sisters when she had finished her pitch.

April chewed her lip, considering the proposition.

"Don't you dare," Hannah warned.

"Oh, go on, April." Sadie poked the driver-sister in the shoulder. "For once in your life, *dare*."

April looked at Hannah.

Hannah held her breath.

The band came to an uproarious conclusion. Then after a moment's silence, began to play a soft, sweet, patriotic tune.

The car began to move. The paper barricade snagged, coming free of the light posts it had been taped to and creating a lovely banner across the Caddie's grille as it eased forward.

Sadie plunked her hat on as someone rushed up and handed her a red balloon.

And off they went.

That was how it happened that Sadie and her sisters came to fulfill their destiny as Solomon's daughters by barging in on the annual Wileyville Fourth of July parade in a yellow convertible, a flurry of red, white and blue streamers with the glorious strains of "The Battle Hymn of the Republic" reverberating in the background.

"Okay, you're so smart." Hannah sank as low in the seat as possible, snapping, "What do we do now, Sadie?"

Sadie swallowed a lump the size of a cherry bomb in her throat and scanned the sea of familiar faces staring at her from the sidewalks. Her cheeks burned. Her eyes stung. And her heart...raced with genuine joyful exuberance!

"What to do? Sisters, we will do the only thing three Shelnutts in an open-air car inflicting themselves on a decades-old Wileyville tradition *can* do. We're going to enjoy it."

"Are you...?" Hannah couldn't even finish her question.

"Really?" April met Sadie's gaze in the rearview mirror, her eyes glittering with the fun of it all.

"Smile pretty girls, and wave!" Sadie did both.

In turn, slowly, so did Hannah, then April.

From her prime spot in front of her family's home furnishing store, Lollie Muldoon cocked her head one way and then the other, clearly unsure what to make of it.

Her son, Kurt, working "crowd control"—as if anything in Wileyville constituted a serious crowd or would submit itself to control in these circumstances—stopped long enough to tip his hat to the passing ladies and call out, "Nice entry, Miss April."

"April has a boyfriend," Sadie teased with a tug at her sister's braid.

Waynetta Cummins did manage to put a damper on things with a simple shake of her head, but that soon evaporated when Sadie caught a glimpse of Claudette and her sons laughing and cheering them on.

Sadie raised her arm and pantomimed scratching that old itch.

Claudette gave her a thumbs-up.

Sadie laughed, but before she could say anything about it all to her sisters, Deborah Danes had appeared out of nowhere, taking long strides to keep up with the slow crawl of the car.

"Don't tell me. That nut Moonie put y'all up to this."

"For your information, that *nut* is not even in town." Hadn't she just told her son recently that smart people didn't stoop to sarcasm? Well how smart could she be, Sadie decided, that she not only got herself into a parade by accident but then decided to take on the likes of Deborah Danes in the middle of said parade? "In fact, we were headed out of town ourselves, took a wrong turn and are just trying to make the best of it."

"You know the saying?" April kept her eyes on the road and her smile on high beam. "When life gives you lemons…"

"Life does not give me lemons, thank you. It does, at times, in the form of people with the last name of Shelnutt, sometimes give me ulcers, but not lemons."

Hannah's head jerked up.

"Now with all due respect, ladies," Deborah said tartly, her smile more of a grimace, "get out of my parade."

"I thought this was the town's parade." *Had she actually said that out loud?*

"It's the whole country's parade." Twisting around in the seat, Hannah gave Sadie a wink and Deborah a stern look.

Something had changed in her sister. Something had shaken loose and awakened. Without asking, Sadie knew what that something was. Hope. It filled her sister's face and fueled her words. For once in her life Hannah had real hope that they would finally know the truth about their mother, that she might finally be let off the hook over that whole left-her-as-a-baby complex.

And it showed when she tossed back her hair, waved to the crowd and announced, "Everyone here has gathered to celebrate the roots of our individual freedom. And I can't think of a better send-off for a journey to find our own family roots than doing something to make our daddy—or as Mrs. Danes likes to call him, *that nut*—proud. Drive on, April."

"Buh-bye, Deborah!" Sadie gave the official beauty-queen wave.

April accelerated just enough to pull away from the parade's irate organizer.

For the first time in what seemed forever, the three of them had acted in unison and for a common goal. Whatever lay ahead for them on this strange and tenuous trip, Sadie told herself to hold this memory in her heart.

They were sisters. They were family. They were on their way to find out the truth, and no matter what, with love and God's help, they would be all right.

Wouldn't they?

❧ Chapter Fifteen ❧

"I can't believe this," Hannah muttered.

"You were the one who told us to always listen to the navigator. April said turn right here, and so I turned…" Sadie spread her hands wide over the yellow convertible sitting nose first in a grassy drainage ditch "…right here."

April pushed the loose strands of hair from her eyes, then pulled her braid free from a dry bush that had ensnared it. She began working her way up the three-foot-deep embankment by the side of the old disused two-lane road, saying, "Right, as in to the right. Here, as in at the next intersection."

"I *know* that." Sadie extended her hand to help her sister back onto level ground. "I was making a joke."

"I think this trip is going to give me a whole new appreciation of Deborah Danes and her whole life-doesn't-give-me-lemons-but-Shelnutts-give-me-ulcers philosophy." Hannah paused long enough from pawing around in the back seat, where she'd been sitting, to hold her hand over her stomach and sigh.

"Just misjudged the distance." Sadie peered off into the growing dusk. "That's all."

"We wouldn't even be on this road if you hadn't taken us twenty miles back toward Kentucky after we left that giant truckers' plaza place and that nice clerk hadn't told us about this way to get on track." Joining Sadie by the side of the road, April turned, her hands on her hips. "Which leaves me with one question."

Sadie dared to give her sister a little shoulder nudge. "Why am I driving?"

"No." April tried to maintain her stern exterior.

Sadie nudged her again and laughed, just a little.

April gave in and joined her in a brief tension-easing chuckle. "That *is* a good question, but no. My real question is, if the three of us can't make this trip without mishaps, what are the odds that Daddy did?"

"They must be pretty good." Sadie gazed at the horizon thick with trees divided by the road that disappeared over the next hill. "We haven't seen hide nor hair of him yet."

"He's probably there already." Hannah picked her way around the side of the stranded vehicle, clutching a paper bag from their last stop along the way. "Meanwhile, we're still ninety minutes away from Alphina and it's getting dark."

"The roadside-assistance man said they were running behind because of the holiday." Sadie pressed a button on her cell phone to check the time. "He should be out here within the hour."

The bag crinkled in Hannah's death grip while she used her free hand to shake some leaves from her once-tidy summer dress. "We should have been there by now."

April folded her arms and shifted her weight. Small rocks and dried twigs crunched beneath her clunky hiking boots. "We'd have made better time if *somebody* didn't have to stop every few miles."

"I'm nervous." Hannah held the bag containing her suddenly indispensable bottle of pink gooey antacid aloft like Scarlett O'Hara swearing she'd never go hungry again, and proclaimed, "When I'm nervous, my stomach gets upset. I'm delicate that way."

"Delicate?" Sadie snorted.

"Right." April clicked her tongue. "I have known you since the day you were born, girl, and I have never seen you go 'delicate' over anything before."

"Well, you've never seen me just hours away from meeting our mother before, have you?" Their baby sister took a swig from the bottle on the spot, and in a very unHannah-like move, wiped the excess from the corner of her mouth with the back of her hand. "I tell you, it's got me all in knots."

Puh-puh-pop.

They all flinched at the sound of fireworks in the distance.

"Can you believe it?" Hannah leaned her hip against the back end of the car and looked skyward. "In a few hours we could be meeting our mother."

April stepped forward. "Hannah, I…"

Sp-pt-pt-fe-e-ee-euw. A bottle rocket screamed high, high up over their heads, then burst into a blinding flash of light.

Sadie put her hand on April's arm to keep her from saying anything more.

"You two do believe that, don't you?" In the dimming last rays of daylight, Hannah's auburn hair looked quite dark in contrast to her pale skin. It made her eyes appear as large and luminous as a fretful child's when she looked to her sisters for reassurance.

Two more bottle rockets pierced the darkening sky.

"Sadie? April?"

The pleading in Hannah's voice cut straight to Sadie's heart. She blinked, and in doing so, freed a warm wash of tears, which softened the image of her younger sister standing there waiting for an answer.

April exhaled loudly and turned her upper body toward the road they had just come down.

"I just can't help thinking, Hannah, that if she really wanted to find us—"

"No!" Hannah's hand went up to demand Sadie say no more.

Sadie pressed her lips together, and for the first time in such a very long time, sought help from a higher source. *Help me to get through this, Lord.* "If Mom was…*interested* in finding us."

Interested. What a strange code word for what they all suspected in their hearts—that their own mother did not want them, did not care what had become of them, did not love them.

A tear fell on Sadie's cheek. She sniffled, looked away from her sister's stricken expression and concluded, "She surely would have found us by now."

"No! Don't say that." Hannah's voice cracked. "Daddy kept her from us. Now if he could keep us from finding out about her, what's to say that he couldn't keep her from finding us?"

"If that was Daddy's goal, he would have changed our names," April said softly.

Sadie raised her head to keep another tear from falling. "Daddy is not the villain in our story, Hannah."

"And Mama is?" Hannah's hand went to her throat. "Is that what you're saying? That our mother is the bad one in all this?"

"No!" Sadie clenched her jaw. "I did not say that."

Why did every exchange between them have to deteriorate so quickly into conflict? Sadie anguished. Even now, when they should all be supporting each other, every word they spoke to one another remained suspect. Like too many things involving the people that she loved, it tore at Sadie's heart. But somehow, standing here with no one but her sisters and the Lord as witnesses, it did not defeat her. Had her short, unimpressive prayer been answered?

Sadie could come to no other conclusion when she marveled at the peace she found when she confronted her younger sister's pain with kind and loving reason. "There are no villains in this situation, Hannah. Don't you see that? There are only people. Flawed, misguided, hurting people."

If you think of everyone you meet as an uncertain, hurting individual, most of the time you'll be right.

Funny, Sadie had never thought to apply Claudette's insight to her own family. Yet standing here with her sisters and knowing their deepest inner yearnings for some kind of closure regarding their mother, she realized she'd been treating each of them as if *she* were the only one in pain and wondering why they did not minister to her. She had shortchanged her sisters in that way.

And Daddy.

"He would have done anything for her," Sadie whispered.

"What?"

"That's what Daddy said when he had his episode in the cemetery. He wished Mama had trusted him more, and wondered if she ever knew how much he loved her."

Boom. Somewhere, not too far away, another holiday celebration had gotten off to a raucous start. A spark of light soared into the sky and seconds later red-and-white sparks formed a breathtaking blossom.

As the aftermath, a shower of sizzling embers fell to earth again. Sadie shut her eyes and hung her head.

"Well I don't believe it. I think she's alive and some plausible reason exists for why she hasn't come to us. Daddy wouldn't have taken off on this supersecret mission to go to her unless he thought he could make a bridge." Hannah scooted up onto the trunk, lying back to watch the show. "That's what I choose to believe."

Hurting or not, Hannah had spoken. And when that woman made up her mind, there was no arguing.

April joined her on the back of the car. "I guess we'll know soon enough."

Pow. Pop. Bang.

Both sisters held out their hands to Sadie and she climbed up beside them. They watched the show overhead for a few minutes, the silence broken only by gasping now and again at the beauty of the display.

Finally, during a lull where they could hear but not see the small celebratory explosions going off in every direction, April spoke, softly and plaintively. "Been a lot of years since the three of us talked about Mama."

"Remember?" Sadie drew in the night air, slightly tinged with smoke and dust. "Those summer nights when Daddy and Aunt Phiz let us sleep outside in the tent and we knew they couldn't hear us?"

"Supermom," Hannah murmured.

"She was going to show up one day out of the blue and rescue us from all the rules and expectations that we hated." Sadie thought of Olivia and how she had gotten that wish—a mom who let her do exactly as she pleased, if only for a little while. Her heart sank to think that she had placed that kind of burden on her own child.

"And she would be bright and beautiful and radiant, and…and perfect in every way." Hannah crossed her legs at the ankle and managed not to get so much as a smudge of road dirt on her sleek sandals. "We sure made her larger than life in those talks, didn't we?"

"We made her who we needed her to be." April laced her arms tightly around herself.

"No, not you, April. You never went in for grandiose fantasies about how our mom could do or say or be anything we dreamed up."

"I just don't remember her that way," April whispered.

"At least you *can* remember her."

"Not much."

"But some. You have something. We don't have anything…" Hannah gestured to include Sadie in her complaint. "Not even a crust of a memory from you, since you refuse to tell us about her."

"I've explained that to you. It was all so long ago, I can't in good conscience promise the authenticity of my recollections."

Sadie touched her older sister's arm. "We're not asking for promises or guarantees, April, we just want—"

"Anything," Hannah begged. "How she smelled. Did she sing? Did she kneel beside the bed at night with you and listen to your prayers?"

"I remember…"

"What?" Sadie and Hannah asked at the same time.

"I *think* I remember when Moonie and Mama got married."

"No!"

"Really?

"You never told us that," Sadie murmured in awe.

"It's such a fleeting image—the church, the flowers, eating cake while sitting on Moonie's lap, and Mama worried that I'd make a mess and him saying, 'That's all right, Teresa. Kids are supposed to make messes. It's part of life—the best part.'"

Sadie leaned her chin in her hand. "You remember that?"

"Well see, that's why I never mention it. It does seem like a lot for a four year old to recall. But I *do*. I think it got fixed in my mind because I remember thinking at the time what a lucky little girl I was to have a new daddy who thought the messes were the best part of life."

"He still thinks that." Hannah curled the bag of stomach medicine close to her chest.

"Bet you don't think you're so lucky now, huh?" Sadie laughed a little.

"Actually…yes, I do."

Hannah rolled just her head to the side and asked, "Really?"

"Y'all, I…I don't know if I should say any more."

"Yes, you should." Sadie's pulse picked up at the promise of knowing something—anything—more about the mother she had never really known.

"Do. Please, do," Hannah pleaded.

"Most of my memories of Mom are not…happy."

"Happy?" The paper bag in Hannah's grasp crinkled. "You mean, like birthdays and Christmas happy?"

"I mean…" Even in the darkness April's eyes betrayed her inner conflict. For a moment it seemed she might close up again and not say any more. Then, slowly, she sat up and looked at her own hands and went on. "The few memories I have of Mom always make me feel so very, very sad—*even* the birthday and Christmas ones."

"Because she's gone?" Hannah's tone begged for that to be the reason.

"Because she was never there."

They all sat silent for a moment, trying to absorb the whole significance of April's simple reply.

Somehow, Sadie knew instinctively what she meant, and it chilled her to the bone.

"Oh, physically, her body was present." April kept her gaze cast down. She fidgeted with the end of her braid. "You've seen the photos, you both know that. But inside she just wasn't available to the people who loved her."

Sadie shivered. She knew that feeling all too well. Finally she found the courage to ask, "Wasn't she ever happy? Didn't she ever…get better?"

"Not that I recall."

Sadie's breath stopped short in her chest. This was their mother they were talking about, not her. April was telling them about the past, not giving a warning about Sadie's certain future.

"My very last memories of her…and, again, I may be mixing all this up with the last stages of pregnancy and her being tired or what have you. But my last memories of her were of her never getting out of bed. Never wanting to see us." April sniffled, which was for her like a great outpouring sob from someone else. She paused, gathered herself, and then in a voice so raw it hurt just to hear it, whispered, "If she'd have just let us in. I'd have…"

"Done anything. If only she had trusted how much people loved her," Sadie paraphrased what Moonie had said that day in the cemetery. "If only she hadn't withdrawn. If only she hadn't let it eat away at her. If only she had asked for help…"

"Sadie?" April sat up, closer now. "Did Daddy say all that about Mama?"

"Hmm?" Sadie blinked and suddenly realized she'd been all but making a confession about her own actions. She shook her head. "No. I was just… I wonder if Mama ever saw a doctor for her condition?"

"Doctor?" April asked.

Hannah cocked her head. "Condition?"

"Well, obviously, that's not normal. Something was wrong with Mama. That's probably why she ran off. And maybe it's why she couldn't try to find us."

"You could be right." Hannah lay back on the hood again.

"Of course she's right." April lay back, too. "The question is, what does Daddy think he's going to do about it now? Why, after all these years, did Daddy decide to try?"

"Maybe the stroke scared him into the realization that he no longer had all the time in the world." Hannah took a deep breath.

"No." Sadie finally lay back on the hood with her sisters even though the fireworks had dwindled to mostly sound and low flashes beyond the trees. "This started before the stroke."

"It started the day of his accident at the bank. You talked to him that day, Sadie. Any insights? Anything stand out in your mind?"

"Just the usual. Had to go down to the VFW and pry him out of an altercation with Deborah over his wanting to march in the parade."

"Too bad he missed our show today." Hannah laughed lightly. "He would have loved it."

"He lectured me on pursuing joy and authentic individualism," Sadie went on.

"Heard it," April croaked like a bullfrog.

"And I told him about the three of us having words—or, not having words. We weren't on speaking terms at the time."

"Oh, no." April put both hands over her face. "You don't think…?"

Sadie pulled at her sister's arm. "What?"

April dropped her hands, pounding them in quick, gentle thuds against the metal of the hood. "Could all of this just be a Shelnutt-inspired ruse to get the three of us talking again?"

Hannah sat bolt upright. Her hands twisted the paper bag around the neck of the medicine bottle inside it. "It better not be!"

"Why?" April asked.

"Mostly because I want to learn the truth about Mom. But also because, if the ruse worked…"

Another firework scaled high, high into the sky above them.

"Oh, no. Oh, no, no, no." In the burst of light that followed, April's eyes reflected her sudden understanding of what was at stake.

"Oh, yes." Hannah nodded knowingly. "Can you imagine? If Daddy discovers this shifty charade has accomplished his goal, what might he try next?"

Sadie chuckled. "Heaven help us."

"Not a bad idea." Hannah set the sack aside and lightly brushed her hands together.

"Hmm?"

"Clearly, now we have no concept of what Daddy is planning or what we are walking into in Alphina. We took off in such a flurry, we didn't even stop to say a prayer for our journey." Hannah held her hand out first to one sister, then to the other. "I think it's about time we did that."

"I said a prayer," April protested even as she accepted Hannah's outstretched hand.

"I did, too, but *we* didn't. Not all of us, together." Another firework went off, and Hannah followed its upward spiral for a second before she lowered her gaze to the hand that remained empty. "Sadie?"

Bang! Boom! Ka-powie! The sky filled with light.

Sadie's entire being filled with…apprehension. She still prayed, of course. She still believed. But…

If only she hadn't withdrawn. If only she had asked for help. The questions she had asked about her mother but that came from the depths of her own pain echoed in her mind now.

Moonie had said he'd have done anything for Mama. Their mother never gave him the chance to prove it.

God had promised He would uphold Sadie in all things and He had not waited for her to admit she needed help, but sent His Son to demonstrate just how far He would go to prove His love.

Hadn't she waited long enough to share her heart with Him again?

"Okay," she said quietly but not without reservation. It had been so long and so much remained unsaid, unresolved. "Count me in. But someone else has to be the voice."

"We'll do that for you, Sadie." Hannah extended her hand farther.

Sadie slipped her hand into her younger sister's grasp, and then into her older sister's. They bowed their heads, and with the fireworks exploding overhead, quietly joined together to pray for their journey, their father and for each other.

And when the roadside-assistance man showed up at last to haul them from the ditch with a "Sorry for the wait, ladies," Sadie smiled and said, "That's okay. Waiting isn't *always* a bad thing."

He strode all the way around the car, smacked his chewing gum, then scratched the back of his neck and looked up at them. "Glad to hear you feel that way, ma'am, because this here looks like it could take a while."

❧ *Chapter Sixteen* ❧

Sadie let up on the gas pedal as the car went skimming past the Welcome to Alphina sign.

"Finally," she muttered under her breath, careful not to wake either of her sisters, who had both zonked out shortly after they'd hit the highway again.

Some lone late reveler must not have felt the same respect for the weary, however. As the car cruised from the darkness through the illuminated circles created by the streetlights, three quick, earsplitting firecrackers erupted nearby.

"What was that?" April jerked into a dazed consciousness.

Hannah groaned and put her hand to her forehead. "Isn't this holiday ever going to end?"

"It already has." Sadie tilted her head toward the Citizens Savings and Loan, where the time and temperature flashed electric red. "Twelve fifty-seven. It's officially July the fifth."

April groaned, stretched, then let out a long, loud yawn. "And too late to do any real detective work."

"Oh, I wouldn't say that." Sadie wasn't sleepy. The whole night had recharged her in ways that she hadn't counted on. During the drive, her mind had not stopped whirring away. Maybe what had been awry with her these last months had not been some failing on her part. Maybe the seeds of her inability to rise above her sadness lay in her family history.

And she had finally come to the place where she could get some answers.

"What do you suggest we do?" April pulled the band from the end of her frazzled braid and started to undo her hair as if already preparing for bed.

"I know my vote." Hannah rested her cheek on the back of the seat. "We check in to a hotel, get a good night's sleep, then in the morning use the phone there to call all the other hotels and see if we can find where Daddy is registered."

"Or…" Sadie stopped at a red light and leaned forward over the steering wheel, peering at a parking lot two blocks away.

"No 'or,' please, Sadie. Last time you gave us an 'or' option, we ended up as the star attraction in a fool's parade." Hannah curled her hands under her chin and fought to keep her eyes open. "I'm exhausted, tired right to the marrow of my bones. I need to rest."

"You're not supposed to be tired," Sadie argued, her energy unabated. "You're the young one here."

"Well none of us is as young as we used to be." April wriggled her fingers through the heavy strands of her hair. The tightly crimped waves clung to her knuckles as she raised her hands and began massaging her scalp. "So I suspect we all could do with a good rest before we tackle what might be the biggest confrontation of our entire lives."

"Or…" The light turned green and Sadie took off.

"Or *what*?" Hannah snapped without opening even one eye.

"Or we could cruise around town a bit and see if we can find Daddy," Sadie said softly.

"Cruise around? Are you crazy?" April disentangled her fingers from her hair with a few crisp shakes. "Three weary women meandering through a strange town looking for one cagey old man?"

"How hard could it be?" A car slowed to turn in front of Sadie, and she eased her foot onto the brake. "He'll stick out in that big white van with Royal Academy and a beauty-pageant tiara painted in red on the side."

"He sticks out plenty enough in this boat of a car around itty-bitty little Wileyville, and half the time we can't find him there." Hannah frowned, her eyes shut even tighter.

"Look, I saw the population as we drove in." Sadie tapped her foot on the gas and sent the car gliding down toward the next turn, which she made with ease. "Twenty-four thousand, a little more than twice the size of Wileyville. It's doable, I tell you."

"No, it's not."

"April's right, we could never, even in our wildest—"

"Here we are." Sadie pulled the convertible to a stop in the empty parking space directly across from a big white van with Kentucky license plates and Mary Tate's logo, big-as-you-please, shining in the overhead light. "Now what?"

April hopped out and went to peek inside the van. "Maybe we should just camp out right here. You know, sleep in the car so Daddy can't slip out without us knowing."

"Sleep in the car?" A lock of hair fell over Hannah's eyes. A tremble started in her lower lip that warned she might just burst out crying if they chose that alternative.

"I say we get a room and deal with Daddy in the morning. We could all use a good night's sleep," Sadie insisted.

"Sleep," Hannah echoed.

"But what about the car?" April argued. "There's no place in this lot we can park it that Daddy won't spot it the second he comes out of his room."

"Hmm." Sadie glanced around to confirm April's assessment. "Okay, simple fix. We all know Daddy is a creature of habit, right?"

"I motion to amend that to a creature of mostly *bad* habits." April grinned. "And I'm sure Hannah will second that, right, Hannah?"

"Sleep."

Sadie laughed. "So it's easy. Daddy gets up at the same time every morning."

"Six-seventeen," Hannah and April said together.

"Exactly. Six-seventeen. So we just arrange a wake-up call for 6:00 a.m., get up in plenty of time to throw on some clothes, dash out here and nab Daddy before he can get gone for the day."

"Works for me. How about you, Hannah?"

"Sleep."

"Is that a yes?"

"Sleep."

"I think that's definitely a yes," Sadie said as she took the key from the ignition and opened the car door. "Let's go crash for a few hours, so we can be ready for whatever Daddy throws at us in the morning."

"We can be ready for anything Daddy throws at us in the morning?" April stood in the open doorway of their tiny room six hours later, staring at the note slipped under their door. "But what about the things even Daddy doesn't control?"

Sadie sat on the edge of the bed staring at the numbers on the bedside clock. "I had no idea we'd crossed over into the Central Time zone."

"Well Daddy did. Or rather, according to his note—" April lifted the page of motel stationery and read aloud "—These old bones rise like them in Bible days—when the good Lord tells them to. With the time change, guess that means I got up a full hour ahead of the normal time on the clock. I was a bit grumpy about the whole mess until I came out to find my car, and the clerk told me three beautiful women had driven it here. Imagine my delight!'"

"Delight." Sadie shook her head. "You have to hand it to him, he never lets up. You or me, we'd hardly have used that word to describe what we felt in the same situation."

April looked out at the parking lot. "We did sort of set him up for an ambush, didn't we?"

Hannah picked through her open overnight bag like a jeweler selecting the perfect tool to perform precision diamond cutting. Finally she withdrew a small bottle of moisturizer and a prepackaged facial cloth, then picked up a towel and bent forward to wrap it around her head. "Not intentionally. We had his best interests at heart."

"Well according to the note he left when he headed out of here, he always had our best interests at heart raising us, too." Sadie had empathy by the armload for the old fellow, but that didn't mean she had suddenly been struck with amnesia. "But I have to tell you, being on the receiving end of those best interests, it didn't always feel *dee-lightful*."

Hannah dropped onto the bed. In her slightly oversize robe, towel turban and pale, crestfallen expression, she looked a bit like a pile of damp laundry. "He could have at least left us the keys for the van."

"'Sorry, girls, can't leave the keys for the van.'" The paper rustled in April's hands as she held it up high to read it in the poor light of the predawn day. "'Royal loaned that van to me.'"

"Royal?" Sadie frowned. "That man! Sometimes I could just—"

"Wait!" April held one finger up. "'To get him off the hook right now, he told me where the keys were, and said I could use it in a pinch.'"

"Like I didn't already feel queasy enough." Hannah rubbed her eyes, then rested her forehead in her hands. "Go ahead, read on."

"'So I pinched them keys…'"

Sadie groaned at the awful pun.

"'…and set off with a mind to take the best of care of the vehicle. Since none of you three have permission, to my knowledge, to access this van, I don't see how I could leave the keys for you. Not to worry, though.'"

"You'd think he'd know by now that the time we worry the most is when he tells us not to worry." Sadie stood and crossed the room to finish reading the note over her sister's shoulder.

"'I have some business in town that doesn't involve you three.'"

"Ha!" Sadie couldn't help throwing her two cents' in.

"'But it won't take too long. I hope.'"

"He strands us here and hopes it won't take too long?"

"What constitutes 'too long' in Daddy's world, anyway?" Hannah rose from the bed slowly, her knuckles white from clutching the bottle in her hand.

"That's a good question. One would think to set a benchmark like that would require a person to have a clue as to what most of us consider too much to endure, too far to go or too long to wait." Sadie inched in closer behind her sister, then went up on tiptoe to get a better look at the rest of the note.

April twisted her upper body around to keep Sadie from reading ahead and went on, "'When I'm done, I'll hurry right on back, and the three of us can talk.'"

Her sister's movements did not deter Sadie. She had set out on this odd little adventure because she had determined the time had come to take action. And action she would take, right down to peeping around her sister's back to finish off the last of their daddy's instructions. "'Until then, the main part of town is due east a couple blocks, and though this strip of road has grown up a lot since we last lived here, I can eyeball plenty of places within walking distance that look to serve a decent meal. It's on me. See you soon.'"

April dug into the envelope with the motel logo on it and withdrew two twenty-dollar bills. "Just like when we were kids, remember? When he used to bribe us with cash not to tell Aunt Phiz anything potentially incriminating or embarrassing during her visits?"

"I have to confess." Sadie ruffled her fingers through her unruly morning hair. "I always told."

April gave a flippant wave. "Oh, me, too."

"Not me!" Hannah fluffed the lapels of her pink robe.

In a flash April's wave turned into an invisible fan, which she flapped under her chin, her eyes batting like a delicate southern belle. "Well aren't you the Miss Goody Two-shoes?"

"More like Goody Toe-shoes." Hannah grinned and wrinkled her nose. "Up until about age seven, I made up songs about Daddy's exploits and sang them for Aunt Phiz while I spun around the den pretending to be a ballerina."

April slapped Sadie's arm with her faux fan. "You're kidding."

"Uh-uh." Hannah's wan face lit up—well, as much as a face can on only a few hours' sleep. "And when I got a little older, I used to make up mock newspapers with articles on all the family doings—Daddy had his own section—and send them to her wherever she was teaching that year and even to her archaeological digs."

"Why, you darling little snitch!" Sadie laughed.

April put her arm around Sadie's shoulder as she told Hannah, "No wonder you're still her favorite!"

Sadie looked to her older sister, and before she could think of a reason not to, rested her head on April's shoulder and sighed. "Well clearly bribery didn't work on us as children. Whatever made Daddy think he could use it now?"

April pressed her cheek to the top of Sadie's head. "Maybe because now we're stranded in a cheap motel in Alphina, Tennessee."

"Stranded and starving." Sadie straightened up.

April slipped inside the open door and let it fall shut at last. There was something final in that action. Something that said that this path—the one they had chosen when they agreed to come on this trip together—was now closed. "Okay, now what?"

Hannah looked to Sadie.

April did the same.

"Why are you two turning to me? Last time I made a decision, we ended up in a ditch."

"Yeah, but the time before that, we got to ride in a parade." Hannah moved to the sink.

April, already dressed for the day, sat in the wobbly chair by the lone window in the room. "And before that, it was your ruling that set us off on this whole adventure, which, despite its obvious flaws, I count as a positive experience."

Water gushed into the basin. Hannah went through her cleansing routine quickly, then bent down and splashed two handfuls of clear water onto her face. Between pats with the towel to daintily dry her cheeks and chin, she concluded, "So with that kind of record, I'd say the chances are pretty good that you'll pick a winning option, Sadie."

They looked at her, and though neither one said another word, Sadie could feel their expectations closing in around her.

What are you waiting for, Sadie? They said it with their eyes and the way they each leaned forward just a little as they watched her intently.

At first their stress over Daddy had got them *not* speaking to each other. Then it got them speaking, if only a little, about their mother. And now this. Hannah and April wanted her to speak for the three of them. Together. As sisters.

It was a monumental moment in their relationship. Sadie didn't dare blow it.

"Okay, well…" She took a deep breath of the motel's stale air. "We came here out of concern for Daddy, right?"

The others nodded their agreement.

"So since we can't go looking for Daddy now, maybe we should think about looking for what he came after?" *What did that mean, exactly?* Even Sadie didn't know.

"Yes. I get it."

"You do?" Sadie asked her older sister, unable to hide her relief.

"Sure." April turned to Hannah. "Sadie is saying we should try looking for information on Mama."

"Mama?" Hannah looked down a moment, then raised her hand to cover her mouth.

She'd honestly been thinking more of plying April for memories of the town, of places that Daddy might want to visit while here. An old church. His former place of business. But this idea—to actually look for clues about their mother….

"Why not?" Sadie's pulse thudded hard in her ears to say aloud the question that Daddy had asked, the question that had helped launch a series of choices that had brought her to this very moment. "We *are* in Alphina. We have a phone and a phone book."

April shifted in her chair to open the desk drawer. The seat squeaked. The drawer squawked. The phone book, though thin, hit the bed with a satisfying *thwack* when April tossed it to Sadie, suggesting, "We could start by calling city hall."

Sadie laid her hand on the tattered cover with its photo of a local landmark. "And ask for what?"

"Records...um, marriage licenses?"

Hannah sank to her knees and placed her hand on the closed book next to Sadie's, her eyes fixed on the oldest sister of the three. "And even if they could tell us something, how would that help us find her?"

April had no answer.

But Sadie did. "We won't find the kinds of things we want through official channels."

"No?" Hannah cocked her head. Hannah liked official channels. They were organized and easy to access without having to rely overmuch on others' help to do so. If Sadie had let her, she'd have gladly spent the day flitting from office to office to library files and back again, gathering information, networking and generally making herself the scourge of Alphina paper handlers everywhere.

"The newspaper!" Hannah clapped her hands together. "Or maybe an old established doctor's office?"

"Chamber of commerce," April added her best guess.

"Nope. Nope. And no. Unless our mother made herself newsworthy or owned a business, the paper and any civic organizations would be out. A doctor might know something, but how would we find the right one, and if we did, would he or she divulge privileged patient information?"

"Not likely." Hannah rested her chin on the bed and tucked her robe in around her feet.

"No, ladies, we need to seek out the collective knowledge of the resident population, the whole body of data accumulated through intense survey and interaction with various locally based denizens, the shared wisdom of the generations."

A slow smile worked over April's lips. "Town gossip?"

Sadie touched the tip of her nose to let her sister know she'd gotten the right answer. "Yup. We need to find Alphina's answer to Lollie Muldoon."

"Well there is a little café across the street. It's just the kind of place locals might gather." April stood and held her hand out to help Hannah up, as well. "If there isn't a good gossip connection there, they could probably point us in the right direction."

"Good thinking." Sadie leaped up, suddenly energized again. "In fact, we could take Daddy up on his offer to feed us, and do both at once."

Hannah rubbed her temple with one hand and clasped her robe closed high at the throat with the other. "Ugh—how can you two think of eating at a time like this?"

"A time like what? Breakfast?" April's braid swung with a spring in her step as she took Hannah's shoulders and gave her a shove to prod her to get ready. "I always think of eating then."

"I always think of eating—period." Sadie pulled at the hem of her shapeless jersey tunic. "Right now I'm thinking pancakes!"

"Pancakes?" Hannah shuddered. "How could you eat something that sweet and sticky and heavy and…" She covered her mouth.

"Hannah, are you all right?" April was at her sister's side in a heartbeat.

"I told you, I'm nervous." She pushed April away, snatched up the outfit she'd laid out and headed into the bathroom, calling through the closing door, "This whole experience is taking its toll."

April leaned against the bathroom door. "I know you're not the type to admit you might have a human failing or two, but maybe you're actually sick."

"Or maybe…" Sadie jumped up and ran to the door, knocking gently before she said, "Hannah, honey, maybe we should take this money Dad left and head to the nearest drugstore to buy a test."

April's face lit up. "Oh, Hannah, you don't think you could be…?"

Silence answered them for a few seconds, then the door slowly opened and their sister emerged, fully dressed.

"Give me that." Hannah grabbed the money from Sadie's hand. "If Downtown Drug is any example, the local drugstore will be just as good a place as any to get some prime gossip—and that test."

᧞ Chapter Seventeen ᧞

"You praying about Hannah's test or sitting there willing the phone to ring?"

"Can't I do both?" Sadie took her eyes off the tan motel phone long enough to smile at her older sister. "That pharmacist said he'd check around, and if he got in touch with the woman he thought might remember Mama and Daddy living here, he'd get right back to us."

The raised green letters of the chain pharmacy's business logo looked stark against the white of the crisp card in April's palm. She flipped it over to the handwritten name on the back. "What a blessing to find someone who had run a drugstore for so many years and sold to a national chain."

"Actually it happens all the time now. The private shops just can't keep pace. This fellow was completely in awe of how long Ed had held out already." Sadie sighed.

"Do you think Ed will call him to talk about the pros and cons of selling the store?"

"Who knows? I told this guy that Ed had recently taken up

golf, and he assured me that was the first step toward dumping the drugstore but…" Sadie wondered what Ed was up to right now. Was he hard at work, maybe pausing now and then to think of or say a prayer for her and her sisters? Or was he on the golf course? Or maybe getting a facial or manicure or total makeover courtesy of Carmen Gomez? "You may find us terribly predictable, April, but I no longer have any idea what Ed will do next."

April set the card aside.

"Can you two turn the TV on out there, I can't…it's too quiet. It's making me self-conscious."

April obliged with the flick of a button.

"Better change the channel." Sadie pointed to the talk-show host announcing the day's lineup of guests. "If you think *we* make her nervous, imagine what that crew would do for her."

After a few more clicks, April settled on an old black-and-white sitcom. "Okay, the TV is on. We are not listening. We won't hear if you are taking the test or talking to Payt about the results. All better, Hannah?"

"Thanks. I won't take long, I promise."

April rubbed her hands together gleefully and tiptoed over to sit on the brown-and-gold bedspread next to Sadie. "Just think—in a few minutes we'll know if we're going to be aunts!"

Sadie leaned back to check under the nightstand, making sure the phone was plugged in properly. "You're already an aunt."

The laugh track from the old TV show roared.

"Oh, yeah, sure." April fingered the collar of her staff shirt from her annual work as a church camp counselor. "And I love Olivia and Ryan. I love all kids."

"You're good with them. You're a born nurturer." Sadie cocked her head and wrinkled her nose. "Is that a word? Nurturer? Born to nurture? Either way, you do good with growing things, plants, puppies, children."

"Thanks." April flicked her braid back, her gaze cast in the general direction of the TV, though she clearly wasn't paying the show any attention.

Sadie wondered if the compliment had been unkind. Was it wrong to remind her sister that she excelled at loving and caring when her life offered fewer and fewer opportunities for her to do so? Sadie thought of just letting it go, the way they always did when things touched on the uncomfortable. But the trip, the circumstances, the talk they'd had last night, had all worked to open something up in her, and she didn't want to just leave things alone anymore, not if there was a chance that she had said or done something that had tapped an aching nerve in April.

"But you're right." This was not easy for Sadie, either, this topic, so she broached it gingerly. She chose her words with care, kept her tone light and reminded herself that this was her gift to her sister, and that she, Sadie, controlled the circumstances. "Being an aunt to a teenager just doesn't have the fringe benefits of being an aunt to a brand-new baby."

"So true." April twisted her neck to speak to Sadie over her shoulder, her expression cautious but her eyes shining with excitement. "There's just something about a new baby..."

"You don't have to tell me." Sadie put her hand up. "And before you ask the inevitable, I am fine with it."

"Hannah is going to be a mom, you know." The mattress dipped and creaked as April situated herself cross-legged in the center of the bed. "Whether you're fine with it or not."

"Ouch," Sadie whispered, more for the hardness of her sister's tone than her actual words.

"I'm sorry if it hurts you to hear it, Sadie, but if we don't take anything else away from this trip together, I hope we can at least do this— I hope we can finally stop walking on eggshells around each other."

Sadie opened her mouth to argue that she never did any such thing, but her heart wouldn't let her mouth form the feeble protest. She took her sister's hand. "I think that's a very good goal, April. I've thought for a while now that we—you, me, Hannah—we're bound as much by what we're afraid to say as we are by those few things we do manage to talk about."

"Let's face it, Sadie, if we get everything about Mama out in the open finally…"

"It will either bring us together finally and forever as sisters…"

"Or tear us irreparably apart." April slipped her hand from Sadie's, her eyes somber. "That's why I feel I had to say what I said. After today I don't know if I'll have the chance again. So I am telling you, the way you've been since you lost the baby scares me. It scares me a lot."

Sadie balled her hands into tight fists. She looked at the phone again, then at the heavily curtained window, then at the mirror over the vanity and sink. She looked anywhere but at her sister as she forced the hoarseness from her voice and said, "It's not like I had a choice, April. It's not like I could just decide to snap out of it. Most of the time it was forest and trees—I couldn't separate the simple everyday problems from the immense, life-changing ones. They were all overwhelming."

"You have to get help, Sadie."

"B-but I'm better now." She whipped her head around. Sadie pushed her hair out of her eyes even as she pleaded with her sister to concede what Sadie wanted more than anything to believe. "Can't you see how much better I am?"

"Oh, absolutely." Her sister actually physically backed down. Her shoulders rounded. She folded her hands in her lap and smiled, though none too convincingly, as she said softly, "Sometimes days go by now and I think 'we have our Sadie back,' but then…"

April chewed her lower lip and cast her gaze to the quilted bedspread.

"No eggshells, April, remember?"

April searched her sister's eyes.

Already Sadie regretted having urged her sister to speak freely. But she said nothing more and simply sat there, holding her breath.

"But then I remember it being that way with Mama, Sadie," April said at last. "Good days and bad. You probably don't have any memory of it, but that made it hard for us as kids."

Sadie exhaled slowly; a long, world-weary breath. "I've made it hard on my kids. I can see that."

"Then promise you'll get help."

"Claudette Addams said I should see a doctor."

"Yes. A doctor and maybe even…maybe drive over to Louisville or Lexington once a week to see a Christian counselor." April recoiled as if she thought Sadie might lash out at her. When Sadie gave no such immediate response, April rubbed her fingers along her braid and rushed to clarify, "You could just see a regular counselor, I suppose, but I was thinking you might want someone who could help you address your spiritual pain."

Sadie's face burned. She put her hands to her cheeks. "Has it been that obvious?"

"That you're a little mad at God? That you've stopped speaking your heart to Him?"

Tears stung Sadie's eyes, but she set her jaw and bid them not to fall. What had seemed a good idea before, now rang hollow in her ears. She did not want a lecture on how she should live her faith. To talk about things that April had observed, their mother, even Sadie's behavior these last months was one thing. But this…her sister simply had no idea how deep it cut into Sadie's soul to have been granted a second chance at motherhood only to have the One she loved and relied on, the One in whom she placed all hope, take that chance away. It was like the Heavenly Father had confirmed to Sadie the very worst of her fears—that she was not good enough. That she would be, given another chance, a failure.

What could she say to God after that?

The theme music for the old TV show blared loudly in the silence.

When it faded, they could hear Hannah talking on her cell phone in the bathroom.

"Thank you for caring enough to speak truthfully to me, April, but can we let it go now?" Sadie pulled her shoulders up. "I need to sort of regroup my emotions so I can give Hannah whatever kind of support she needs, you know, whatever the outcome of her test."

"Sure." April turned to face the television and began searching again for something suitable to watch.

Sadie fixed her gaze on the phone. She blinked, and though the tears slipped from her eyes, she did everything possible to keep from showing her pain.

After a second and without moving to look at Sadie, April set the channel changer down. "Sadie? About Hannah."

Sadie cleared her throat before asking, "What about her?"

"She doesn't really think we are going to find Mama alive and well and living in Alphina, does she?"

"That's our Hannah. She always wants to believe the best possible outcome."

"What about you?"

"I know better. That is, I know that whatever the outcome, we have to accept it."

"I've never said this to anyone, Sadie, but I accepted a long time ago that Mama…isn't here anymore."

Mama, dead? That's what Sadie believed, and had believed for a very long time now but, like April, could never bring herself to say it out loud to anyone. Maybe now that they had vowed to speak frankly to each other—

The phone rang.

Sadie seized it. "Hello?"

"Hello? Is that better, Payt?" Hannah stepped out from the bathroom with the cell phone hidden under the waves of her tousled hair.

Sadie stuck her finger in her ear. "You'll have to speak up—there's a lot of interference coming from this end of the line."

"Don't worry, I'm taking this outside." Hannah headed for the door in long, brisk strides. Her hand slipped on the knob at the first try, but when she flung the door open, sunlight came streaming in.

Sadie shaded her already smarting eyes.

Hannah giggled.

The door fell shut.

That didn't matter. Sadie did not have to see her baby sister's body language to know the news she was giving Payt was better than the news the local pharmacist had called to give to Sadie.

"No, that's all right. I understand." Sadie hung up.

April glanced at the closed door, then back to Sadie. "Well?"

Sadie just shook her head and hung up the phone.

"What does that mean?" April mimicked her sister's gesture. "That he didn't find anything out or—"

Sadie held one finger up to ask her sister for a moment. "Just let me make one more call. Maybe two."

"Why? Can't you give me an answer?"

"I can give you part of an answer," she said. "But it's the part that will only lead to more questions."

Outside, Hannah squealed in delight.

April stole a quick look in the direction of the door, then glared at Sadie and whispered, "Spare me the soap-opera dramatics. Just tell me what the man said."

"In a minute." Sadie had already slid her own cell phone from her purse and punched in an all-too-familiar number. "Hello? This is Sadie Pickett, the cemetery superintendent? Can I please speak to the sheriff?"

"You're calling Kurt Muldoon?" April's eyes went wide. She curled her fingers into the hem of her camp shirt. "Why are you calling Kurt Muldoon?"

"I'm going to ask him if he has a girlfriend." For the first time in a while her natural sarcastic streak buoyed Sadie's spirits. In this long journey back from whatever darkness had seized her, the presence of mind to crack wise—no matter how much she knew she shouldn't give in to the impulse—had been one of the first signposts of her old self returning.

From the look on her face, Sadie could tell April did not appreciate that subtle distinction.

"Why are you calling the Wileyville Sheriff's Department, Sadie?"

"Because...yes, I'll hold." Sadie lowered the mouthpiece to better try to keep the two conversations separate. "Because..."

"Guess what, y'all?" Hannah burst into the room looking green around the gills and radiant all at the same time.

"We're going to have a baby!" April leaped up and rushed to take her youngest sister into a big hug.

"We?" Sadie scoffed, but with a tentative smile. "Remember that commitment around the twelfth hour of labor, Hannah, and see if you can't get her to do her share of having the baby then."

"Oh, Sadie, you're such a..." Hannah kept one arm around April and held the other open to her other sister. "Weren't you on the motel phone a minute ago?"

"She's trying to reach Kurt Muldoon in Wileyville," April said, her eyes narrowed at Sadie.

"Whatever for?"

"She won't say. She got a call from that pharmacist and won't tell me what she found out, but apparently has no qualms about calling a stranger to discuss it with *him.*"

"Kurt is hardly a stranger, April." Sadie strained to listen to the noises on the other end of the line as they transferred her call from the switchboard to Kurt's office.

"What are you up to?" Hannah put her hand on her hip.

"I am up to getting out of here so I can talk to the man in peace." Sadie stood, and like her sister before her but with much less enthusiasm, went to the door of their room to step outside.

April snagged her by the elbow. "You can't walk out of here until you tell us what you know about Mama."

"I know… Yes, Kurt, I have a favor to ask of you. Can you hang on just one sec?" She pulled her arm free and crossed the threshold to the sunny sidewalk, then turned, and seeing the sweet expectant glow on Hannah's face, sighed. "I know where Mama is, and if you give me a few minutes to pull some strings, I hope to be able to tell you how she got there."

❧ *Chapter Eighteen* ❧

Hannah was crying.

Well of course she was crying. In the duration of a few short minutes she had learned of her own impending motherhood and of the death of her own mother almost thirty years ago.

April was stoic.

April was always stoic. But in this case it went beyond a state of mind or way of carrying one's self in an uncertain world. Now it seemed to sink into the lines around her hard-set mouth, to have gotten under her skin. Her face looked gray, her eyes devoid of light—and of tears. She had followed Daddy's chosen biblical admonition and girded her loins, and in doing so she had thrown up such a wall of defense around herself that she had blocked off the tentative new inroads she and Sadie had made earlier.

Sadie felt…

It didn't matter what Sadie felt. She'd have plenty of time for mulling over the news she had heard and trying to make peace with it all. Right now Sadie had a job to do.

"Come on, y'all. It can't be far now. Daddy's note said the old downtown was just a couple blocks away, and the desk clerk at the motel said that the cemetery where Mama is buried lay just across the railroad tracks that run behind the old courthouse."

They reached the town square. Alphina, for all its population advantage over Wileyville, looked deserted, almost ghostly. They had not kept up the old buildings. Most of them sat empty. Some looked in real disrepair. There was no quaint café. No antique mall to reclaim the ruins of what must have once been thriving businesses.

Things called superstores and retail chain pharmacies, quick-stop markets and the fast-food restaurants that had lined the highway into town must have taken the place of what had once been the hub of the community. Even the government buildings looked shabby. And the town monument to its fallen veterans stood lonely and unkempt amid what could have been a lovely garden.

Seeing this made Sadie appreciate her quirky old Wileyville more than ever. Walking along broken sidewalks past padlocked doors filled her with a longing to be back home again. She didn't kid herself. The circumstances that she and her sisters now found themselves in only fanned the flames of that longing.

"Tell me again, Sadie, what the death certificate said." Hannah wiped her nose and pulled her shoulders back as if to reassure her sister she could withstand hearing the coroner's finding again.

"Overdose," April said without a single spark of emotion.

"*Accidental* overdose," Sadie corrected. "Of a prescribed medicine."

"Did it say which one?"

Does it really matter? Sadie wanted to bark. Instead, she swallowed the lump lodged high in her throat and shook her head. "Hannah, honey, I did this all long-distance and quick. The death certificate came from someplace in Arizona, and I told you everything the local cemetery superintendent told Kurt."

As a daughter, she probably could have gotten a look at the burial permit and pertinent information required for it without having gone through the Wileyville Sheriff's Department. But that would have taken time and cutting through who knows how much red tape. Because of her job, she had known exactly what to have Kurt ask for, and she had her answer, such as it was, within the hour.

"And Daddy knew?" Hannah sniffled but did not break down again. "Do you think he knew?"

"I don't dare speculate, Hannah. The information listed no next of kin to notify. It showed Mama as divorced."

"Divorced. That's the part I don't get." April lifted her chin and stared straight ahead. "Daddy never mentioned divorce."

"Yes, but you didn't think… If you suspected that Mama was alive, you didn't actually think they would still be married, did you?" Not that it mattered, of course, beyond it being yet another piece of a puzzle that Sadie was reluctant to try to put together without more information.

"I guess not."

"Daddy's pride would never have let him confess that Mama divorced him." Hannah spoke without looking at either of them.

"Not pride." Sadie couldn't help thinking back on the pain in her daddy's face when he had mistaken Sadie for his beloved wife, a woman who obviously had always been, and now would always be, unreachable to him. "He loved her. He still loves her. You know he taught us that marriage means forever. Maybe in his heart they never really got divorced."

"Poor Daddy." Hannah began to cry again, but this time without making any real sound, just tears and sniffles.

"Poor Hannah." Sadie wanted to join her in those tears. "Poor tenderhearted Hannah. Whatever happened between Mama and Daddy, he's dealt with it as best he could."

"And now it's our turn to do the same." A strand of hair blew across the bridge of April's nose. It was the closest thing to change that fell across her unwavering features.

They walked on another half a block before Hannah spoke again. "Since no one knew to notify us…"

"We were kids," Sadie reminded her, thinking back on the date of the certificate.

"Okay, since I assume they didn't notify Daddy, does that mean she was buried in an unmarked grave?"

By unmarked, her sister meant a pauper's grave. She wanted to know if their mother had died unnoticed, unclaimed and alone. Suddenly she thought about the serene stretch of land where she and Daddy had last looked for Mr. Green, and her father's empathy for the indigent man became all the more poignant to Sadie.

"No, Hannah. She had two plots in her name there already. Bought when she and Daddy lived here, I'd imagine. Guess that's why she didn't end up interred in Arizona. She must have left instructions to send her body back to Alphina."

"Maybe that's because she was…happiest here." Hannah's hand brushed Sadie's. Her fingertips felt like ice, but there was warmth in her trembling voice as she finished her simple, heartfelt thought. "You know, because we were born here. We were a family here, if only for a little while."

"I'd like to think that."

It was a hot, humid day. July in Tennessee was rarely anything but. Yet somehow, Sadie felt a chill that settled deep into her bones.

They crossed the street on green, and as soon as they reached the other side, April came to a halt, her arm out stiff to hold them back. "There it is."

"We don't know this town at all. It might not be the right cemetery. Maybe we should have done some more research," Hannah said.

"It's the right one," Sadie whispered.

"How can you know?"

"Because…" Sadie reached out to guide Hannah forward by giving her shoulder a push, but instead her hand curved around her sister's upper arm. Without overthinking the need to make contact, Sadie slid her palm down until her hand fit nearly inside her sister's. She cleared her throat, but that did not make her voice strong when she gave Hannah's hand a squeeze and said, "Because Daddy's car is parked on the far side of the fence."

"This is it then." April stared emotionless in the direction of the spot at the end of the block.

"What do we say to him?" Hannah asked.

"I'm more worried about what he's going to say to us," Sadie said. She had to shut her eyes to keep from searching the quiet graveyard for the solitary figure of her father.

"Why?" Hannah took a step and then another, her hand trailing away from Sadie's.

"Because, Hannah, what can he say to make this all right?" April's tone was sharp. She did not follow her youngest sister's movement toward the goal they had come so far to find. "Mama is dead. And maybe at her own hand. She didn't run off from us. She's *dead*. Daddy lied to us."

"April, that's enough," Sadie snapped.

What had they done? The bond of silence between them all had been broken. They could not go back. They could no longer create elaborate fantasies to quell their fears that their mother might be out there, that she might one day come back to them. They could not pretend that their father was simply some eccentric victim of his own charm who never meant anyone any ill will.

As of this moment, everything had changed. It had been on the pathway to change for some time now. But here and now, when they walked up to that cemetery, looked into their father's eyes and waited for him to tell them why he had done what he had done, nothing in their lives would ever be the same.

"What are we going to say to him, Sadie?" Hannah asked again.

"Why are you asking me? I can't talk to my Heavenly Father Who has only wanted the best for me. What makes you think I know what to say to this father, the one who has deceived me my entire life?"

"You'll know what to say, Sadie, because you've waited on the Lord to prepare you for this moment." Hannah held her hands out to beckon her sisters to come on with her. "I've watched you this summer. I've seen how you've come around, how you've taken on new challenges and made every effort to fix your mistakes. I've seen you grieve and I've seen you grow."

"True enough," April said with a nod. She took Hannah's hand.

Hannah gave her oldest sister a quick hug. "April here, she's not the one to approach Daddy. She's our warrior. She's girded up good in her Godly armor. April is the one we'll need in the aftermath."

April hugged the youngest girl right back and murmured, "Peace, be strong, Hannah."

"See? That's me. In the midst of this, I'm here to bring peace and strength. It's not for me to confront Daddy."

"Confront Daddy," Sadie said under her breath. A trickle of sweat snaked down under her collar. "I'm not…ready."

She had said ready when in fact she'd meant *worthy*. Who was she—an awful mess of a person—to confront anybody about anything?

"You *are* ready." Hannah shook her dark red hair back off her face. "You've got what Mary Tate calls 'the fire' in you. You'd lost it for a time there. But it's back. At least enough to do this thing."

Sadie started to shake her head no, but Hannah threw her hand up to stop her.

"You've waited on the Lord long enough, Sadie. You're ready."

Worthy! She wanted to scream it in correction. No amount of waiting would ever make her worthy. Why couldn't anyone see that?

Sadie lifted her eyes to scan the graveyard at last. "It's going to change everything."

"Well maybe it's about time something did." April held out her hand.

"What are you waiting for, Sadie?" Hannah's hand reached out, as well.

What *was* she waiting for?

It didn't really matter now. They had arrived at this place of no turning back, and her sisters had chosen her to speak for them. She would face their father and somehow she would find it in herself to open her heart and ask him to finally tell them the truth.

❦ Chapter Nineteen ❧

How long have you known? How can we ever trust you again? What else have you kept from us? Why, Daddy? Why?

Question upon question tumbled over one another in Sadie's mind. Her pulse rose like the heat in her cheeks, until her head throbbed and her thoughts swirled into a muddy mess. What could she say to her father upon finding out that he'd lived most of their lifetime in lies? Where could she find the inner strength to look into the eyes of the man she thought would never hurt her and ask him why he had betrayed her?

She placed her hand on the wrought-iron gate surrounding the small, silent cemetery and closed her eyes. And in that moment uttered a prayer so simple that anyone hearing it might have accused her of being glib in her approach. But to Sadie it was a start. All things start somewhere, and here at this site of grief and confusion and, yes, even power and calm in the renewed relationship with Hannah and April, here Sadie chose to start, at last, to speak to God about herself again.

Lord, please, be with me now. Be in me. Speak through me. Do not desert me. Amen.

The gate creaked. She stepped across from smooth sidewalk to a well-worn stone path.

Hannah and April closed in behind her.

Daddy did not look up.

The sisters stopped and took a collective breath.

Only a hundred feet away or so, Moonie was in another world. One inhabited by only himself and the unyielding marble stone that he knelt beside. Now and again he brushed his trembling fingers over the small white marker. His little gray hat lay on the ground. His shoulders rose and fell. More than once they shook, his head bent low.

"Sadie, maybe we should—"

"Shh, April." Sadie raised her hand to stop her sister from voicing their shared misgivings. "We're here now. We have to go forward with this or go back to pretending, to never really talking to each other, to always wondering. And I can't go back."

Hannah gave Sadie's shoulder a squeeze. "What will you say?"

The questions bubbled up to the surface of her consciousness fast and furious. She squared her shoulders and lifted her head.

How long have you known? How can we ever trust you again? What else have you kept from us? Why, Daddy? Why?

But when she reached the solitary figure kneeling in the shade of a gnarled old tree beside the grave bearing their mother's name, all Sadie said was, "'Why seek ye the living among the dead'…Daddy?"

"She was a woman of faith, your mother. Some might look at her choices and conclude otherwise. But I want you girls to know that she held firm to her spiritual beliefs. *Always.* She never let go of them. It was this world she couldn't seem to keep a grip on." He struggled to rise, his aging eyes rimmed in red.

"Let me help you, Daddy." Hannah stepped up first and took one arm.

April moved in and took the other arm.

"Don't know why you'd want to help the likes of this old man. I've made such an awful mess of things."

"I'd deny that, Daddy, but after having chased you through two states only to end up staring at a headstone with Mama's name on it, I don't see how I can." Sadie hoped he heard acceptance, not accusation, in her tone.

Moonie patted Hannah on the cheek, then April on the hand as he extricated himself from their aid. Bending down, he reached out and rubbed his fingers over the chiseled name on the stone. *Teresa Owens.*

Sadie's eye was drawn to the dates below the name. "She was so young."

"Thirty-one," April murmured.

"Yes. Almost the number of years since she passed." Daddy ran his weathered fingers under the final date.

"How long have you known, Daddy?" Sadie had to ask.

"So young." He shook his head.

"Daddy?" Hannah lurched forward.

Sadie put her hand out to stop her younger sister from prying further. There was too much pain here now. The grief in their father was as fresh as if it had all just happened. Moonie would tell them everything, but they could not force it from him. Sadie understood that now, and despite all they had suspected he had done, she still trusted her father.

She bent and picked up the familiar gray hat from where it lay in the thick green grass. "Let's go, Daddy. There's nothing more for us here."

"Now…now that I've found her again after all these years…" He folded his hands and bowed his head. "I hate to leave her."

"It's all right, Daddy," April said, her voice hushed. "She's not here now."

"And besides—" Hannah stood over the grave, her face emotionless but her eyes filled with tears "—she left us a long time ago, even before she died."

"Your mama didn't abandon you. *I* left *her*."

"What?"

He looked at the grave. "Your mother insisted."

"Daddy, all my life you've told that story of how Mama ran off in the night." Hannah stepped backward and crossed her arms as if to hold back the inevitable ache inside her as she added, "With me just three weeks home from the hospital."

April and Sadie closed ranks around their sister. Sadie looked at their father and went into her role to speak for them all. "We've heard it a thousand times, Daddy. Mama ran off. Now you say *you* left *her*, taking along her blood child, a toddler and a newborn? That doesn't make any sense."

"Sadly that's about all it did make, was sense. It sure didn't make us happy."

April took a step toward Moonie. "I don't recall Mama as ever being happy."

His head snapped up. His gaze searched his stepchild's. "She was, April, sugar." Then he looked away. "At times. But…your mama was what we called back in those days 'fragile.'"

"She suffered from depression, didn't she, Daddy?" April persisted.

"I don't know the right term for what had a grip on her, but suffer with it she did. Merciful heavens, girls—how your sweet mama did suffer."

Silence enveloped the shaded plot.

Beyond them the sun shone in almost blinding light on the abandoned buildings and empty, weed-infested lots.

"The baby blues," Moonie finally whispered.

"What, Daddy?" April leaned in to better hear.

"I recall that's what Phiz called it when she came to help out." Daddy nodded as he spoke, his head cocked slightly. "Said your mama had a bad case of the baby blues."

"Postpartum depression, like Sadie…" Hannah started to point to her older sister, then froze midgesture and let her hand fall to her side. "That's what it's called, Daddy."

Moonie looked to his middle daughter and nodded knowingly. "Phiz claimed Teresa might have fared better if she hadn't had you two girls, Hannah and Sadie, so close together."

Sadie tried to remember how she had felt after giving birth to Ryan and Olivia, desperate to find a pattern that might bring the answers she had sought for so long. "So are you saying it all started when I was born?"

"Pretty soon after. Yes, I think so." Moonie glanced down again, then motioned toward the old convertible waiting beyond the side entrance. "I always carried some guilt over that, but back then, we didn't know. We just thought she needed to perk up."

"Or pray harder. Or put it behind you." Sadie knew all the suggestions by heart. And she knew the greatest fear she had felt when she could not live up to the simplistic, well-intentioned suggestions. The all-encompassing sense of failure. Her greatest fear that those she loved the most would finally see her for what she was: flawed and ineffectual, a waste of time. Worthless and then…

She shut her eyes and pulled the warm summer air deep into her lungs. She asked the Lord again not to desert her and in that same instant asked her father the one thing that she now had to know from him. "But if she suffered so much, if she was that 'fragile,' as you put it, why would you leave her?"

Their father edged close to Sadie and, extricating his beloved hat from her white-knuckled grip, said calmly, "Like I said, she insisted."

"Why?"

"For the sake of you girls."

"How could anyone come up with that, Daddy?" Hannah held back and did not follow the rest of them. "All our lives we missed out on having a mama because you two had split up. What possible benefit could anyone have seen in that?"

"That it spared you having a mama right there in front of you every day who couldn't give you the most simple basic daily care that you three needed. And to spare you, I see now, the pain of losing that mama so young."

"You don't think she asked you to leave because she planned to...?"

"Kill herself? No." He started again for the car. This time all three sisters followed, surrounding him to hang on every word. "I don't believe that for one minute. But I do think she lived every day in a world of hurt, so much so that there weren't enough tranquilizers and pain pills in the world to dull it."

"There are so many things they'd do differently today."

"I wish I'd done things different, that's for sure. But your mama, she had one wish in this world, and I had to honor it."

"That you leave her?"

"That I keep you girls together."

"Why wouldn't you keep us together?"

"Oh, I *would*. But there were some who said... To understand it, you have to remember that your mama had her good days and her bad ones."

"I do remember that, Daddy," April said. "I remember more bad days than good."

Moonie nodded, his eyes cloudy. "I wish I could say the good days were a blessing, but in some ways they only served to remind her of what she might do—and give and have—if only she didn't wrestle with that monster, that, tell me again that thing you called it—post…?"

"Postpartum depression," Hannah said.

Moonie sighed as if the very term weighed heavy on his bones. "It was one of those days, one of those bad postpartum ones, that made up her mind. It came on the heels of a respectable spate of days so good that life almost seemed…"

"Magical?" Hannah asked.

He shook his head, slowly. "Doable."

Sadie shut her eyes and mouthed the word again, feeling the full weight of understanding for her mother for the first time in her life.

"On one of those days your mother called me at the insurance office and asked me if I'd be willing to adopt April."

"Which you did." April moved ahead of them, probably intending to open the gate for Daddy when they reached it. "And then?"

"No. I never did. I never legally adopted you, April, honey."

She stopped, blocking the path. "Daddy, yes, you did. I have your last name. All my school records show you as my father."

"I fudged the documents. It wasn't so hard to do back then. But I didn't adopt you. I couldn't."

Sunlight brightened the top of her head. She squinted and ran her fingers down her braid. "Why not?"

"Because we waited too late. Starting up the adoption proceedings brought your mama's fragile state to the attention of the child welfare."

Sadie started to give the proper name for the agency that might have come to investigate their home life, then thought better of it. Her father was finally telling them everything, and picking at details wouldn't make things easier.

"Teresa was pregnant then with our little Hannah. And weak as a kitten and withdrawn. But not so much so that she didn't grasp the severity of the situation."

"What situation?" Hannah pressed.

"That if a social worker looked too hard at our family, she might not like what she saw," April said.

"She feared she'd be judged an unfit mother, unworthy of and unequal to the task." Moonie studied his hat.

Sadie's knees wobbled. How well she knew that feeling! Until this very moment "Mama" had remained an abstract to her way thinking. A concept, bittersweet and beautiful, but just not real. Intellectually Sadie understood that they shared the same DNA, but now to hear they also shared the very same fears and failings?

She could hardly breathe for imagining her mother carrying that pain…and all alone.

"And Teresa wasn't far wrong. There was talk around town, and some said maybe they should take you girls away—or at least April, as she wasn't my blood kin." He reached out and took the eldest girl's hand. He held her gaze only a moment before he turned his beseeching eyes on the others. "I couldn't let that happen, don't you see? I couldn't let my girls get torn apart. I couldn't let them take you away, April."

"So you took us and left town?" No emotion colored Sadie's question. She felt stunned and angry and afraid all at once.

"At your mother's insistence," he reiterated.

"In a station wagon in the middle of the night," April whispered.

"Well, after dark, but you were already in your pajamas, so it probably seemed later to you."

April blinked, still fingering the end of her braid. "And we stayed at a motel with a park, with horses on springs and teeter-totters."

"How'd you ever remember that?"

April pressed her lips together, a softness coming over her expression. "And Mama came to see us once. I remember her in that park."

"Yes, to tell me she wanted to go away to get better and that we should move on, find a town and make a home and that she'd come when she could. When she drove off that day, I had no idea I'd never see her again."

"Then Mama *did* leave us." Always the stickler for details, Hannah gave a curt nod to emphasize the correctness of her assessment.

And though it humbled Sadie to admit it, she felt just as smug and satisfied with that conclusion as anyone. Daddy had not walked out on a woman in pain—he had done what he thought he had to in order to rescue the children he loved. It was a small distinction and not one she'd have thought noble at the time, but it was all they had, and so much time had passed since he'd made his own Solomon's choice that she simply could not dwell on "what ifs."

"That's right," Sadie said with the finality of closing a door to the past. "Mama left us."

"I…I suppose. But the way she was… I don't think she felt she had any choice. It was this thing that consumed her that compelled her to leave, don't you see? It wasn't the woman I loved who left. It wasn't your mama." Moonie turned his head to try to make sure each girl understood. Then he whisked one open palm along the brim of the hat in his hand and shrugged as if trying to get out from under a heavy mantle. "Got divorce papers in the mail a couple years later. I didn't want to sign them, but I had to protect you girls. I couldn't leave an open end. I had to let Teresa go."

It wasn't their mama who had made the choice, the depression had chosen for her. Sadie had to take that away and consider it more before she could either accept or reject it. But one thing she had to know and she wanted to know it now. "And the news of her death, when did you get that?"

His watery eyes met her gaze. He winced, just slightly. Then he looked down at his hat and in a shaky voice confessed, "About an hour before you did."

"Today?" Sadie looked around them at the cemetery surrounded by decades of decay. "You can't have just found out today!"

"I suspected, yes, but that's why I came to Alphina." He cleared his throat. "I came to make sure. Old insurance man, me, I'd bought these plots for your mother and me as a wedding present."

"Wow!" Sadie crossed her arms and glanced at the tombstones around them. "And I thought *Ed* lacked the knack for romance!"

She got a chuckle out of her daddy. That eased her heartache, just a touch.

"Your mother asked for the plots in the divorce," Moonie went on. "Teresa loved Alphina, and she knew we had settled in Kentucky, so…"

He started toward the car again.

Hannah dogged his heels. "So why didn't you try to find out what happened to her before now?"

He stopped in his tracks but did not turn to look at his daughters. "Because as long as I stayed away, as long as I didn't know if she'd found use of this little piece of land, I could dream."

The three of them shared a guilty glance. They all knew that feeling all too well.

"And now…" He threw back his shoulder and started to walk forward again, this time with the uneven gait left over from the car accident. "I can't anymore."

Hannah dashed to his side. "If it cost you your dreams, Daddy, why did you come now?"

He stopped, and again did not look directly at them when he said, "To keep my girls together."

"What?" Petulance finally broke in April's usually steady voice.

"I saw the signs in Sadie." Now he turned on her. He could not hold her gaze, but he did lift his eyes time and again as he spoke. "I saw the sadness, but I thought as long as she had her family, nothing bad could befall her."

"Because they wouldn't leave me." Sadie wished she'd shared his faith. But then he was her daddy, the last person who would ever see how truly undeserving she had become of the people who loved her.

"Then she told me that you three had quarreled and weren't speaking. And Hannah had these plans to go off with Payt to who knew where and I thought…what if they lose touch? What if the greatest sacrifice their mother and I ever made ended up for nothing?"

Just like when they were little and the pieces of a puzzle they worked on finally began fitting together, Hannah had to be the first to announce her version of the whole picture. "So you came here knowing we'd follow?"

"I came here knowing it was time to tell you the truth, the whole of it. But until today, I didn't have that, I only had the pieces that I had saved and the ones that I had wanted to believe still existed." He looked out toward their mother's grave again, his face pinched and worn in the bright sunlight. "Can you forgive a foolish old man who only wanted the best for his children?"

"Why didn't you tell us before now?"

"Because you girls seemed reconciled with your mother's absence—not content, mind you, but that you'd made your peace with it. I just didn't see how dredging it all up again could do anyone any good."

April's lips went thin. "It might have done Sadie some good. She might have had some warning that she had a predisposition toward depression."

"Sadie? Oh, darling, I didn't know. I thought if I lived my life with joy and exuberance, you three would learn by my example. I had no idea it was a medical condition. You understand that, don't you? I didn't…"

His mouth continued to move as though forming words, but no sound came. His eyes fixed on something in the distance and yet showed no sign of seeing anything at all. He raised his hand toward them, almost clawing the air, but without a sense of desperation, like a man reaching for a handrail or for help getting up out of a chair.

"Daddy?" Hannah tried to grab his hand, but he flailed and pushed her away.

"Daddy, are you all right?" April bent to try to look into his face.

He twisted away from her. He struck his arm out. The hat in his hand fell to the ground.

"It's happening," Sadie said. "It's happening again."

"Is this…the transient ischemic attack? Is this what you saw last time, Sadie?"

Sadie bent down in front of their father, her heart racing. "Daddy, can you hear me?"

His head turned in her direction. He did not appear to recognize her.

A strangled sob caught high in her throat. She put her hand to her mouth.

Hannah stepped in behind him and braced him with her arm around his shoulders. "Daddy, can you sit down?"

He nodded.

"He's responding." Cautious relief washed over April's expression.

"Can you walk to the car?" Hannah asked.

He coughed into his fist and nodded again. "Why? Are we going someplace?"

"Yes. We're going to get out of this graveyard. I know how you hate them," Sadie said, moving ahead to get the gate.

"Why see the living among the dead?" His lips managed a wan smile, but his eyes had that old Moonie Shelnutt spark in them again.

"Come on, Daddy, let's get to a hospital." She took his hand and began to guide him to his beloved old car. "You may have left Mama because she insisted, but her daughters are not going to let you go without a fight."

❧ *Chapter Twenty* ❧

It didn't take the doctor long to check out Moonie and reach the same conclusion they had come to in Wileyville. Nothing we can do here and now. Get to your regular doctor as soon as possible and discuss options in treatment, management and indications for future health issues.

That hadn't satisfied Hannah, who had promptly gotten Payt on the phone and asked him to get all the details and information from the doctor in Alphina. While that transpired, April took the time to duck into a hallway and call the store to make sure Olivia and Mary Tate had opened up without any difficulties. Then they planned to settle the bill so all of them could hit the road home.

That left Sadie and Moonie all alone sitting on unforgiving plastic seats in the sparse, cold waiting room.

"So let me see if I got this right, Daddy. All these years, your acting up and speaking out, going over the top and generally creating chaos around every corner, you intended that to teach us how to stay happy by example?"

He ducked his head a little. "Maybe I didn't think that through so good."

"You actually thought that running us ragged, driving us batty and making us constantly fly by the seat of our pants to try to keep up with you would somehow make us better sisters, better mothers, better equipped to handle the harsh reality of the world around us?"

He stared at the hat in his hand.

"Well I just have one thing to say about that." The way Sadie saw it, this was her opening. The time had come at last to consider all that her father had done and said over the years and finally give Daddy exactly what he deserved.

A second chance.

"Thank you, Daddy."

He jerked his head up. His eyes searched hers for any sign of her trademark tendency to use sarcasm in a pinch. "But, Sadie, honey, I did so many things wrong."

"Join the club, Daddy." She took his hand, smiled, then leaned back in the chair and watched the medical staff at the nurses' station busy themselves with charts and phone calls. "I can see how it would be hard for you to recognize depression, Daddy. To understand it. You're just so vital. So full of joy."

"Joy? Is that what we're going to call it today?" He harrumphed in gracious good humor and balancing his hat on his knee, stroked his chin to underscore his insight. "Because it isn't such a very distant time ago that I recall you using some other choice words for my uncompromising quest for authentic individualism."

He'd nailed her without compromise and it made Sadie laugh lightly. "Aren't we a pair, Daddy? You always make me smile…"

"And you could always break my heart if I thought for one moment I'd let you down." He placed her hand in his open palm.

She curled her fingers around his. "You never did."

"Oh, I think I did, more than a few times, darling." The lines around his eyes creased more deeply. His smile held a tiny tremor. "But I always hoped you'd forgive me my shortcomings."

"I always knew you'd overlook mine."

"You had that much faith in me?"

"Yes."

"And in your family?"

She looked away, anxious that her eyes would betray her. She thought of Ed and how his inattentiveness had started to panic her.

And Olivia and how she'd let her daughter ride roughshod over the household because deep down Sadie knew the time was fast approaching when her child would leave. Sadie hadn't trusted her firstborn to love her mother even if she didn't like the rules that mother set down for her.

And her sisters, how they had chosen silence over sharing secrets.

Her faith in those she loved the most had been small indeed.

"And God?" Moonie pressed on.

"I still believe," she said. "With all my heart, but…"

"That's the kind of sentence that shouldn't have a qualifier, sugar."

"I know. I *know* that, Daddy. But…" Her father had told her the truth today and in doing so had risked shattering her faith in him. She owed him the same kind of stark honesty.

No, strike that. She owed it to herself. And to everyone of late who she had not fully showed faith in. And to her relationship with God.

"Daddy, here is what I feel." Tears stung her eyes. Her chest constricted until she could hardly speak. She had never said this aloud to anyone, and the last person on earth she could have imagined herself confessing to was her father. But he was the one who had told her she had to start somewhere, so she took a deep breath and jumped on in. "It's not scriptural or divined by study or the result of any kind of serious soul-searching, you understand. It's just…it's just what's in my heart."

"And it's safe with me, Sadie-girl."

She nodded. She sniffled. She laid her head back against the wall and spoke, finally. "After a lifetime of waiting for things to turn out my way and never seeming to have that happen in full, I'm afraid."

He shifted his weight, and she knew he wanted to pull her into a hug.

But she just wasn't ready for that yet.

She held up her hand to keep his kindness in check and shut her eyes. "I'm truly terrified that if I ask for what I really want for myself, God will take a long hard look at me and find me…unworthy."

"So like your mama," she thought she heard him whisper.

She swallowed hard but did not let herself stop until she had said all she had to say. "And if I push it or ask for more or bare my pain before God, He will see me as a grubby little ingrate who doesn't understand how undeserving I truly am and He…He will abandon me. Just like my own mother did."

"Oh, Sadie." This time he ignored her attempts to block him out. He wrapped his arms around her as if she were a child again, and kissed her cheek and even rocked her slightly while saying her name again and again, "Sadie, Sadie, Sadie."

The tears came at last. Not racking sobs but the quiet, long-overdue tears of finally having let go of her greatest and most dreaded secret. "Oh, Daddy. It hurts so much to live like this."

He pulled away and placed his knuckle under her chin. "Then you get help, Sadie. Learn from what happened to your mama. You get help."

"I will, Daddy."

"You promise?"

She nodded.

He pulled a hankie from his pocket and wiped away her tears. "You have that all turned around, you know, Sadie-girl. God already took that long hard look. He looked at all of us and, just like you suspicioned, He found us all wanting and plenty unworthy. Beggars in filthy rags, to be specific. That's why He sent His Son to take our place. Because unworthy sinners though we are, God does not intend to ever abandon us."

"I know all that, Daddy." She let out a shuddering breath. "But why is it the things I hope for with all my heart never come to me? When I pray and believe and nothing comes, how can I not feel rejected?"

"God is not like some mail-order catalog there to fulfill your latest whims, honey."

"But they are more than just whims, Daddy. I thought you of all people would understand that. Didn't you ever pray that Mama would get well? Didn't you ever pray that she would come back to us?"

"Of course I did. Now blow your nose."

Sadie obeyed. In fact, she did such a good job of it that it made her hair fall over her eyes. She looked around, more than a bit chagrined.

Moonie let out a belly laugh and pushed her hair from her eyes. "Oh, Sadie, yours are the kinds of questions of faith that people have asked of all times. Why did God let this happen? Why does one person prosper and another fail? Why am I sick or sad or alone, when others have health and wealth and more people than they can count to love and admire them?"

Sadie laid her head on his shoulder. "What's the answer, Daddy?"

"I don't know, honey. But that doesn't mean I stopped believing. God is always good. And there is always good to be found in our lives if we look for it."

"That's why I feel so guilty. I recognize that I have so much, but all my mind dwells on is what I lack."

"Let me tell you, as a lifelong practitioner of dwelling on things I can't do a thing about—guilt don't get the billy goat fed."

Sadie managed to smile at that.

"There's my girl. I knew she was under all those tears." He stroked her cheek. Then raised his head to glance around them at their sterile setting. "Sadie, if I had known there was some kind of medical connection between the way your mama was and what you've endured of late, I'd never have kept it from you."

She folded the handkerchief in half. "I know that, Daddy."

"And do you know why you know that?"

Sadie had no idea what he was driving at but felt she should. She shook her head no, but with reluctance.

"Because I'm your father and I love you and you don't doubt my love for one single moment." He slapped her knee and grinned. "You know I want everything wonderful for you, don't you, girl?"

"Of course."

"Just like you want for your children."

"Yes."

"But not everything your children want for themselves is going to make them happy or help them grow into strong, loving, or dare I say wise, individuals."

"Wise? That may be asking a bit much." She sniffled again and wiped the last of the tears from under her lashes. "And I know what you're driving at, Daddy. God sees the bigger picture. And if my prayers are not answered as fast or as fully as I want, that doesn't mean God isn't listening."

"He's listening…if you are willing to talk to Him."

"What happened to 'Wait on the Lord?'"

"Wait on the…?" He chuckled softly, lifted his hat from his knee and plunked it on his head. "Oh, honey, when I chose those verses, I was a single man with three small daughters. You were my impatient one, always wanting what you wanted when you wanted it."

She folded her arms and looked down the hallway for her sisters to finally return. "Well, that much hasn't changed."

"But it has changed, Sadie. You've changed. You're entering a new phase of your life. Seeing your children grow up and no longer needing you can make you feel that you're losing something, but take it from someone who has had the privilege to watch his girls grow into wonderful and, yes, *wise* women—there is still so much to gain."

"Really?" Maybe it was the cry. Or maybe it was the confession. Or maybe it was the comfort her father had heaped on her in every form from cliché to handclasp, but Sadie suddenly believed him. And her heart felt lighter.

"Did having an empty nest slow this old buzzard down one bit?"

She laughed.

"Try looking at it a new way—think of all the new adventures awaiting you and Ed soon."

"Well, me, anyway. Ed seems determined to have his own adventures."

"I won't speak to that, honey. I don't think it's any of my business, but I will tell you, I never once thought the verse I picked out for you as a child defined you. If you need a verse to do that, find your own, Sadie-girl. And let God help you do it."

"I bet if you had a verse, it would be that proverb, 'A merry heart doeth good like a medicine.'"

"I don't suppose the modern translation of that would be, 'A man with a merry heart can be a real pill?'"

"No, but that does sound more suitable, doesn't it?" She adjusted his hat just as Hannah strode up to them with April only a few steps behind.

"The doctor says Daddy can go, but that he needs to get to his own physician as soon as he gets home."

"I say let's get going, then. If there's nothing holding us here." Their father stood and looked down at her. "Sadie?"

She stood reluctantly. Was there nothing for them here? It felt as though she still had something left undone.

"Okay, here's the plan then." No surprise that Hannah had a plan. Hannah *always* had a plan. "Two of us drive back with Daddy in the van."

Moonie opened his mouth, but before he could launch any protest, Hannah cut him off, her hand to his chest.

"Don't even start with me, Daddy. The van is the most practical way for you to travel. And we need two people with you because…" Obviously it was because they were all terrified of him having another attack and none of the three of them wanted to have to go through that alone while driving a classic convertible down the highway. "Because you are more than any one God-fearing, Christian woman can handle."

She'd found the one thing their father couldn't argue with.

He shut his mouth and tipped his head to show everyone he acknowledged that she'd bested him—this time.

"Now let's get going." Hannah clapped her hands together. "I'm anxious to get home."

Sadie could just imagine. She could practically see the wheels turning in her younger sister's head. It wouldn't be a week before Hannah had dug up everything she could, gotten together records and files and done as much research as possible to piece together the missing years of their mother's life.

All while battling morning sickness, the complications of combining impending parenthood with the possibilities of taking on a seasoned foster child and always managing to look calm and cool and expertly coiffed.

"'Peace, be strong,' eh, Hannah?" April bent at the knees to put her arm under her father's, letting him lean on her.

Moonie chuckled, "Did I ever tell you why I picked out that verse for you, Hannah? Or yours for you, April?"

"Tell me walking, Daddy," April ushered him toward the door with Hannah on his other side.

Sadie watched a moment, her emotions still tender and twisted from all that had transpired.

Something was yet undone here, and she couldn't go until she'd seen it through.

Chapter Twenty-One

Half an hour later at the motel, when Daddy had gotten settled into his seat in the van—shotgun, he called dibs on it the moment they pulled into the parking lot—Sadie held back.

"Y'all go on ahead." Sadie dropped her overnight bag into the back seat of the yellow convertible. "I want to drive through town once before I go—you know, to sort of clear my thoughts."

"Sadie, if you need a few more minutes, we can hang around until you're ready."

"It's okay, Hannah. Between the mama-to-be needing to stop every few miles and the daddy-too-bossy wanting to direct every driving moment, I figure I'll catch up with you in time for all of us to have lunch together." She pulled her cell phone from her purse and waved it. "We can arrange the details later."

"Sure thing." April tried to smile, but it wouldn't hold.

Hannah tilted her face up just enough to bathe it in mid-morning sun. She scrunched her eyes shut and wrinkled her nose. "Going to get hot today. Don't hold back too long."

"I won't." Sadie tried to tote up the amount of time she'd need, but since she really didn't have a clear notion of what she had to do, she couldn't.

"Okay, then. We'll catch up later." April looked at the van and then at the motel and finally at the ground, where hiking boots, high-fashion sandals and scuffed sneakers stood toe-to-toe.

Hannah's feet shifted restlessly at first, then inched forward to wedge her place solidly among her sisters.

April put one hand on the back of Hannah's neck, then stole a peek over her sister's shoulder to the van before leaning in to form a closed circle between the three of them. "You're going back to the cemetery, aren't you?"

Sadie rested her forehead against April's so lightly that she doubted it even smashed her hair down. And yet the touch united them sufficiently that when Sadie found the power to speak in a dry, feeble whisper, she knew the others heard her. "I have to go. I just…have to."

Hannah wrapped both hands around Sadie's arm. "Sadie, are you sure that's wise?"

"Of course it's wise." Sadie raised her head, all queenly and confident, and she smiled. "Don't you know? We're Solomon's daughters, girl. We're just brimming over with wisdom born of authentic individuality."

"You trying to roast me alive in this van?" Moonie leaned over and beeped the car horn three shorts and a long. "Come on, girls, let's get going!"

"Oh, all right, we're Solomon's daughters born of having put up with *that* all our lives." Sadie jerked her thumb over her shoulder to their father, who was at that very moment tapping his fingers on the steering wheel as though he just might take a mind to slip into the seat and start them off on another adventure. "If that didn't give us some kind of horse sense, what else could?"

"You got that right." Hannah swept her hand through her hair and somehow managed to actually improve the already flawless style. "We're coming, Daddy. But if you honk that horn again, you'll be riding on the luggage rack."

"And lovin' every minute of it," he hollered back, waving his hat in the air.

April laughed.

Hannah groaned. "You sure you don't want to take the first shift driving Daddy?"

"I have enough to cope with, if you don't mind." Sadie gave her sisters a quick hug. "Now go. I'll be okay."

They all stepped apart, but no one really moved to leave their circle.

"Okay, then," April said again.

"Okay." Sadie lifted her hand in a halfhearted wave.

Hannah started to walk away, then suddenly turned and gave Sadie a hard, emotion-fueled hug, murmuring, "Tell Mama goodbye for us."

She broke away as quickly as she'd started the embrace and rushed to get into the driver's seat of the Royal Academy van.

Sadie took a deep breath, her eyes watering, nodded to April, then hurried to the old convertible and drove away.

Outside the cemetery she pulled into a spot not easily seen from the main road.

Now what?

Why not?

What are you waiting for, Sadie?

The old questions came at her even as she sat in utter silence.

Now what?

Do what she had come to do. To try to make some sense out of all she had learned today and all she had gone through since losing her baby.

Postpartum depression. She had never thought of it happening after a miscarriage. That's what Claudette was telling her without using the words. She knew that now. It helped to know she had someone to go to who would understand—and someone Sadie thought would be perfect for taking over the reins as the president of the Council of Christian Women.

Oh, Waynetta would have a fit. "It just isn't done, stepping down midterm."

And Deborah Danes would sniff and sneer about duty and commitment. On second thought, after the parade stunt, Deborah might have already started a recall, or even an out-and-out revolution to remove Sadie from any seat of honor, ever.

Lollie, of course, would needle and pry, slopping sugar to cover up her quest to uncover the "who, what, where and why" behind Sadie's sudden decision.

"Let her ask," Sadie muttered, gripping the steering wheel with both hands. "And maybe if she asks straight out, why, I'll look her in the eye and give her the kind of answer I learned at Daddy's knee—why not?"

Why not?

Why not start something here and now?

She whipped out her cell phone and hit the speed dial for the pharmacy.

"Ed? I just realized that because of the time difference between here and there, you are probably making your Saturday run to the bank." So this is what it had come to between her and her husband. After almost twenty years, the best way she knew to get through to him was to shout a message through her cell phone for him to hopefully pick up on his voice mail.

Nice.

She took a breath and vowed not to let it undermine her determination. Ed would get the message. One way or another.

"I'm still in Alphina but should be on the way home soon. I know it's Saturday and you're busy and we have to get things laid out for church tomorrow, and maybe you have golf plans." She was rambling. Well, why not? It was sure a lot easier than just blurting out what she really wanted.

But isn't that why she had called? *To blurt?* To be honest with her husband? To tell him what she wanted and trust that he wanted the same?

"Anyway, I was hoping…" As honest blurting went, that was a pretty pathetic example. She cleared her throat and began again. "No, I am more than hoping, Ed, I am *counting* on seeing you when I get back, and not just for a minute as you rush back to work or off to golf. We need to talk. So set aside this entire evening. I'm through with being last on your list. I believe our marriage deserves better than the leftover scraps of our lives. I just hope you feel the same way."

She hung up and waited.

The sky did not grow dark and dreary.

Lightning did not strike from out of the blue.

The earth did not crack open at the center and swallow Sadie up, yellow convertible and all.

People kept on walking.

Cars kept right on driving.

Sadie batted her eyes and exhaled long and low, unaware she had been holding her breath at all.

"Well what do you know? I told my husband what I wanted from him, and the world did not cave around me."

Of course, she thought, always ready with a darker viewpoint, Ed hadn't actually heard what she had asked of him. Maybe he wouldn't even check his voice mail before she got back to town. And what if he did and decided he didn't feel the same way she did?

Her world might just fall in on her yet.

Or not.

Sadie sighed. She started to lay her head on the steering wheel and retreat when her phone chirped out the tune Ryan had programmed especially for her.

"Aw, c'mon, Mom, you gotta admit, the 'Monster Mash' is the perfect song for 'Fraidie Sadie the Cemetery Lady," he'd told her.

She tried to argue the inappropriateness of it, but when she heard it, well, it always made her smile. And how could she deny her son the not-so-small pleasure of making his mother smile? Sadie knew, sitting here, that she'd have given the world for such a privilege.

She punched a button. The song stopped. She put the phone to her ear. "Hello?"

"Oh, Sadie." It was Ed. "I just got your message. Are you…are you okay?"

"I'm at the cemetery in Alphina."

"You said."

"We found Mama—she's here."

"I guessed. Do you…do you need me to come down there? I can be out the door in—"

"No." Her heart lifted. "No, Ed. It's enough that you offered."

"Sadie…you're still my sweet Sadelia, you believe that, don't you?"

He was asking her if she still had faith in him, in their love and their marriage.

"Yes, Ed," she whispered as she battled to keep the wellspring of emotion from overwhelming her. "I believe."

"When will you be home?"

"As soon as I…" She looked around at the run-down properties and the little patches of greenery among the graves. This cemetery was larger but much less lovely than hers.

Her cemetery? Hmm, maybe all those folks who said she was meant for the job were right. It certainly had gotten under her skin. Of course, it wasn't the job so much as the opportunity to feel useful again. To know that what she did with her days made a difference.

How it pained her to think Mama had never known that kind of simple satisfaction. At least Sadie thought it had pained her. She still hadn't quite taken up the notion of her mother as anything but a fantasy creation.

Had they really been so alike? What might each of their lives been if only…

"I'll start for home as soon as I take one last look at Mama's grave, Ed."

"I'll be waiting for you whenever you get here."

She didn't know when she'd ever heard sweeter words from the man she still adored after all these years.

"Thank you," she murmured, then as an afterthought added, "You might say a prayer for traveling mercies for Daddy and the girls…and me, if you think of it."

"I have been. In fact, you may not realize it, but you've been carried along this whole time on the prayers of all the people who love you."

She thought of her mother's fate and of her own and of how things had played out to reunite her family these past two days when it might well have gone the other way. "I do realize it, Ed. I do."

They said their goodbyes and Sadie climbed out of the car.

This was it. Whatever *it* was.

She shook her hair back and brushed her hand down her clothes, an act that neither dewrinkled her outfit nor smoothed her ruffled emotions.

The screeching of the wrought-iron gate didn't help put her at ease, either.

Why had she come here, really? What had she hoped to find? The living among the dead?

Had her mother retained her personal faith in the face of crippling depression? Sadie didn't know. She probably never would.

Her shoes crunched over the broken path. She wound her way to the headstone she had only glanced at earlier in the day. But when she reached it, she didn't know what to do.

Teresa Owens.

That's what she had come to see.

It had bothered Sadie more than she could ever let on to Daddy or her sisters that Mama hadn't kept the name of Shelnutt. The unfamiliar name mocked her and stood in silent testimony that Mama had truly left them—in every possible way.

Sadie's fears were not ungrounded. She *had* been abandoned. All her life she had wondered if she had been a better child, if she had not been the impatient one as Daddy described, would things have gone another way? Sadie had spent her life waiting for the answers and the understanding to come to her. Standing here looking at the grave of her mother, dead by her own hand even if by accident, Sadie finally had to accept—maybe they never would.

Maybe, just maybe, instead of living her life waiting for the big picture to be revealed, she would just have to take it day by day, hour by hour, from one moment to the next and every one of them with nothing more to stand on than faith.

And that, Sadie finally decided, standing there alone in among the graves, would be enough.

What are you waiting for, Sadie?

"I'm *not* waiting anymore, Mama." She folded her hands and cocked her head to speak to the marble marker. "I'm going on with my life."

Sadie looked up. "Do you hear that, Lord? I'm not waiting for life to come to me anymore. I'm not waiting for everything to be perfect before I come to You and lay my burdens at Your feet. I'm flawed. In fact, I'm a great big bundle of unresolved issues and complaints and confusion and bad habits and big hips and a smart mouth and…and…enough faith to remember that You love me anyway."

She looked again to her mother's grave, her emotions raw but at peace, and whispered, "Amen."

At last she knelt to touch the marker, to take away with her some final, visceral memory of having made contact with her mother. And then she saw it. Words she had not seen before, small and cramped and all but hidden by the grass that grew over the edge and sides of the flat rectangular stone.

Wife and Mother.

The simplest of epitaphs. Ordinary. Unremarkable.

Except to someone for whom those words meant…everything.

Wife and Mother.

Mama had not forsaken them. In the end, *that* was how she wanted to be remembered—as Moonie's wife and Sadie, Hannah and April's mother.

It was not a perfect, tidy answer to Sadie's every prayer. But it was an answer. One that she had waited all her life to find.

Her heart swelled.

If she cried, it came unbidden. She did not feel like crying. In that moment she felt…like Sadie.

At last, after so long and even with so much unresolved, she felt the hint of her old self again. And it felt good.

She kissed her fingertips, placed them on the newly uncovered words and whispered for the first time she could ever recall, "I love you, Mama."

Then she got to her feet, unsteady and yet completely sure of herself, walked to the car and headed home to start living the next chapter of her life, the one she had waited too long to begin.

Don't miss the further adventures of the three Shelnutt sisters.
Hannah's story will be told in the Christian mom-lit novel
MOM OVER MIAMI,
coming from Steeple Hill Women's Fiction in July 2005.

Look for Sadie's reappearance in Steeple Hill Women's Fiction in
December 2005.
And April Shelnutt will find romance in
Steeple Hill Love Inspired in the winter of 2006
in
APRIL IN BLOOM
And now, turn the page for an excerpt from
MOM OVER MIAMI
by Annie Jones

Snack mom.

It had all sounded so harmless when she'd been saddled with the task at the first parents' meeting. All she'd have to do was buy in bulk and show up, right?

Ah. How young and foolish she'd been three weeks ago. That was before she'd learned that in the cutthroat arena of middle-class American child-rearing, not all the competition remained on the soccer fields.

School. Car pools. Extracurricular activities. Even church. All were littered with potential land mines of mommy-one-up-manship. And Hannah had stepped—no, been *thrown*, really—into the very center of it all.

Hannah Bartlett believed that Loveland, Ohio, was the friendliest city on the face of the earth. And living there was going to be the death of her.

Okay, death might be a bit strong.

But standing in the barely broken-in kitchen of her darling new house on this dank August afternoon while twelve

eight-year-old boys who'd been rained out of soccer practice—again—played "quietly" in her unfurnished living
room, knowing their parents wouldn't pick them up for at
least an hour, the term "suffocating" did keep popping into
her mind.

She would probably survive the experience of living in the
upscaleish suburb. Perhaps she'd even grow stronger because
of it. If she wasn't killed with kindness first. Or smothered
under the weight of her own powerlessness to tell nice people
"no." Or stifled by her need to please and show everyone—i.e.,
her husband and cutie-pie extraordinaire, Dr. Payton Bartlett,
M.D., her older sisters, who still treated her like an inept,
gullible child, and her much-adored daddy—that she could
handle anything life threw at her.

Yes, *anything.* Even volunteering at her small—"small
on the attendance rolls, large in the eyes of the Lord," as
her new minister liked to admonish—church. And even
learning the ropes of foster-parenting Payt's eight-year-old
distant cousin while mastering first-time motherhood at
the age of thirty-six. Luckily, at six months, her daughter,
Tessa, impressed easily. A game of peekaboo and a lullaby
and the girl was eating out of Hannah's hand...well, or
thereabouts.

And Sam, Hannah's foster son...

"You don't know anything." Sam bumped shoulders with the
kid sitting next to him.

"Do so." The boy leaped up to tower over Sam.

Hannah held her breath.

"Nuh-uh," Sam retorted, his expression the sole province of
prepubescent boys—something between a teenager's I-know-
everything sneer and a kindergartner's you-are-a-big-doody-
head-and-I-don't-have-to-listen-to-you face.

Sam's combatant hunched his slender shoulders, obviously working up to a scathing, witty comeback. "Uh-huh," he said.

Hannah rolled her eyes and tried not to laugh.

Sam wrinkled his nose. His lips twitched.

"Hey, uh…" Hannah hated to single Sam out by calling for him to knock it off without at least saying something to the other boy. Kyle, Hannah thought the kid's name was…or Cody. Colby? She glanced down at the enormous can of "American-cheese food product" in her hands as if it might jog her memory. Cheddar? Gorgonzola?

Okay, neither of those were kids' names…probably. But since most of the adult conversations she'd had in the last week had taken place primarily in her head, she wasn't going to feel guilty about a few cheesy thoughts. She sighed, shoved the can under the blade of the electric can opener and opted for distraction over inconsequential discipline.

"Hey, Sam?" She kept her tone light. "Will you come help me a minute, please?"

He shot the boy—whose name might be…Monterey Jack?—one last warning glance, then hurried around the half wall that divided the two rooms.

The can opener whirred under her hand for a good thirty seconds before clunking to a jarring stop.

Sam's rival melded into the knot of arms and legs and striped blue-and-white shirts with numbers on the back.

Hannah wrestled the can away from the opener.

"What can I do?" Sam leaned both elbows on the gleaming black granite countertop, though he had to stand on tiptoe to do it.

She stared at the big dent that had stopped the whirring blade cold. "Got any ideas for getting cheese out of a half-opened can?"

"If you melted it first, you could just pour it out."

"Great idea," she said, and was rewarded by a light in Sam's eyes that wasn't there as often as it should be. "Except…" She tapped one finger against the metal side.

"Oh."

"It won't microwave."

"And you don't know how to cook the regular way?"

"Do so." Hey, eight year olds didn't own the patent on the brilliant retort.

"Yeah, but in the time it would take you to figure out how to melt the stuff inside the can…" He leaned back and looked at the dozen boys decked out in brand-spanking-new soccer regalia writhing in a heap vying for the attention of the family dog, a rescued racing greyhound with the affectionate and all-too-apt nickname, Squirrelly Girl.

"I see what you mean. If we don't feed them soon, it may turn out like…" She was going to mention the grisly story of that soccer team in the mountains turning to cannibalism but caught herself in time. A reference to *Lord of the Flies* also sprang to mind, followed by a flashback of her first PTA meeting. She shut her eyes and reminded herself to think like an eight-year-old boy now and use his frame of reference. "It might turn out like one of those reality survival shows."

"I know who I'd vote off the island first," Sam muttered.

"Let's hope it doesn't come to that." She held the can up and peered through the jagged slit already cut around the rim. "If only we could pry that back just enough to—"

"I got it!" Sam yanked open the junk drawer, rummaged a moment and pulled out a huge screwdriver—the one Hannah had used to fish a pot holder out from behind the refrigerator. Before that, she'd used it to stab holes into the plastic covering of a microwavable lasagna, and before that she'd even used the heavy wooden end of it to pound nails for hanging a picture. Sam waved it around as if he'd freed the sword Excalibur. "Old trusty!"

"Old trusty." Hannah smiled weakly and took the tool from his hand. She pushed a lock of dark auburn hair from her eyes, stuck out her tongue and pried the lid from the can with a screwdriver. At least none of the other mothers—the polished, poised, professional women who had caught her on a good day and immediately accepted into their ranks—could see her now.

* * * * *